INTERCEPTS

a h o r r o r   n o v e l

T.J. PAYNE

Intercepts: a horror novel
Copyright © 2019 T. J. Payne
All rights reserved.

Published by Tunnel Falls

ISBN: 978-1-954503-04-5

Cover Photo by Stefano Pollio on Unsplash

PROLOGUE

I see nothing.

Just blackness.

But even blackness, when there's nothing to contrast it against, is it truly black? Or is it just... nothing?

I also *feel* nothing.

I might be lying down.

But I cannot feel the hardness of the floor against my back.

I might be wearing clothes.

But I cannot feel their fibers brushing against my skin.

My mind tells my leg to kick.

But I am unsure if my leg receives the message.

My mind tells my arm to rise.

Even as my mind strains, I do not know if my muscles have responded. Perhaps my arm is up, as I have commanded it to be. But I do not know.

My mind tells my hand to touch my face.

Maybe it has.

Maybe it hasn't.

I tell my hand to hit my face, to slap it hard.

Nothing.

I tell my hand to stretch out its fingers and *dig* its nails into my cheek.

To scratch. To claw. To rip away the flesh. To find the nerve-ends and pluck at them. To pull away the muscles and the tendons until they find the bone. The jaw bone. The cheek bone. *Any* bone. Find something.

Fingers, I say, wrap yourselves around that bone.

Now rip it out.

Pull.

Keep pulling.

Deliver me a pain that I can feel.

Let me know that I am alive.

But I still feel nothing.

Fingers, I say, feel my face. Find my eyes. Now, press down. Dig hard. Reach through the pupil. Reach to the back of the nerves. Dig until you stimulate some sort of sense.

Maybe my hand is complying. Maybe it is digging through the flesh on my face like a mole digs through dirt. Maybe it is shoveling out chunks and throwing them aside.

I do not know.

I may never know.

I scream. Not from pain, but because my ears can't hear what I say. And so, I scream louder. I'm shouting. I'm telling myself to shriek. Any pitch, any frequency that might penetrate my dead ears.

But I hear nothing.

Maybe I never screamed at all. Maybe I never stopped screaming.

I cannot even hear the quiet hum of a silent room. I cannot hear my heart beat in my ears, nor the air pass through my nose and into my lungs. I cannot feel that air either.

Sometimes I worry that maybe I am not breathing. That I am suffocating. I panic. I think that I gasp for air at these times, but there is no way to know how my body has responded. There is no way for my body to report back to my mind that, yes, I am in fact still alive. Still breathing. Still pumping air through these lungs and blood through these veins.

I do not know how long I have been here. Been like this. Unfeeling. I am no longer tethered to the concept of space and time. I remember that I am *somebody*. Or *was* somebody. But I do not remember who.

It is easier to forget. It hurts less.

I held onto memories for as long as I could because they were the only foundation that my mind had. Even if they were not tangible, they were something real. Something I could imagine myself standing on to make sense of who I am — or was — and my place in this world.

But those memories slipped away long ago.

I only remember that I once *had* memories.

Now there is darkness.

Only darkness.

Well...

Not *only*.

It starts out faint, like a single buoy a mile off in a pitch-black sea. Just a speck of light, bobbing up and down. It is small. So small. I'm not sure it's really there. Perhaps it is only a spot on my eye, an echo of a pigment that my brain has held onto.

And then I hear a sound. Muffled and far away.

It is as if a train, made of sound, is racing toward me at incredible speed. It gets louder and louder, rattling the inside of my head as it approaches.

I scream out, and for once I hear my screams.

The sound stabs into my ears like ice picks.

That little light suddenly grows big and bright, flashing a kaleidoscope of color and movement that fills my vision. It hurts and I try to shut my eyes, but I cannot. I am used to my body not responding to my mind's commands, but this time it is different. I can *feel* my eyelids trying to close, trying to clamp shut to block out the searing bright light, but something presses against them, forcing them to remain open. The more I try, the more the stabs of pain ripple through my eyelids.

I then realize that there are hooks prying my eyelids open.

They must have placed the hooks there.

They are making me watch.

I can feel them holding me down. Their grip digs into my skin which tingles then throbs in pain. The spigot on my nerve endings has been turned on, and pain — burning, blinding pain — shoots through my skin, my veins, my muscles like gale winds whipping an already blazing inferno.

My tongue tastes the inside of my mouth. It is filled with mint and bile. The taste overwhelms me so that it sends my stomach churning. I feel my innards retching and convulsing, and soon an acidic water bubbles into my mouth, sending its foul smell up into my nostrils, where it lodges itself and begins the nauseous cycle anew.

They make this happen.

They open my eyes to burn them with light.

They open my ears to stab them with sound.

They open my nerves to set them on fire.

I do not know who *they* are.

From the corner of my eyes, if I focus, I can see them. It is hard. It is so bright that my eyes cannot see. My mind retains the

T . J .   P A Y N E

faintest fragments of the concept of Hell, and sometimes that's where I think I am. Being tortured by an Evil so profound that my weakened mind cannot fully grasp its form.

But as my vision clears ever-so-slightly, I can tell that these aren't monsters or demons who toy with me so.

These are men. These are women.

Sometimes I hear them call each other by their names.

They don't know I am listening. They don't know I understand them. They don't even know that I faintly recall the concept of *names*. Of *identity*.

They call out one name in particular.

"Joe."

"Joe Gerhard."

He controls this place.

They answer to him.

They bring me this pain on his orders.

When my pain ends, and I return to the blackness, I search for Joe Gerhard.

No matter how long I must search, no matter how far my mind must travel to get there, I will find Joe Gerhard.

I will find those he loves.

I will torture *them*.

I will bring pain to them.

Then I will bring pain to him.

To Joe Gerhard. The master of my Hell.

CHAPTER 1

Carson was in a rush.

He maneuvered his cart, which was too wide, through the stainless-steel door, which was too narrow. There was barely a half-inch of clearance on either side of the cart, and, of course, he had to lift it over the small lip at the bottom of the door.

Carson complained frequently that the "diaper pails," as all the nurses called their work carts, needed to be redesigned for their purposes. Something smaller, lighter, more maneuverable in these tight work spaces. Not having to wrestle these damned things through every airlock would shave several minutes off each orderly's rounds, and just that little bit of time — multiplied over several days, weeks, and months — meant that hundreds of man-hours would be saved. Just with new carts.

But despite how loudly and how often he mentioned the design flaw, nothing ever changed.

Someone once told him that it was easier to get a bill passed by Congress than it was to get an equipment authorization passed by the Company. Studies would need to be conducted, auditors sent in, and then the covert funding would need to be procured and funneled through various shell companies.

It was a miracle that anything ever got done, Carson thought.

When he started this job two years ago, Carson assumed that he worked at a place with unlimited resources; the months-long background check he endured probably cost tens of thousands of dollars by itself. But once he actually started working, he realized that everything was held together by duct tape and twine, not for lack of technological know-how, but because duct tape and twine were cheaper and easier than dealing with the crippling bureaucracy.

He finally finagled his cart into the small chamber and let the stainless-steel door shut behind him.

Now, he waited.

The lights in his little airlock chamber flashed red. Behind him, the door he just entered through hissed and whirled with the sound of an air-drill. A gasket in the door inflated to insure a full airseal between this room and the main facility. It would take a minute.

Carson sighed as he waited.

He wore a watch, but he couldn't see it. It was hidden beneath the sleeve of his blue "moon suit."

As he waited for the door to seal, and then for the airlock chamber to achieve sufficient high pressure, he went through the routine of grabbing the yellow, coiled hose that hung from the ceiling. He plugged it into his suit.

With another hiss of air, his suit filled with oxygen and inflated with air pressure. He looked like a blue Marshmallow Man.

The air, hissing into his suit and hood, drowned out most of the other noise and made him feel as though he were a deep-sea diver.

He thought this whole charade was absurd. The Facility had borrowed their design, equipment, and procedures from the Bio-Safety Level 4 labs that were used to study bio-warfare pathogens like Ebola — viruses that were highly contagious and thus deserved levels of extreme caution while interacting with them.

But there were no such pathogens at *this* facility.

That wasn't what they did here.

The designers had simply cobbled together labs, checklists and procedures that didn't quite match the mission. It was probably easier and cheaper. But Carson also wondered if the designers were even told what exactly they were designing. Or if they just winged it.

Typical.

The cut-corners of the past were now mucking up Carson's present. Each little obnoxious delay — none of which would exist if anyone higher-up actually listened to Carson — threatened to make him late for his date.

Carson desperately wanted to impress the girl he was going to see tonight. Her profile pic was cute. Cuter than most who responded to his messages, at least. And the texts he exchanged with her showed a fun, sarcastic personality.

Definitely out of his league.

If Carson were going to win her over, though, he needed to clean himself up beforehand. That meant he needed to finish work early enough that he could scrub down and catch the 17:30 elevator to the surface. If he had to wait for the 18:00, he wouldn't have time to get home and take a shower.

The suit's hood and mask made his head sweat and his hair turn greasy. Plus, he always left the Facility reeking of shit and bleach. Maybe the smells were simply embedded in his nostrils and she wouldn't notice, but just to be safe, he wanted a little time to make himself presentable.

The Company didn't exactly forbid dating. Not even online dating. But the staff always murmured that the Company watched and vetted all such interactions. Carson had noticed that occasionally he'd meet a girl on an app only to have her mysteriously cut off all communication. He knew that "ghosting" was a thing in the real world, but Carson often wondered if the invisible hand of the Company had run a background on the girl, deemed her untrustworthy, and then swooped in and denied further access.

Some fellow staffers had gone as far as to theorize that the Company remote-activated the microphones on their cell phones and eavesdropped on their dates. In this line of work, it wasn't uncommon to be issued a vague citation/warning that one could only assume was because of something uttered in private.

But Carson didn't buy that story.

The Company wasn't all-powerful. If they were, then they would have purchased more maneuverable "diaper-pail" carts for their employees by now. If anything, Carson found them too inept. Powerful, yes. But also disorganized, clueless, and too secretive to be efficient.

The light on the airlock finally changed to green.

Carson disconnected the yellow oxygen hose from his suit, letting it coil itself back up toward the ceiling. He approached the second stainless-steel door. As he was trained to do, he glanced through its square glass window to assess the room before entering.

Everything in the next chamber seemed in order. No danger, no imminent threat.

He swiped his key card at the pad beside the door. With a loud click, the door unlocked.

Carson cranked the handle and pulled open the airlock door, having to strain slightly as the air-pressure differential tried to shut it on him.

With the door open, he grabbed hold of his cart and maneuvered it into the room.

He stepped in and inspected his surroundings.

Near the door ran a long viewing window that looked out at a corridor where other staffers went about their business, pushing their own diaper pails as they performed their rounds in other chambers. Occasionally, an armed guard wandered past on patrol. None of them paid attention to Carson; they all had their own duties.

Carson hooked into a new oxygen hose as the door clicked and sealed behind him. The hissing of the oxygen filled his ears again. He stepped across the room, his boots leaving slight indentations in the white, padded floor. It was like walking on a soft gym mat. Early in his career, the combination of the bulky suit, the hose tether, and the soft floor made him trip and stumble, but he had grown accustomed to the nuisances of the job by now.

He looked at the woman in the hospital gown who lay on the floor. "Afternoon, Bishop," he said. "I hope you don't mind I'm early. I got a big date tonight. The babe's a total dime."

Bishop lay on her back, lolling her body from side to side. Her eyes were open and staring out of her bobbing shaved head. She didn't seem to be focusing on anything in particular. Not that she could. She couldn't see a thing.

Her hands, strapped in protective mittens that looked like oven mitts, waved around, scratching and pawing at the air. Occasionally, her hand fell toward her face and pawed at her cheek and then her eyes, but after a moment, her hands moved on to other destinations.

Her mouth stretched a few times, opening and closing in some motion that couldn't seem to decide if it wanted to form words or chew down hard on something.

A soft moan escaped from her mouth. The moan rolled around her lips for a few seconds then quickly built in intensity before transforming into a piercing, agonized shriek. It was the type of sound that Carson imagined a mythical banshee might make. But as quickly as the scream rose, it receded back to a moan.

The sounds used to really bother Carson. Sure, he laughed it off during his staff orientation. He even mimicked their moaning wails during lunch a few times. His department head lectured him and then wrote him up for that little act. Not that any future employer would ever see that citation. It vanished into the same void that every paper, email, or instruction manual slipped through in this place, never to be seen or referenced again.

But the sounds — the choking, warbling screams these things made — wormed their way into Carson's subconscious. For months after he started this job, whenever the wind rolled over the roof of his apartment, Carson swore it was building to a shriek. Every time he heard a semi-clogged bathroom drain make a *glug-glug-glug*, like Bishop did when her throat gagged on her own saliva, Carson expected a scream of intense agony to come out of the drain next.

Over time, he managed to ignore the sounds they made, although he never fully managed to block them out. He convinced himself it was just the way they were. In fact, the moaning and screaming was probably good for keeping their lungs and vocal muscles active. They'd sure need them at some point.

He figured Bishop could wail away. It wouldn't slow him down one bit. He dug in his cart then turned and faced her. He held a pack of baby-wipes in his left hand and what looked like an IV bag of apple sauce in his right.

"Bath first? Or dinner?" he asked.

Bishop continued rolling on her back from side to side as she swatted at the air like a drunken cat, oblivious to Carson's presence.

"I'm feeling bath time first," he said for her.

He set his things back in the cart and wheeled it all over to Bishop. "Let's make a deal. You don't like this routine; I don't like this routine. Why waste time dealing with restraints? You're a good girl, right? What do you think about us just getting right to business?"

Her mouth stretched into a wide, gaping oval. She screamed.

"Totally agree," Carson said in response. "Cool, no restraints then."

That would save him a few minutes. Having to take the time to strap their arms and legs to the rings embedded in the floor felt like yet another procedure that served no real purpose here. Maybe it was a good idea if he were working in a prison, or mental institution, or any place where the patients were actually dangerous. But here? These things were harmless. He never even saw one of them stand. They just spent all day rolling on the floor and flailing their arms. Apparently, allowing them to use their muscles in those sporadic movements helped them live longer, but Carson sure didn't think it made them dangerous.

He bent down beside her. In a firm, practiced motion he held down her kicking leg with one hand as his other hand slid up under her hospital gown.

"So, what you got for me today?"

He pulled a thick diaper out from under her gown.

"Yummy."

He flung the diaper with a one-handed hook shot. It arced through the air and landed with a clang into the trash bin of his diaper cart.

"Two points!"

Then, with a sanitizing wipe, he reached back under the gown and cleaned her. He went through one wipe... two wipes... three wipes... four wipes before the little square of damp tissue came back without a single brown streak. He bundled up the wipes in a plastic bag and tossed them all into the bin.

With that, he pulled more wipes from his cart. He firmly grasped Bishop's right arm, stopping it from waving around. He undid the strap that held her safety mitt in place and slid it off her hand.

Her now-freed fingers stretched and clawed at the air.

He wiped down her arm, taking care to give her muscles a massage as he did. He hummed softly to himself, blocking out Bishop's moans and occasional screams.

When Carson finished, he moved to perform the same task on Bishop's right leg, releasing his grip on her arm.

Bishop's mouth twisted up.

"I feel nothing... They did this to me... *He* did this to me..."

Carson looked up, startled. "What?"

"He loves you, Kate... You are his weakness..."

For a moment, Carson sat there, unsure how to proceed. He had only heard them speak — form actual words and sentences — during the tuning sessions. Otherwise it was just mumbled gibberish and screams.

At first, he figured that maybe his mask and the hissing of oxygen through his suit had played a trick on his ears. Or maybe it was a prank. Someone was screwing around on a walkie-talkie, pretending to be the voice of Bishop. Carson didn't want to overreact. He didn't want to do anything that might make him the butt of some lame joke.

And so, he sat at Bishop's side, slowly scrubbing her leg while keeping his gaze firmly focused on her lips. Her mouth twisted and contorted. These were common muscle movements, although that didn't make the bizarre grins that formed any less eerie.

Then Carson saw it. Bishop's jaw, lips and tongue moved, but not in some random assortment of shapes. She formed words.

"I know you know him. His name is Joe. Joe Gerhard," she said, her eyes still staring at the wall as though there was someone else in the room she was talking to.

Carson glanced up at the camera mounted in the corner of the room. Did the control room hear this?

He grabbed his walkie-talkie from the cart and held it to his hood. "Hey, Control? I'm in Bishop's cell and she's saying some really freaky shit."

"Like what?" said the voice on the other end.

"Well, she's saying things like—"

He looked back down at Bishop. In the moment it took for him to grab the walkie-talkie, her entire posture had changed. She didn't loll or swat anymore. Her head had stopped moving. Her eyes seemed to stare at him, right through him, in fact. Even though her eyes couldn't quite focus on Carson's face, he could *feel* the gaze.

"I see you," she said directly to Carson.

And then, Bishop's right hand — still free of the safety mitt — swung out.

It latched onto the hood of Carson's suit.

"Let go! Bishop, let go!" Carson shouted.

In a sudden, firm motion, she *ripped the hood and mask from his face.*

Carson heaved in panicked breaths of the room's air. He stood and ran toward the door.

"Help! Somebody hel..." The words slurred in his mouth.

With each breath he took of the room's air, his legs became more like gelatin. They crumpled under the weight of his body. He collapsed to his knees. With all the strength he could force, he rose back to his feet. Only a step later and his muscles gave out entirely, sending him tumbling back to the floor. He tried to pull himself forward, but his hands merely flopped about as if they were dead fish.

"Helpth meeth... pleastht..." he tried calling out. His mouth couldn't form the words, and his lungs couldn't push enough air out to make them more than a whisper.

His vision blurred.

The darkness closed in from the sides, narrowing down until there was only a pinprick of light in front of him. It was as if his world became one of those old televisions that maintained a slight ghost image of the picture for a second or two after the power shut off. He tried to focus on that image, tried to use it to ground himself to the urgency of the task at hand.

He couldn't hear Bishop's moans anymore.

He couldn't hear the hissing of the air through the vents.

All he could hear was a single high-frequency note, unwavering in his ear, but slowly fading out. It hung in the darkness of his mind as though he were floating in a black sea, listening to the horn of a ship as it sped off into the distance.

Until finally, nothing.

Silence.

Blackness.

For a brief moment, Carson thought he felt something on his back.

First it was a sharp pain.

Then it felt like little more than an itch.

Then just a tingle.

And then, he felt nothing.

Whatever had been on his back must have left.

Carson was now adrift in that sea, feeling, hearing, and seeing nothing.

***

As Carson lay sprawled on the floor, Bishop had thrown herself on his body.

The swatting motions of her hands, which had been so erratic and almost playful, now had a firm and violent purpose.

She propped herself into a sitting position and clawed furiously.

Her free hand dug into his suit. Again and again, faster and faster, until her fingers tore through the fabric. She was like a mole digging through dirt, constantly moving. She threw all of her meager weight behind her gouging hands.

She tore through his outer suit and then progressed quickly through his t-shirt underneath.

At last she reached the flesh of his back.

Her hands, never slowing, clawed at the flesh, tearing out large chunks of skin as she went. She ripped out bone and organ.

Never pausing.

Just burrowing.

Digging a hole straight through the man's body.

Red lights flashed in the room and in the corridor outside.

People in the hallway screamed and shouted orders.

But Bishop kept digging.

Her face remained blank. Her eyes continued to roam around her head, unable to see or lock onto any object in particular.

And down she dug.

Through skin.

Through muscle.

Through tendon.

Through bone.

She dug and clawed until she had reached the padded floor beneath Carson's shredded body.

And still she didn't stop.

CHAPTER 2

Joe Gerhard paced his office.

Although, in all honesty, "pacing" constituted a total of five steps of his massive frame in one direction before he reached a beige concrete wall. Then he would turn around and pace the five steps in the other direction.

The office was tight, windowless, and always a little too cool from the recycled air. But at least it was an office. A place for Joe to practice his little speech in private.

"It's my duty to let you know that my boys ain't had a..." he stopped his pacing and made a note to correct his phrasing, "... *have not* had a weekend off since March."

He shook his head and repeated to himself, "'Ain't' ain't a word. 'Ain't' ain't a word. 'Ain't' ain't a word."

For the past twenty years, he'd been in a state of constant battle against his West Virginian accent. One of his coworkers, Hannah, had joked that Joe needed a swear jar for every time he said "ain't" or "y'all." He laughed it off, but he knew it was true. No matter how persuasive his arguments and counter-arguments were to the brass up in D.C., if he let a single *y'all* slip, it would remind them that he wasn't Yale, Harvard, or West Point like them. They'd see him as some yokel who they kept promoting because he was damned good at his job.

But a non-college-educated yokel, all the same.

"My colleagues have not had a weekend off since March," he said to himself, beginning again while trying out what he considered an Ivy League accent. "This is manufacturing a work environment of unsatisfactory quality."

He paused.

"Jesus H. Christ, that's stuffy as shit," he said. "Oh, fuck it."

With a shrug, he began again. "Look here, y'all, I respect the challenges of staffing a place like this as much as the next man, but when I put in position requests, they get sucked into some black hole over yonder in your offices. Coming up on two years now, I've had three open janitorial spots listed as 'pending review.' You've got me using doctors — souls with honest-to-god M.D.s — on their hands and knees bleaching the shit off the floors. This is unacceptable. Morale is low and sinking like an iron turd. So, don't stonewall me on this anymore. I gotta protect my team. These people are my brothers and sisters. Who do I got to talk to if I wanna pry open them purse strings?" He paused. "You tight-ass, hoity-toity, sons-a-bitches."

He smiled to himself.

BEEP!

The walkie-talkie that was propped on a cradle on his desk sounded. Joe picked it up. "This is Gerhard."

"Joe! Something happened in Bishop's cell. Carson's hurt!" The voice belonged to Dr. Hannah Chao.

Joe went to his desk and turned on his computer monitor.

Security feeds filled his screen. Most of the images were of people lying on their backs in padded cells, swaying and swatting at the air. The feeds of the corridors, though, showed a mass panic. Staff members — many in nurse scrubs, but some in body armor and holding rifles — raced to and from the scene of the emergency.

In an instant, Joe processed all the information.

He enlarged one particular security feed; on the screen, in the center of the room, Bishop clawed through the mushy lump on the floor. She dug out handfuls of red, gooey material, throwing it behind her as she went in for more. A pool of blood grew around her on the nonabsorbent padded surface.

Hannah's voice came through the walkie-talkie again. "I'm at the outer door. I'm masked up. I'm going in."

"Hold position, Medical," Joe said. "Security, where are you?"

"We're in the Cell Two airlock," a man said over the walkie-talkie. "Field masks on. Door is unlocked and room pressure is optimized. We are ready for incursion."

Joe glanced at his monitor. A team of three guards, all armed and wearing gas masks, waited at the airlock. Their leader's hand gripped the handle, waiting only for the green light.

"Security, you are to enter Cell Two," Joe said. "You are not authorized to use lethal force. You are to restrain the Antenna, but under no circumstances are you to terminate or injure her. Do you understand?"

"No lethal force. Affirmative."

"Proceed," Joe said.

"Entering Cell Two."

With that, Joe watched as the gas-masked guards pulled open the door and stormed into the room. They swooped in on both sides of Bishop before grabbing her and pulling her off of Carson.

Bishop didn't resist. She didn't even seem to recognize they were there. Even as they held her to the ground, her limbs continued to claw and dig at the air, but her motions seemed almost playful and innocent.

"My mask's on," Hannah announced. "I'm going in."

"Medical, hold position in corridor," Joe said. "Do not enter until Cell Two is secure."

"Jesus, Joe! Lemme check on Carson!"

"Hold position."

He glanced at the security feeds. Hannah stood in the corridor with her mask on. She paced with her hands on her head, staring in the cell's main observation window, but she obeyed orders and made no motion to enter the room.

"Security, check Mr. Phillips vitals at first opportunity," Joe said.

A long silence overtook the radio.

Joe watched the feeds. Two of the guards strapped restraints onto Bishop's wrists and ankles. The third knelt by Carson's body.

"There's no way. Not with this blood loss," the guard said. "He's gone. I'm sorry, Hannah."

Joe watched as Hannah, seemingly overcome by it all, knelt down and took a seat in the middle of the corridor. She bowed her head and held it in her hands.

"Shit," she said softly over the mic.

Joe took a deep breath. "Control, keep on recording for another thirty minutes. I want that file to have our unedited response and cleanup. Then transmit it to HQ."

"You got it, boss," came the response. "And what about Case 10598?"

"What about it?" Joe asked.

"Everything is set up in Cell Eight. Should we proceed?"

Joe clicked away from the bloodbath in Cell Two to the work that was proceeding in Cell Eight.

Medics, orderlies and technicians stood around a man who was strapped to a chair. The man had sensors attached to his body. An array of large screens had been propped just inches from his face. Clips held the man's eyelids open. The man didn't notice or care; his eyes roamed around his head, looking everywhere and focusing on nothing.

Joe picked up his phone and hit the intercom button.

"Attention, staff," he said.

He could hear his voice echoing down the hallways as the speaker system broadcast his message to every room and department in the Facility.

"This is Site B Supervisor, Joe Gerhard," he continued. "There's been an incident on Level Two. Due to that, we'll be gathering no intercepts today. Break down your gear and equipment. Nonessential personnel, clear Level Two."

He clicked off his intercom. He thought for a moment before reaching out toward the intercom button again. After a brief pause, he turned it on.

"For those of you who don't know, yes, there's been a loss-of-life," he said, trying to keep his voice steady and dispassionate. "It's a sad day for our little family. I know you're all aware of the rules, but I'm gonna remind you anyway. You are not to contact the deceased's family without Company approval. No money, no cards, no phone calls. Wait 'til HR holds a staff-wide briefing on appropriate conversation topics. If you feel you must do something..."

He immediately regretted even starting that last sentence. The Company wouldn't allow anyone to do anything. Carson's employment records were sure to be scrubbed. There were rumors that during situations such as this, the Company hired actors to pretend to be the deceased's coworkers and supervisors. Those would be the people attending the funeral and paying house visits to the relatives. Joe didn't quite believe the Company went that far, but he did know that anyone who actually worked with Carson would be prohibited from communication.

After a long, expectant pause, he finally muttered into the microphone, "If you feel you must do something, say a prayer for him."

With that, he turned off his intercom again. Then he picked up his walkie-talkie. "I'm comin' down."

Joe pushed himself up from his desk and marched out of the room.

CHAPTER 3

Joe stepped out of his office and into the hallway of Level One. With the practice that came from putting out hundreds of fires over his ten-year career, he speed-walked with a briskness that never actually became a full jog. As the many posted signs on the beige walls explicitly said, running was forbidden.

Level One was the office level of the Facility where the white-collar members of the staff toiled. Or in Joe's case, the blue-collar workers who found themselves promoted to white-collar jobs; it was always easier to promote from within.

Bright fluorescent lights illuminated the hall from cages mounted to the ceiling. The bulbs, toned to a cool "daylight" temperature that was meant to invigorate workers by mimicking natural sunlight, fooled no one. The lack of windows and the hum of fans constantly recycling the air made it hard for any staffer to forget that they were several floors underground.

For all intents and purposes, it was a bunker — a concrete tomb buried in rock.

The place always had a strong scent of bleach that lingered from the nightly scrub-down. Joe's shoes, as fast as his feet were moving, squeaked against the sealed and spotless linoleum floor. With nothing to catch the sound, and every office door having to remain closed at all times, the squeaking of Joe's shoes bounced around the hall, making the place feel even emptier.

As he neared the elevator door at the end of the hall, he passed large posters hanging from the walls. They were designed in the style of classic World War II posters, the *"Loose Lips Sink Ships"* and *"We Can Do It!"* variety.

But these posters depicted modern people.

The messages were simple:

"Your Work Saves <u>Lives</u>."

"If You Wouldn't Tell Chairman Kim, Don't Tell <u>ANYONE</u>."

Joe blew past the posters. He had walked by them so many times over the years that his mind barely registered their existence or their message anymore.

He reached the elevator and swiped his ID on the console.

As Joe waited, his gaze fell on the final poster as it often did when he found himself waiting for the obnoxiously slow elevator.

The illustration simply depicted a woman and her daughter sitting at a dining table. They smiled as they ate their dinner. The text read, *"Do your job. Keep <u>them</u> safe."*

HQ had sent the poster for installation at about the same time that Joe was promoted to Facility Supervisor. He never thought much of it at the time despite the fact that he often found his eyes lingering on it. Then, at one point, he realized that the mother in the photo parted her long black hair down the middle only to have it curl back upwards around her shoulders. It was exactly the way Kate, his ex-wife, wore her hair.

The smiling child in the drawing was a complete tomboy, wearing her hair in a simple ponytail, exposing a joyful face full of freckles. Just like Joe's daughter, Riley. The little girl was the same age Riley had been when Joe accepted his promotion. That must have been ten years ago.

Before the divorce.

Joe often wondered if HQ had specifically commissioned that poster for *his* benefit. *His* eyes. To constantly remind Joe of the purpose of the Facility and the stakes of his job.

At first, the thought seemed absurd. But then Joe heard a story from one of his security officers who had been in the Air Force. The man told him that the onboard computer on most fighter planes knows when the plane is in an unrecoverable nosedive. It flashes warnings at the pilot to eject. But pilots are tough guys, the best of the best. Through overconfidence, or basic masculinity, the pilots believed that they could correct the dive and save the plane, often dying in the attempt.

The Air Force realized they were losing far too many pilots to crashes when they didn't have to. And so, they tried something new. When a plane began an unrecoverable dive, instead of a detached computer voice ordering the pilot to "EJECT! EJECT!" the pilot simply heard a pre-recorded little voice say, "Daddy... please eject."

The sound of their children broke through every tough-guy impulse. Pilots were suddenly willing to ditch their planes and save themselves.

That was the power of parenthood; the protective instincts overrode everything else. That's why Joe was certain that HQ had purposefully designed *this* poster for him specifically. And they placed it for him to see every... single... goddamn... day. A reminder that he needed to perform his job to keep his family at home safe.

And, without fail, whenever his eyes found a spare moment to gaze out at the poster, he felt a mix of joy and sadness.

DING!

The elevator doors opened and Joe stepped inside.

The elevator only had three buttons: Lobby, Level One, and Level Two.

He pressed the button for Level Two.

The doors closed, the gears spun, and the large service elevator descended even deeper beneath the ground.

After several seconds of journey, it coasted to a stop and the doors opened.

Joe stepped out into the Level Two corridor.

The holding chambers ran along both sides of the hallway, six to the left and six to the right. Each chamber had a door and a large observation window that looked into the room and its occupant.

The design of Level Two consisted of a bizarre amalgamation of a laboratory, a hospital, and a prison. With the large glass viewing walls, the level had been given the nickname "The Aquarium," much to Joe's displeasure. He didn't know why that particular nickname bothered him. Maybe he worried that comparing the valuable Antennas to some sort of freakish fish betrayed the importance of the work they performed here.

At the far end of the hallway, Joe glimpsed the armed guards and medical staffers clustered around the observation window of one of the cells.

With his well-practiced speed-walk, he made his way in that direction.

As he passed the various cells, he glanced to his left and right, checking in on each of the occupants. It was a force of habit. Anytime he walked this hall, he tried to take in as much visual input on the health and well-being of the Antennas as possible. He knew that behind his back, many staffers made fun of his peculiar head-swinging walk, but their giggles and imitations of "The Gerhard

Shuffle" was something he took in stride. He liked the example it set. Always be alert. Always be observing the Antennas.

His practiced glances revealed no abnormalities.

In each cell, the Antennas — all with shaved heads, hospital gowns, and protective mitts on their hands — lay on their floors, gently rolling from side to side.

Some barely moved. This was normal.

Some moved in furious bursts of clawing and kicking, like a mouse in its final death throes as a predator pins it to the floor. This was also normal.

Some of the Antennas moaned.

Some screamed.

Some spoke slurred gibberish.

Normal, normal, normal.

Hanging over each of the large observation windows were homemade signs. The flowery, ornate signs, with names carved into the wood in cursive, seemed more at home in the front yard of a third-grade teacher who enjoyed collecting bird houses.

The signs identified the occupant of each cell:

"Hello, my name is DIETRICH."

"Hello, my name is FROST."

"Hello, my name is VASQUEZ."

"Hello, my name is DRAKE."

Joe proceeded past them all and toward the cell at the end.

"Hello, my name is BISHOP."

The closer he got, the more apparent the carnage became. He stopped looking in on the other cells. The horror of the scene in Bishop's cell began to sink in.

The cells were lit by fluorescent lights that bounced off the white walls and white padded floors. It reflected through the large observation windows, making the hallway particularly bright, almost like daylight. Coming out of the elevator, Joe often found himself taking a moment to adjust to the brightness. Not that it bothered the Antennas; their eyes couldn't register light waves even if they stared directly at the sun long enough to burn out their retinas.

However, the light coming from the cell at the end of the hall was dimmer. It had a red tint, as if the sun had set in that room and that room only. It was the color of light reflecting off liters and liters of blood.

Joe passed the final few cells. He expected to hear the habitual hum of conversation from the gathered medical staff and guards, but mostly they were quietly staring in shock.

He slowed his walk and approached the group.

"We don't all need to be here, people," he said.

Everyone turned and faced him. No one disputed that point.

"Anyone who hasn't got a specific assignment from your department head needs to wrap up your business and get on back to Level One."

With heads nodding in agreement, and a few last sorrowful glances at Bishop's cell, the staffers migrated down the hall toward the elevator.

"Hustle it up, folks," Joe said as he lightly clapped his hands together.

As the staff always did, they obeyed. The pace quickened and everyone dutifully left the area.

Joe pulled out his walkie-talkie. "Control, this is Gerhard. I'm clearing out non-essential personnel from Level Two. From here on out, put the elevator on lockdown. No one comes to this level unless requested by me."

"Affirmative, Joe. Elevator locked until further notice."

The hallway had suddenly become so quiet that Joe could hear himself sigh. What a day. What a mess. What a waste.

With a deep breath, Joe took the final few long, leaden steps toward Bishop's cell's observation window. He stood there, taking in the sight.

Inside the cell, some of the orderlies tried to soak up the blood with towels. They mostly just smeared it around, though. Some of the guards performed a thorough examination of the door, windows, and restraints.

Bishop, meanwhile, lay in the corner — restrained and under watchful guard. She stared off while trying to move her bound legs and arms. Blood drenched her white gown. It had splattered on her face and clung between the short hairs of her shaved scalp.

Her hands and arms — tugging against her restraints as she swatted playfully — were dyed that same dull red. For a moment, Joe wondered why Bishop's nails were so long. They looked as though she had gotten a manicure; they were long and curved, like the fake nails at glitzy salons. Then the nails flapped as she waved her hand. Joe realized it wasn't her nails he was looking at but long strips of Carson's flesh that had become stuck and embedded onto her fingers.

The skin fluttered about with her movements, like flags at full-staff on a rolling ship.

Joe finally glanced to Carson's body in the center of the room. Carson lay face down. His entire back had been hollowed out. Bishop couldn't have emptied his torso any better if she had used a shovel.

One of the staffers firmly grasped Carson's shoulder and rolled him onto his side, revealing Carson's face to Joe. It surprised Joe that the face had no expression, just blank eyes. The muscles around the mouth and cheeks, which should have been pulled tight in fear and pain, were loose and relaxed.

Considering the condition of the rest of his body, the dumb-cow look on the man's face seemed almost comical. It didn't match the situation.

At least Carson didn't feel anything, Joe thought.

Except fear.

"Joe..."

The voice rattled him.

Dr. Hannah Chao sat on the floor in front of one of the neighboring cells, purposefully having positioned herself so she couldn't view the cleanup. She was in her forties, but the way she sat on the floor, tucking her knees to her chest, made her seem almost like a teenager.

As Joe looked at her, he realized that this was the first time he had ever seen her rattled. That made him feel better. If Hannah Fucking Chao, M.D. could be rattled, then Joe had permission to be rattled too.

He felt his spine immediately relax and his shoulders slump. The features on his face pulled their way down, and Joe suddenly realized the effort he had been exerting to maintain a neutral expression.

"Hiya, Hannah," he said softly.

On any other day of work at this busy, noisy place, the volume of those words would have been too quiet to penetrate the constant thrum of moans, screams, conversations, and equipment.

But today, they found their target. Hannah looked at him, and he looked back at her.

Their warm gaze seemed to hold an entire conversation, not of anything of substance, but a general, *What a fucking mess.*

"Sorry I was a dick to you on the radio," Hannah finally said.

"Oh, that's alright."

"No, it's not. Your staff shouldn't question your authority during a crisis. I was out of line. You were right and you handled things well."

He smiled at her. "I appreciate that. I really do. But honestly, you 'n me, we're fine. Ain't nothing to apologize for. Now, just tell me what happened."

Hannah shrugged. "I'll have to review the tape. Best I can tell, Carson didn't restrain her before administering her bed bath. I don't know why he'd shirk like that. He was in some sort of rush. I'll schedule a workshop with my team to stress the need to use restraints even when they don't think it's necessary, but... fuck... I dunno. I can't explain it. Unless it's an issue with the gas."

"I'll check with Tariq. But I'm pretty sure he'd notice if the levels were *that* off."

"Well, my report just might say, 'Orderly took a shortcut. Had bad fucking luck.'"

"Bad fucking luck." Joe stood quietly, shaking his head.

His walkie-talkie beeped. A guard's voice came through. "Everything in Chamber Two is secure. You can send in the stretcher team."

Joe clicked on his walkie-talkie. "Control, send down a stretcher team."

He stepped over and looked in the observation window at Bishop.

She was still restrained to the floor. Her eyes darted around in their sockets, zigging and zagging from end to end. Her teeth chattered and then suddenly snapped together, like an animal trying to snatch a bone from a handler.

Bishop looked very much like the other Antennas. From the shaved head, to the hospital gown, to the protective mitts. Her face, just like the others, had gone pale, maybe even a little jaundiced, from lack of sun and nutrition.

Joe stared at her.

"I think we may want to consider a full system reset," Hannah said.

"That's a big ask."

"There's something not right about this."

"HQ'll flip their shit," Joe said. "They can't stand to have us offline."

"You're the supervisor. Just do it."

Joe looked away from her. He didn't respond.

Hannah pulled herself off the floor and walked over to stand beside him. "There was no way that she should have known that Carson was there. She doesn't react to any somatosensory stimulation."

To prove her point, Hannah suddenly slapped her hand hard against the glass. The loud bang ricocheted around the hallway, making Joe flinch. But not a single muscle on Bishop twitched. If anything, the edges of her mouth pulled back, straightening out the sagging skin that hung from her cheeks and twisting her entire face into what could only be described as a grin.

Despite his conscious effort to never react to the weird faces and gestures the Antennas frequently made, Joe found his own mouth pulling itself into a disgusted grimace at the sight.

Hannah continued, "I examined her yesterday. I can poke her. I can shout at her. I can flash a light in her eye. She doesn't sense a thing."

They stood and looked at her for a moment.

"But if you saw her... if you watched her doing it... she *knew* she was killing him," Hannah said. "She was conscious of it."

"You really think so?"

"I don't know. But it's fucking weird."

Joe sighed. "I'll put in a request with HQ."

With that, he gave one last look to Bishop.

Then he turned and walked off back down the hallway.

He stepped to the side to let the stretcher team pass. His eyes lingered on that empty stretcher as it went by. It would soon be stacked with the remaining chunks of one of Joe's young staffers.

Bishop was probably still smiling, mumbling her gibberish to herself.

Joe turned and walked off, letting his head swing from side to side as he checked on the other Antennas.

Bad fucking day.

CHAPTER 4

Joe sat at his desk.

Video of the attack played on his computer in an unending loop. He hadn't eaten lunch. Now, having to continually watch a kid's organs get tossed around, he was probably going to skip dinner too.

As the video played and played and played, Joe wrote up his report of the incident, describing as many details as he could. He double-checked all the procedures and made note of which ones Carson had skipped. He watched the moment when Bishop grabbed Carson's gas mask again and again.

Did she know what she was doing?

Chuck in the Control Room had said that Carson was in the process of reporting something that seemed to have unnerved him. Moments later, the kid was dead.

Joe leaned in close.

He could see Carson bend down and listen to Bishop. Her head tilted away from the camera. Joe tried cranking up the sound, but her voice was too soft. All he heard was the hum of the ventilation system pumping Bishop's cell full of the specially-formulated, debilitating nerve gas.

What a weak fucking security camera.

For a high-tech installation that's sole purpose was to record each and every intercept the Antennas received, the actual security cameras and microphones were shittier than something Joe could get at Best Buy. Someone, somewhere, at some time must have shaved off a penny or two from the building costs for the Facility by choosing cheaper cameras.

Joe leaned in closer, his face just an inch from his screen.

What was she saying?

What had Carson heard?

And why did her head jerk suddenly, as though she realized that someone was eavesdropping?

Joe stared at the screen until the image became pixels.

RIIIIIING!

He jumped.

It was only his desk phone ringing.

He caught his breath and picked it up. "This is Gerhard."

"Hello, sir. I have a call coming in from an outside line. A Principal Green."

Joe checked his watch. He often lost track of whether it was day or night in this windowless cave of an office. He was surprised to see that it was still only afternoon.

"Put him through," he said.

Principal Green? Riley wasn't the type of kid who ever got in trouble.

The phone clicked as the call was transferred. "Principal Green, you're on with Mr. Gerhard," the front-desk guard announced to both of them.

"Hello, Mr. Gerhard. I'm, uh, calling about Riley."

The moment Joe heard the man's voice — that halting, stumbling, uncomfortable voice — he knew something was wrong.

"First, I just want to say how sorry I am," the principal continued. "Our sympathies go out to you and your family. District policy says that we can't dismiss Riley without her guardian's approval. I see here that you live two hours away. I was wondering if you've made any arrangements and if you could just fill us in on those."

"Arrangements? For what?"

"Oh, well, Riley has been sitting in our office since she was given the news..."

"What news?"

There was a long pause on the phone.

"The police haven't called you?"

"No. Should they?"

Another long silence. Joe could practically hear the principal's throat go dry on the other end.

"What's going on?" Joe asked.

"I, uh... well, we, uh, we got a call from the police..."

"And?"

"Well... they responded to a call to Riley's mother's house... Katherine Gerhard... or I see here she goes by Kate..."

The principal paused as he collected his words. It might have only been for half-a-second, but time didn't seem to be moving in the normal sense for Joe. Each breath, each pause, each delay allowed enough time for a hundred thousand thoughts to flood through Joe's brain.

"And?" Joe said again.

"She, uh, she had a gun. And the, uh, the details are hazy. I didn't get the complete story. So, don't quote me on any of this. You might want to contact the police. The officer who called us... his name was, uh... oh, I have it here..."

"*What happened?!?*"

"Your ex-wife shot herself. In the head."

Joe didn't move.

"She's, um, she's dead. Suicide. I'm so sorry to be the one to tell you this. It was, um, about two hours ago."

After all the thoughts and scenarios that had run through his brain just moments before, Joe somehow didn't have the computing power to process what had just been said. And so, Joe simply sat, the phone pressed firmly against his ear. All of the sweat that had been forming along his body turned an icy cold.

The principal seemed unnerved by the silence. "I thought they would have called you by now. That *is* your ex-wife, is that, um, is that right? Kate Gerhard?"

"Yeah," Joe said, his voice robotic.

"And you're Riley's biological father?"

"Uh-huh."

"Well, so Riley's been sitting in the school office since we found out. We don't want to send her back to that house now. There's no telling what she might see. And if she sees any reminders of her mother at this time... well, gee..."

Joe stared off. *Kate? Dead?*

"But you live so far away. And we're closing up shop here soon. Are there any other relatives that can come pick her up? Aunts? Uncles? Grandparents?"

"This here's what we're gonna do," Joe said. His voice found itself as his mind switched into work-mode. He'd handle this like any other problem he faced on a daily basis.

"Riley shouldn't be hanging out in some old high school office being comforted by secretaries and guidance counsellors and the like. She needs to be comfortable. Her best friend's name is Silvia

Vargas. I've met the family at all sorts of barbeques and birthday parties. Good folk."

Joe paused for a breath, then went on.

"Mrs. Vargas works from home. Call her up. I'm sure she'll put up no fuss if she's asked to come pick up Silvia and Riley. You have my full permission to send Riley home with the Vargases. The girls can hang out. It'll be the best environment for her. I'll get into Linville soon as I can, pick her up from the house. Sound like a plan?"

Principal Green seemed caught off-guard by the directness of Joe's statement. "That, um, that sounds like it'll work."

"Thank you for letting me know," Joe said.

Joe hung up his phone, not even waiting for a response.

He leaned back in his desk and stared at the bare concrete walls. The room spun slightly. His eyes struggled to focus. He didn't know if he should cry or even *could* cry. A numbness had settled into his bones and he struggled to will his muscles to move. Part of his brain, the logical part, recognized that he was in shock.

Kate was alive this morning.

She was alive when he picked Riley up last Friday and she was alive when he brought her back late Sunday night. *Very* late Sunday night. Kate had yelled at him. They fought on her doorstep. Like old times.

But just like that, with the suddenness of a two-minute phone call with a high-school principal... Kate was dead.

She had taken her own life.

Joe couldn't wrap his head around that.

That wasn't the kind of thing Kate would do.

He pushed himself up from his desk.

He walked to his office door. After a single step, he leaned over, grabbed his garbage can, and vomited.

***

Ding!

Joe stepped out of the elevator and into the Facility's lobby.

He was now above ground for the first time since he punched in at 7 a.m., but it sure didn't feel like it. The lobby, like every other area of the Facility, was windowless.

The lobby was relatively small, functioning solely as the elevator's guarded entrance and exit. The door that led to the outside world stood on the far side. To get there, one had to walk alongside long glass partitions that encased the guard booths. A dozen or more well-armed guards monitored both the lobby and the extensive security camera footage of the outside area.

The center of the lobby split into two paths — a metal detector/x-ray machine for all employees who were arriving and a similar set-up for all employees who were departing. Helpful footprints were painted on the concrete floor to act as a guide.

Joe swiped his ID card at a console. A screen mounted to the ceiling flashed his name — "JOSEPH GERHARD, CHECKING OUT: 17:32."

With a green light signaling him to proceed, he stepped into the x-ray machine. He spread his legs and raised his hands above his head. A scanner twirled around him, taking a 360-degree image.

An armed guard waved him through. "Good evening, sir. You're all clear."

"Thanks, Dave," Joe said as he nodded his head. He waved to the guys behind the glass wall as he passed, "G'night, boys."

They waved in response.

Joe walked up to a bank of lockers by the front door. He pressed his thumbprint onto a pad and a locker clicked open. Joe reached inside and pulled out his wallet, cell phone, and keys.

Then he walked to the door which unlocked with a *bzzzzz* as he approached.

He stepped outside.

The late afternoon sun made him squint. He wasn't used to leaving work this early, especially considering the situation that had just unfolded on Level Two. The evening frogs had begun croaking in chorus from wherever it was that they lived. Their belching mixed with the rustling of the wind stirring through the spring leaves. He could detect the sweet fragrance of blossoms on the air, as well as the rustic scent of grass that had grown tall during the winter rains and, now that late spring had arrived, had begun to dry into an earthy-smelling hay.

Moments like these reminded Joe how much he liked the location of his work. The smells and sounds reminded him of his summers in Boy Scout camps as a teen. Back then, he thought that he might like to become a professional scout leader, or maybe work for the Forest Service. He couldn't pinpoint the moment he veered away from those goals, other than the fact that such careers couldn't pay the bills.

With a sigh, Joe trudged his way to the parking lot.

The gravel of the unpaved path crunched beneath his feet.

The Facility wasn't much from the outside. Its above-ground portion looked like a concrete box in the woods, smaller than many single-family homes. Hills rolled off to either side of it, causing Hannah to once joke that they worked in the literal butt-crack of

West Virginia. About a football field's length to the south, atop one of those hills, rose an array of antennas and dishes.

If a foreign satellite were to take an image of the Facility — and they most certainly did — it would look like any number of similar listening stations or relay stations scattered throughout the globe. However, judging by the dozens of vehicles in the unpaved parking lot, they might surmise that this particular location housed something special.

Joe had actually once put in a request to obscure the number of employees at the Facility by constructing an underground parking lot, or at least by hanging canopies so the vehicles weren't visible to the world. (It was actually Hannah's idea because she didn't like her car getting too hot in the summer sun. Dust also tended to settle on the morning dew, making everyone's car perpetually filthy.)

The request sat in circulation for three years before someone at HQ quietly deleted it and sent Joe a standard reply: *Thank you for your idea. We will take it under advisement.*

That's how it went. It was impossible to get anyone in the Company's bureaucracy to sign off on new spending. Joe didn't know where the money for any of this came from, but he assumed that it was all secretly cobbled together from various branches of the military and government. A little from this pot. A little from that pot. To a degree, Joe understood that altering these streams of funding was a complicated affair, but come on, how hard would it be to install a canopy for the cars?

Joe climbed into his hot, sun-heated pickup and immediately turned on the A.C. He slipped it into reverse and pulled out of the lot.

Time to go get his daughter.

Joe usually enjoyed the drive to pick up or drop off Riley from her mother's house.

For most of it, the two-lane highway stayed nestled in a tall tunnel of oak trees. In the fall, the red and yellow leaves came down so thick that it was sometimes impossible to see the lines on the road. The highway did some switch-backs up the Allegheny Mountains. The view, whenever it managed to peek out from the tree line, became only more impressive as one ascended.

Near the summit, Joe passed the High Knob Trailhead.

As he often did when he passed it, he made a mental note that one day he should actually hike that trail. Maybe with Riley.

Riley.

What would he say to her?

What *could* he say to her?

He hadn't had time to really process this all for *himself.*

His truck reached the peak and then descended the Virginia side of the mountains.

The sun set behind him, throwing the long shadow of the Alleghenys onto the farmland below. Joe realized that it would be dark by the time he and Riley began their journey home. As much as he enjoyed the trip in the day, the road seemed long, twisty, and narrow the moment the light wasn't there to showcase the beauty of the area.

He didn't like driving in the dark.

But it was what he had to do whenever he dropped off or picked up Riley.

***

Joe pulled to a stop, climbed out, and walked up to the house of Riley's best friend, Silvia Vargas. He rang the bell.

A moment later, Silvia's mom answered.

"Uh, hey," Joe said, suddenly feeling uncomfortable. "I'm, uh—"

"Riley's father, yes I know," Mrs. Vargas said. She clutched a hand over her heart and her eyes teared up as she stared at Joe. "I am so, so sorry for your loss."

"Uh, thanks," Joe responded. It was all he could think to say.

"If you need anything..."

"I appreciate that."

"Anything at all."

Joe looked past her and into the house. "Um, can I see Riley?"

"Yes, yes, yes. Please, come in. You can keep your shoes on," Mrs. Vargas said as she stepped aside and waved Joe into the house.

Joe walked through the entryway and into the living room.

Facing away from him, two teenage girls sat on the couch and played some first-person shooter game. All those games looked the same to Joe. He never understood the appeal. But, then again, he just spent his afternoon surrounded by guys-with-guns and blood-and-guts; maybe that was why he never wanted to spend his free-time with more of the same.

He watched for a moment. Riley's dark hair was the exact same shade that her mother's had been when Joe first started dating her. Today, Riley's hair had been pulled back into dual braids that ran behind each ear. For the life of him, Joe had never been able to figure out how to do French braids like that. Kate was a pro at braiding hair, though. It was the one reason that she said she wanted a girl instead of a boy.

Riley always wore her hair like that for softball practice and games. It kept the hair out of her eyes. But now the braids frayed. Dozens of stray hairs escaped the rubber band.

A wave of sadness hit Joe.

His daughter must have woken up that morning and done her hair expecting for a normal day of school and softball. Between the moment when she did her hair and now, everything in her life had changed.

The girls didn't talk and didn't gesture wildly with their controllers. They seemed almost robotic as they moved their avatars around the screen, shooting at enemies. The volume was turned up loud. Excessively loud. Joe wasn't sure if the loud game was a legitimate excuse for why Riley didn't seem to be aware that he had arrived.

Or maybe she was purposefully ignoring him.

"Riley," Mrs. Vargas said. "Your dad is here."

Riley put down her controller. Immediately, bullets thudded into her character on the screen. She didn't seem to care.

Silvia paused the game.

Riley stood and looked at Joe.

He was surprised at how normal her face looked. The same beautiful, freckle-faced girl he always knew. Her eyes weren't red or teary, but there was an emptiness in her gaze, not too different from the empty face of her dead character on the screen. She seemed detached and drained, like she had just stepped off some long red-eye flight.

They looked at each other for, perhaps, a single second, but it felt much longer.

"Hey, Riles," Joe said.

"Sup, Dad."

Something about saying that word — "Dad" — seemed to unpin some emotional grenade in her. Her legs wobbled. Her mouth twisted into a mix of shock and complete despair. Before Joe knew it, he had his arms wrapped around his daughter, who suddenly felt smaller and more fragile than any teenager should feel.

She pressed her eyes into his shirt and sobbed.

Silvia and Mrs. Vargas stepped off to the side and silently left the room.

Joe guided his daughter to the couch.

They sat down together.

He held her as she cried.

CHAPTER 5

Riley stared out the window of her dad's pickup as they sailed past miles of rolling farmland.

They were going back to his place.

The sun had finally retreated behind the western hills, and the world clung to its last hour or so of blue, dusky light for the day. In the distance, Riley could make out shadowy black cows, ambling along as they munched on their evening grass.

They passed the occasional farm house and church, but Riley mostly kept her gaze focused on the powerline poles, zooming by one at a time. She sometimes marveled at the infrastructure in this country, how each of these poles was essentially a tree that had experienced decades of life, only to be cut down, soaked in some sort of resin, and then jammed in the ground to hold up maybe a hundred feet of cable. It was a lot of work to bring power and roads to everyone.

Why doesn't this country build big, ambitious shit like that anymore? she wondered.

She could feel her dad glance over at her from the driver's seat. She knew he wanted to say something, to reassure her somehow, but there wasn't much to be said. Besides, her dad was many things, but a comforter was not one of them.

At this particular moment, Riley wanted nothing more than to stare out the window and muse about the lifespan of telephone poles.

Anything else might make her cry.

She already felt a bit of shame that she had cried so hard in front of her father. Her father had always been so strong, so cool, so collected under pressure — and, yes, so detached emotionally — that Riley felt she had somehow betrayed him by shedding those tears.

"You wanna listen to music?" her dad asked, his voice cracking a bit in his attempts to soften it.

Riley shrugged. "Whatever. I don't care." She truly didn't.

He reached toward the radio but hesitated a moment, then he withdrew his hand. "We're, um, we're going to be heading into the Quiet Zone anyway," he said, almost apologetically.

"It's cool." Riley kept looking out the window.

What her dad said was true. Just over the West Virginian border was a vast area of restricted radio signals. Radio stations had to decrease their range. TV was practically impossible to receive over the old rabbit ears. It was one of the area's many secrets/not-secrets. It was the kind of bizarre intrusion that people shrugged away and accepted as part of life living near major NSA facilities and military installations. The residents of the small town near the Facility simply paid for cable TV and moved on with their lives.

"If you want to talk about anything...," he said, letting his voice trail off.

"It's cool," Riley said.

They sat quietly for another full mile or two of road.

Riley sensed her father's mind churning, trying to figure out something to say. At that moment, she wished that they *did* have music on because the quiet hum of the tires on concrete created an emptiness that her father somehow felt obligated to fill, even if neither of them wanted him to.

Pretty soon, she was sure that he'd start pointing out the trailheads as they passed and talking about how they should do a hike together. Then he'd veer off into some story about Boy Scouts and how he always wanted to be a forest ranger but had a job to do and a family to raise.

Her father didn't bring it up as some sort of intentional guilt trip. It was just the small talk that his mind circled around to on these long drives between Riley's two homes. She knew he wasn't allowed to talk about his work, not that Riley cared about his work even if he could have talked about it. He seemed proud of what he did, though. So, instead of talking about the job he had, he talked about the job he didn't have.

But Riley didn't want to talk. There was nothing to say. She simply wanted to stare out the window at the cows and fields and telephone poles.

Her dad cleared his throat. "I reckon that over the years, I mighta said some things about your mom that weren't very nice," he said in a steady, low voice that made Riley wonder if he had been hashing this little speech out in his mind during the past few miles. "But I respect the hell out of her and you should too."

Riley didn't have much to say to that. She wanted to come up with something more substantive than her standard "it's cool" response, but her brain was fried. As much as she searched for something to say, it just made her tired.

So, she glanced over at her father, nodded, and simply said, "It's cool."

She turned back to the window and stared out for a few quiet miles.

The road curved around to the right. The tree line began to thicken as they started a gentle ascent up into the hills. The world loomed darker up ahead as the trees blocked out the last moments of dusk.

Riley rested her head against the shoulder strap of her seat belt. Her eyes felt heavy and the emotional exhaustion of the day began to fully settle in.

She had a sudden twinge of a headache. It was an aching pain at first. The pain crept backwards, through her head, until she could feel the sharpness in the back of her neck. She reached back and massaged her shoulder muscles, momentarily wishing that one of the guys from school — Brian Holgate, perhaps — were here and she could flirt him into giving her a backrub.

The pain must be from stress, she figured. Had she been clenching her shoulders all day? Her mom used to sleep with a mouth guard to keep from grinding her teeth at night. Riley often worried if such weird, old-person, stress-avoiding bullshit was also in her future.

The saliva in her mouth suddenly turned thick and creamy. It tasted of metal. Or was it blood?

What was happening to her?

Maybe she was dehydrated. When did she last drink water? She didn't know. She couldn't remember. Perhaps she hadn't had anything to drink all day.

With that thought in her mind, she suddenly desperately wanted a drink of water.

She glanced over to the center console. No bottles there. Her dad might have some under his seat, but she didn't want to ask.

The dull ache sharpened into a knife of pain, stabbing behind both her eyes and at the base of her skull. A high-pitched tone then filled her ears. It was a constant whine, blocking out all other sounds.

As if someone had their hand on the volume control inside her head, that tone steadily became quieter and quieter. Before Riley knew it, all sound became a distant murmur, as if she were sitting at the bottom of a swimming pool.

While concentrating on her hearing and the pain in her head, she barely noticed that her hands had grown numb. She could no longer feel her fingers pressing into the knot on her shoulder. She couldn't feel her other arm resting on the pickup's door or the seatbelt pressing against her cheek.

Was this a heart-attack?

She shut her eyes.

Just as she was about to say something...

Click.

It all went away.

The numbness, the ringing, the pain in her head. The weird sensations had flown through her and subsided as quickly as they had arrived.

She pressed her thumb into her temples to try to recreate the pain, but nothing felt out of the ordinary. Whatever it was had passed on through and left. She hoped her dad didn't notice. The last thing she needed was for him to be all awkwardly concerned about her health.

Riley took a breath and then rested her head against the seatbelt again and stared out the window.

That's when she saw *her.*

The area didn't have streetlamps, and so it was only the headlights of her father's pickup truck that illuminated her.

A woman.

Standing alongside the road.

Her white hospital gown reflected the light from the headlights. Her long, black hair fell down past her shoulders. It was so straight, and seemingly oily, that the cars zooming by didn't blow enough air to move a single strand. That greasy black hair framed and accented a ghostly pale face. Unnaturally pale. It was as if this woman hadn't an ounce of blood flowing through her capillaries.

The woman stood straight but then began to twist at the waist. Her hands and arms shook and twitched. Despite the movements of her limbs, her gown remained perfectly still, incapable of catching the faint breeze.

Her head, meanwhile, swiveled on her neck and tracked the pickup as it sped past. Her eyes didn't move, didn't flutter, didn't focus in on anything. They simply stared straight at wherever her head and neck were pointing them. And, in this case, it was directly at Riley.

Riley jerked upright in her seat so fast that the seatbelt locked into place and forced her shoulder back.

"What is it?" her dad asked.

Riley loosened her seatbelt and spun her head around to look out the back window. She saw only darkness.

"You okay?" He looked over at her.

"You didn't see that?"

"What?"

She settled back into her seat. "Sorry... it's, um... it's nothing."

"What did you see?"

Riley rubbed her eyes. "I think it was a, like, a scarecrow. Or something. It was like a woman, but she didn't look real."

Her dad looked in the rearview mirror. "Weird. Didn't see it."

"It was creepy as fuck." Riley caught herself swearing. "Sorry."

"Don't worry 'bout it." He continued to glance at his rearview mirror. "Was it off in a field?"

"It was only like ten feet away. I swear, it was a woman just watching cars." Riley took a deep breath and shook her head. "Or maybe I'm seeing things. Maybe I'm fucked up."

A silence overtook the pickup. She regretted saying anything. She knew her father wouldn't know how to respond. She could practically hear the thoughts churning in his head.

"Riley..." he finally began.

"It's cool, Dad. I'm tired. I need to take a nap."

With that, she leaned back against the window and shut her eyes. He didn't say another word. He just kept on driving.

After a moment, when she was sure that her dad had stopped glancing over at her, she slowly opened her eyes again. She kept them glued out the window.

She suddenly didn't feel safe with her eyes closed.

CHAPTER 6

For the remainder of the trip, Riley drifted in and out of consciousness.

She finally awoke when she felt the pickup take the familiar sharp right onto the unmarked, gravel road.

Navigation apps could never properly locate the house. More than a few of Riley's childhood friends and their parents ended up circling the area for half an hour trying to find it. But that was back when Riley was really young.

After the divorce, Riley and her mom moved to Linville, a few hours away. Her parents promised her the distance wasn't too far, especially with social media. But to a middle-schooler, it quickly became insurmountable. Somewhere in a drawer back at her mom's home, she had a small box with a collection of half-heart friendship necklaces... and friendship rings... and friendship letters. They all promised the then seven-year-old Riley that her childhood friends would be her friends forever.

What a load of bullshit.

There was no one big, climactic moment that symbolized the end of the friendships. No fight, no jealousy, no nothing. Just a slow-drying cement around Riley's ankles that prevented her from putting forth the effort to bridge the growing gaps. She stopped inviting those old friends over, and no one seemed to mind.

These trips "home," and this turn down the long gravel driveway, no longer filled her with excitement and nostalgia. At this point, she simply considered the weekend trips to Dad's house as a break to escape the nagging tongue of her mother.

The thought then crept into Riley's mind that she had now *permanently* escaped the nagging tongue of her mother.

A massive lead balloon seemed to inflate in Riley's stomach. She tried to push it away.

The drive from the main road to the house was about a mile of gravel driveway. No one else lived off this street. There probably wasn't another house for miles.

Tall trees grew on all sides, completely tucking the house away from random eyes. Riley's mom had once flippantly commented that the trees made it difficult for satellites to see when Joe was home or not. When Riley, who was about twelve at the time, asked her father what that meant, his face turned cold and stern. He excused himself from dinner and went off to his office. She could hear him yelling over the phone at her mother, calling her all sorts of names.

That might have been the last time Riley ever dared ask her father a question related to his work or life.

The pickup finally migrated its way around one final bend in the road and came to a stop. Her father's house was an elegant, modern design, although not particularly large. Riley always took the house for granted until she and her mom moved into their dumpy two-bedroom starter — and finisher — home.

"I'll grab your backpack," her dad said. "You go settle in."

Without saying a word, Riley climbed out of the truck and ambled up the path to the front door.

"You got a key?" he called after her.

Riley gave a thumbs-up without even turning to face him.

She walked up to the door and put her key in the lock.

For some reason, she hesitated. She felt goosebumps on her arms despite the fact that it wasn't particularly cold out.

She glanced around at the woods. She had wandered these woods at night many times before, but she couldn't recall it ever seeming *this* dark. It felt as though a filter, some impossible-to-see membrane, had been placed over her eyes and was blocking out the texture of the world.

At that moment, she felt that something was out there in the woods. Something that she couldn't see. But it could see her. And it was watching her.

With a shiver, she turned the key in the lock, opened the door and—

A black Labrador burst from the shadows of the darkened house and scurried through the door. It whined in terror as it galloped past Riley and into the woods.

"Jesus! Goddamnit, Moby!" she screamed as the dog careened past the pickup and raced off into the trees.

Her dad ran up to her. "What happened?"

"I opened the door and Moby went ape-shit!"

"Did you step on her?"

"No! She just jumped out!"

"Was she greeting you?"

"No, she *jumped out!*"

"Are you sure she wasn't just greeting you?"

Riley glared at him. She hated the way he casually twisted conversations into interrogations, as if Riley were incapable of discerning events for herself. "She *never* greets me like that," Riley said, her voice hissing more than she intended.

Her dad stared out at the darkened woods and sighed, not even seeming to notice his daughter's annoyance. "I'll find her. You go settle in." With another sigh, he turned and plodded back down the driveway, calling out, "Moby! Moby! Here, girl!"

Riley took a moment to catch her breath.

Then she stepped inside the house.

An alarm pad had been chirping since Riley opened the door. It now chirped faster and louder. Even from a young age, Riley's parents had drilled into her how to deal with the house's extensive alarm system. She pivoted around and entered her personalized passcode into the system.

The chirping went quiet.

The flashing red light on the pad turned to green. A small LED screen on the alarm scrolled her name along with the date and time.

Riley glanced around the living room.

The lights were all off and the trees in the area were too thick for moon-light, but Riley knew the layout by heart. Her dad may have no design style, but he also wasn't one to leave a mess. There wouldn't be any tripping hazards.

She stepped across the darkened living room, past the department store coffee table and cheap (but nice-looking) leather couch that always stuck to her skin and squeaked when she moved — no matter whether or not she was sweaty — to the lamp by the hall.

When she flipped it on, the lamp's soft orange glow lit its small area of the room.

It wasn't much light, but it was enough.

Enough for Riley to see her.

She was just within view of the corner of Riley's eye. The light couldn't penetrate too deeply into the hallway, but Riley could see that white gown.

The woman stood there.

Silent. Unmoving.

Riley froze, hand on the lamp and eyes looking at the floor. Only her peripheral vision could see the woman. Riley couldn't bring herself to look fully, but she was sure that she wasn't alone. Thoughts pounded through her head as she stood with her hand on the lamp.

Do I look?

Do I scream?

Do I run?

Do I grab the lamp and swing it as a weapon?

Finally, she called out, "Uh, Dad? Did I leave my phone in the front seat?"

Without taking another breath, she turned her back on the hallway and, one quick step at a time, hurried from the house.

As soon as she emerged from the front door, her speed-walk transformed into a full sprint.

Her dad still paced up and down the driveway, calling into the forest, "Moby? Come on, Moby!" He turned as he saw the urgency with which Riley ran toward him.

"There's someone in the house," Riley said, her voice low and urgent.

For once, her father didn't question or doubt. His body went rigid as he fixed his eyes on the house. "Get in the truck," he said quietly.

No further urging was needed.

Riley ran to the passenger side, ripped open the door, and jumped in.

Her father wasn't far behind. He started the truck, kicked it into reverse, spun it around the driveway and zoomed off down the road.

She had never seen him drive so fast. Gravel shot out from under their spinning tires, clanging into the wheel-well. He took the final turn so aggressively that the truck skidded, and Riley feared they might even roll into a tree.

But he kept the pickup steady. He turned onto the main, paved road and kept his foot on the gas for a while longer. After another minute, he finally slowed and veered onto the shoulder, coming to a complete stop with the engine running.

He turned to Riley. "Alright, now, tell me what you saw."

"There... there was a woman."

"Where at?"

"In the hall. She was just standing there."

"She trip the alarm?"

Riley thought. "Uh, no? No."

"You sure?"

"Yes! I went in. It was doing its little warning beep. I entered the code. It stopped."

His eyes narrowed as he examined her. Riley could read the look on his face — he doubted her.

"You're *absolutely-positively sure* you saw someone in that hall?" he asked.

"Yes."

"Not just some reflection of light from the bathroom? Or some curtain, or something?"

Riley looked at him. Her gaze was firm. "I saw someone in the house."

He nodded. But he didn't make any other motions.

"Just call the police!" Riley said, her voice cracking a bit.

"My job's got certain protocols on how to handle situations like this. Once I make the call, I can't take it back. And so, tell me, are you one-hundred percent sure it wasn't some trick of light? It wasn't that you're tired? You saw someone *in* the house?"

Riley gulped. Her mind replayed the entire scene, everything she could trawl from her memory. She looked at her dad. "Yes."

His face stayed firm. "Well, okay then."

He pulled out his phone and dialed a number. Someone answered immediately.

"Tyler, it's Gerhard. 459, Code 2. My house."

***

At the base of the hill by the Facility, tucked away in the trees, stood a garage. The door of the garage rolled up. Two white, windowless vans pulled out.

They sped off down the road.

The vans rolled through town, honking loudly as they plowed through an intersection without slowing.

The locals knew enough to stop their cars and not ask questions.

The police knew enough to not interfere.

Within four minutes, the vans arrived at the turnoff to Joe's driveway.

They sped down the gravel road and screeched to a halt in front of his darkened home. The back and side doors of the vans opened and two teams of guards — dressed all in black and armed with submachine guns — streamed out in perfect military precision.

One team went through the front door.

The other looped around the sides.

CHAPTER 7

Riley looked out the window of her dad's truck as they rolled to a stop in front of the house. Portable floodlights lit the driveway and the nearby forest as armed guards patrolled the grounds. Every light in the house was on. More guards moved around inside. Riley could see them in the living room as they inspected every cabinet and checked behind every curtain.

One particularly large man, whose black uniform had no rank or insignia, approached the pickup and held the door open for her dad. Riley watched from the passenger seat as her father climbed out and warmly shook the man's hand.

"Whatcha got for me, Tyler?" her dad said to the large man.

Although Tyler stood ram-rod straight, he gave her dad a slight smile, his entire posture conveying both a respect for her dad's authority and a closeness to the man. "Building is clear. No signs of forced entry. We're combing the perimeter now. No footprints in the soft dirt surrounding the house. No suspicious vehicle tracks along the road."

Riley watched her dad's stance tighten and his face flush a bit. "I see," he said. He bit his lip, seemingly disappointed. Or embarrassed.

Riley glanced around. All the other men had stopped working and now kept their eyes on her dad and Tyler, awaiting their orders. Riley always suspected it, but now she knew — her dad was someone important.

"We dusted your computer. No prints, other than yours," Tyler said. "I checked the logs. Don't seem to be any strange logins or obvious signs of system penetration. I'd like to check your security camera feed, see if maybe it caught something."

Her dad stepped around Tyler and turned to stare at his house.

Riley looked too. There was a lot of movement, a lot of lights, and a lot of guns. And yet, the urgency seemed to have subsided in the actions of all the guards. At this point, it looked as though they were just going through the motions.

"What exactly did you see, sir?" Tyler asked.

Her dad let out a sigh.

He turned toward the pickup and motioned for Riley to come join him.

With a gulp, she slowly opened the door and stepped out.

It felt as though all the men ceased their movement, and everyone glued their eyes to her — the crazy girl who called the false alarm.

"My daughter's the one who saw it," he said.

She tried to walk up to his side, but he angled his body away to face her. *Everyone* was now facing her.

"Riley, this is Tyler Whitfield. He's our head of security."

Tyler gave her a friendly smile "Good evening, ma'am. Would you mind telling me what you saw?"

"I, uh, I saw a woman in the hallway."

"Mmm-hmmm. And can you describe this woman?" Tyler said as he took out a pad and pen, jotting down some notes.

Riley shifted her weight and looked at the ground. "Umm... uhhh..."

"Take your time," Tyler said, but the way his eyes stared at her made her feel as though she really didn't have much time to take.

"It was... it was... just a woman."

"And you're sure it was a woman?"

"I... I think."

"Ethnicity?"

"White? I think. Or maybe... Her face was kinda... it was dark in the hall."

"Okay." Tyler scribbled down notes. "Clothing?"

"It was like a, um, white dress. Or something."

Tyler's eyes flitted up and looked at her. "So, a person, possibly a female and possibly white, broke into the house and stood in the hall while wearing a white dress."

He was trying to keep his face neutral and pleasant, but she caught him glance over at her dad who responded with an apologetic shrug.

"That's, um... that's what I... I mean, I didn't really get a good look." Her arms went up and hugged herself. Her eyes drifted down, staring into the ground as her toe dug a little hole in the gravel. She wanted to make the hole deep enough to fall into and vanish.

The silent stares of the annoyed guards felt interminable, although it probably only lasted a few seconds. A few seconds of silent staring and judgment from a dozen large men with big guns. Her father finally stepped over and put his arm around her shoulder.

"I'm sorry, Tyler," he said. "She must've gotten spooked."

"No need to apologize, sir. Happens to the best of us. Besides, it's good practice for the real emergencies, ain't that right?"

"Thanks for understanding."

Tyler motioned Riley toward the front door of the house. "Let's give this little lady a walk-through. Put her mind at ease."

Riley forced a nod.

She followed behind Tyler as they all walked into the house.

They passed guards stationed at the door. The towering men watched her every step. She wanted to hold her head up high and meet their gaze defiantly, but her neck felt permanently bent downward at this point.

A heat seemed to flow up from her chest and settle behind her cheeks. Soon, she could also feel its fire emanating from her forehead and neck. She was sure her face glowed a bright crimson, but she tried to shut it down and keep her mind focused on her own slow-moving feet. *Don't trip on the front step. Don't trip on the front step*, she thought.

They stepped into the house.

Riley finally glanced up.

All the lights were on. The well-lit hallway was empty.

"Pack it up, boys," Tyler announced to the men.

They muttered to themselves as they stowed their gear and proceeded out the front door. Riley could hear various whispered comments—

False alarm.

What was that all about?

Kid thought she saw something.

Tyler had Riley stop in the middle of the living room. He pivoted around, pointing his hand to all 360 degrees of space. "Everything in order, ma'am?"

"Yes," Riley muttered.

Tyler strolled over to a curtain and peeled it back. "No monsters hiding behind here," he said. It wasn't intentionally patronizing; it seemed like the niceties of a man who couldn't tell that there was any sort of cognitive difference between a sixteen-year-old and a six-year-old. But Riley's face still burned with an embarrassment that quickly turned to frustration.

"It's cool. I take your word for it," she said.

"Better safe than sorry," Tyler said as he walked to the coat closet, opened it, and made a show of shining his flashlight around. He pushed the coats out of the way, leaving no inch unchecked. "Nothing in the closet."

"I'd like to just go to bed," Riley pleaded.

"Allow me to perform a walk-through first," Tyler said as he marched off down the hallway.

Riley looked over at her father. Her face pleaded with him to end this mortifying act. She tried to forcefully push the thought into his brain, *Please stop it. I fucked up, okay. You're killing me now.*

But he simply looked down on her with a sympathetic smile, as if he were going along with the charade because it seemed like the best way to put his daughter's fragile mind at ease.

"I'll go first," he said as he walked off down the hallway after Tyler.

Riley lingered in the living room.

"All clear," Tyler's voice announced from her bedroom.

With her head down and arms clutched together, Riley stomped off down the hall. She took a right turn and joined Tyler and her father in her bedroom.

AND THERE SHE WAS.

Riley's mouth hung open. She felt her face, which had been burning with embarrassment only moments before, suddenly turn cold. Her hands, wrapped around her chest and clutching herself, clenched tight. She wanted to scream, she wanted to run. But her muscles seized. Her legs and even her mouth felt like distant islands, too far away for the panicked messages that raced through her mind to reach.

THE WOMAN IN THE HOSPITAL GOWN STOOD BESIDE RILEY'S BED.

The woman's mouth stretched open, then closed. Open, then closed. It was like a fish gulping for air. Her eyes roamed around her head like two unmoored pinballs. The rest of her stood rigid.

Tyler walked past the woman.

He knelt to lift up the bed-skirt and take a look. "No monsters down here," he said.

Riley stared at the woman.

Did no one else really see her?

"Make sure the window's locked," her dad said.

Tyler got off the floor, walked past the woman again, peeled back the curtain and gave a tug on the window. "Window's locked. Alarm sensor is in place and responsive."

The woman's roaming eyes suddenly stabilized. They locked directly onto Riley. The woman's pupils focused. There was now no mistaking it — she was looking at Riley.

This woman *saw* Riley.

Her mouth continued twisting and stretching, but Riley now knew that the woman wasn't making involuntary, random movements. She was trying to get the muscles of her jaw and tongue aligned. She was trying to speak.

When the woman found the words, they escaped her lips in a whispered hiss. "I can't feel it," she said.

Riley just stared.

Meanwhile, her father and Tyler continued inspecting the room. Tyler walked over to the foot of the bed and opened Riley's closet. He shone his flashlight inside and slid some of the clothes around. "All clear," he announced.

Riley barely registered that he had spoken. Her eyes were now locked with the eyes of the woman.

"I can't feel it," the woman said again.

And then, the woman, whose body had been standing so perfectly still as to almost seem as though she were just some Halloween decoration suspended from the ceiling, lifted her hand.

She took her fingers and touched them to her own cheek.

"I can't feel it."

The fingers danced around her face, poking and prodding at her cheek, her chin, her nose. Her hand moved faster and faster as she pressed and dug her fingers harder into her face.

"I can't feel it!"

She flashed her fingernails and dug them deep into her own cheek, scraping out a chunk of flesh. Blood rushed to the slit she created on her pale face. It ran down her white cheek and splattered to the floor in a thick stream.

"I CAN'T FEEL IT!"

"I think we're all good here, sir," Tyler said.

"Thanks, Tyler. Sorry for the inconvenience."

"No inconvenience at all, sir."

The two men shook hands, oblivious to the woman beside the bed who was now clawing furiously at her face with both her hands. She was in a frenzy. Her fingers dug in and tore out large strips of flesh.

"I CAN'T FEEL IT! I CAN'T FEEL IT!" The woman's screams drowned out all other sounds.

Blood poured from her wounds. She was down to the tendons and the muscles, ripping and tunneling through her own cheeks like a rat through newspaper.

As suddenly as she began, the woman stopped.

She looked directly at Riley.

Her face hung in tattered shreds, but her voice became calm and clear with no hint of the slurring, hissing that had enveloped it before. "What have they done to me?"

Riley could only shake her head. It was a movement so slight that no one noticed.

"What do they want from me?" the woman asked.

Riley stood petrified. No answer.

"Why can't I feel it?" the woman's voice rose. She was getting worked up. She held her bloody hands out, reaching toward Riley. "WHY WON'T THEY LET ME DIE?"

The woman shrieked out a horrific scream of anguish and anger as she seemed to fly across the room, lunging at Riley.

The suddenness of the movement rattled Riley from her frozen, terrified state. She didn't have the strength to bring herself to scream and instead released a quick gasp and raised her hands to protect her face as she stumbled backwards. She tried to run, to get away, to put distance between herself and the bleeding banshee.

The horrible scream echoed around Riley's head.

Riley's feet tangled, unsure if they wanted to turn and run or continue stumbling backwards. They twisted among themselves and locked up. Her body weight carried her a bit further, and soon she toppled.

She felt herself falling in slow motion, like in a nightmare.

She tried to tell her feet to keep running and carry her away, but they didn't respond. She tried to tell her arms to get underneath her and catch her fall, but they also didn't respond. A million miniscule muscle corrections flashed from her brain down throughout her body, but nothing could stop her downward momentum.

Despite all the thoughts running through her conscious and subconscious mind, the scream penetrated it all. It was all she could hear as she toppled to the floor.

WHUMP!

The moment she landed hard on her butt in the hallway...

Silence.

The screams were gone.

Riley sat on the floor, looking around the hall. Her eyes darted back and forth. Her breaths were sharp and fast. The woman wasn't there.

Her father and Tyler rushed to her side.

"You okay?" her dad asked, crouching down to face her.

"You didn't see anything?" Riley asked.

"In the room?"

Riley nodded her head vigorously.

Her dad's brow furrowed as he studied Riley for a moment. Then he glanced up at Tyler who stood in the doorway to the bedroom. Tyler's massive stature filled the doorframe. If there was a threat, *this* man was sure to be the first to confront it.

Tyler maintained his poker face, taking everything about this situation seriously. "Empty, ma'am. Your bedroom is clear."

Riley gulped. She craned her neck to peek through Tyler's legs and into her room. She leaned slowly, ready to bolt to her feet and scamper away.

Bit by bit, inch by agonizingly slow inch, the room revealed itself to Riley.

Empty.

No woman. No blood. No nothing.

Riley blinked, not sure what to believe.

"Did you hit your head?" her dad asked.

"No, no," Riley gasped out.

She leaned back against the wall, closed her eyes, and lowered her head into her hands. She sat there quietly, taking deep, calming breaths.

"Let's call it a night, Tyler," she heard her dad say.

"Yes, sir. No shame in a false alarm." Tyler paused and knelt beside her. "Ms. Riley, ma'am? It's really okay. Nothing to be embarrassed about. This is our job and we're blessed to do it. Now, you need anything else — you get spooked, you get scared, whatever — don't you dare hesitate to call for help again. It's what we're here for. Worst thing that can come of a false alarm is when they make people stop raising the real ones." He tipped his hat to Riley. "You have a wonderful evening, ma'am. Get some rest."

"Thank you, Tyler," her dad said.

The two men walked off down the hall together.

Riley kept her head buried in her hands.

Even as they crossed through the living room and approached the front door, she could still hear their parting conversation.

"Is she... okay?" she heard Tyler say.

"She had a stressful day. Something happened to her mom."

"Oh, well, I'm sorry to hear that, sir."

"Thank you. It's... it's a bit of a mess. I might be taking some time off. Sortin' everything out."

"We'll all cover for you, sir," Tyler said. "I'm sure we can keep your machine well-greased and churning."

"I appreciate that, pal."

They bid goodnight.

Then her dad closed and locked the door.

Riley hadn't moved from her spot on the hallway floor.

She could hear her dad slowly walk over to her. And then, with a stiff bend of his aging knees, he plopped down beside her. He hesitated there, fidgeting slightly. Finally, he extended his hand and awkwardly place his arm around her shoulder.

"How you feelin'?" he asked.

She looked up, but not at him. Instead, she simply craned her neck and stared into her room. Her mind raced to piece together just exactly what the fuck was happening to her. She took a deep breath and suddenly felt calmer. No tears, no trembles.

"I think I'm fucked up," she said, her voice remaining level.

Her dad patted her back. It was a little too firm and forceful, like a robot petting a dog. He opened his mouth a few times, trying to think of just the right words to say. He cleared his throat. Finally, he said, "It's not your fault. None of this is your fault."

"I saw someone. It wasn't light reflecting, or a curtain moving, or some stupid shit like that. I saw *her*."

"Get a little sleep. You'll be fine," he said.

Riley stared off. She had been spending the past few minutes desperately trying to block the image from her mind, but now she tried to grasp the memory in all its excruciating detail.

"She... she had black hair. Down to her shoulders," Riley said. "She was very pale. It... it wasn't a dress she had on... it was more like a hospital gown. She was, um..." Riley gulped, disturbed by the memory. "She was digging her fingers into her face. She was scraping off her skin."

Her dad withdrew his hand and stared at her.

"She kept screaming," Riley continued. "'*I can't feel it... I can't feel it...*' Over and over, she kept screaming that."

They sat quietly. Finally, he said, "Riles, the day you've had would mess with anyone."

He leaned over and kissed her head.

Then, with a little bit of effort, he pushed himself off the floor and rose to his feet.

"You wanna sleep in my room?" he asked. "Or we could both sleep in the living room. Have us a little campout, like we used to do when you were young."

"No."

She pushed herself off the floor. Her dad hung around, watching her. It made her uncomfortable, as though every action of hers at this point was part of a psychological evaluation. Trying to act calm (and sane), she took a cautious step to her bedroom door. She bent her head around the door frame and looked in.

The light was on, the room was well-lit, and she was alone.

"I'm okay," she said to her dad, trying to sound casual, but not taking her eyes off the empty room. "Go to bed."

He lingered for a bit, then shuffled off.

Riley stepped into her bedroom.

She crawled into bed but stayed above the covers. Her eyelids felt heavy, though she couldn't bring herself to shut them. So, instead, she stiffly lay on her bed, her head propped up against the headboard, allowing her eyes to dart from one end of the room to the other. If the woman returned, the one thing Riley couldn't bear was to be surprised.

She considered changing into pajamas, but she didn't want that moment of vulnerability when she would have to pull her shirt over her eyes. What would be waiting for her in that split second of blocked vision?

She certainly couldn't *shower* for the same reason.

And sleep was definitely not an option.

So, she determined she would stay on guard for as long as she could.

Her eyes jumped from her dresser, to her closet, to the wall, to beside her bed, to the dresser, to the closet, to the wall, to beside her bed, to the...

***

Joe stepped into his bedroom and locked the door.

He went to his computer. He was tired, and he hated logging in at this late hour. The login system was so arduous. It required passwords, security questions, a PIN sent directly to the user's cell-phone...

But he had to know.

He had to see what had happened for himself.

When his computer unlocked and loaded up, he opened his home security system. He didn't have a camera in Riley's room; he had fought the consultants tooth-and-nail to *not* put one there. Her bedroom and the bathroom were off-limits. At the time, they assured him that the system was a closed loop that only he could access, but he had an inkling that the feed was beamed elsewhere. He refused to subject his young daughter to that sort of observation.

So, he loaded up the video of Riley arriving at the house.

There was a fish-eye view from the living room ceiling. Riley never knew that a secret camera existed behind that recessed lightbulb.

The video showed — in clear night-vision — Riley step into the house and enter her passcode on the alarm. Then she walked across the living room toward the lamp by the couch.

As the lamp clicked on, Riley clearly tensed. Her entire body language angled defensively toward the hall. It was abundantly apparent that, at that precise moment, his daughter saw *something*.

Joe paused the video.

He clicked around to another feed — a wide-angle of the hallway itself.

The act of turning on the lamp had caught the camera in a transition between night vision and regular vision. The screen had washed out with a white blur. And yet... a strange shadow hovered in the dimly lit hall.

Joe leaned toward the screen.

He advanced the video, one frame at a time...

As the camera adjusted to the light, the shadow vanished.

Nothing there.

His finger clicked at the left-arrow on the keyboard, scrolling the video backward, frame-by-frame.

Still nothing. A trick of light.

He nodded, content.

With a weary sigh, he turned off his computer and crawled into bed. He'd deal with this tomorrow.

CHAPTER 8

Joe didn't have a good night's sleep.

He had crawled into bed soon after checking the security cameras but never did relax. Ordinarily, he conquered his sleepless nights, and they were many, by pulling out a book and reading until he dozed off. But when he tried at 2 a.m., his mind kept wandering.

After he found himself reading the same paragraph three times, and the words *still* didn't enter his brain on any cognitive level, he finally gave up and resigned himself to a bad night.

As he drifted in and out of consciousness, he thought he heard a rustling in the house. A kitchen drawer opening. A door closing softly. But the sounds never continued, and he wasn't sure he actually heard them.

Every time sleep seemed to almost take hold, his mind would dredge up Kate's face. All he knew was what Riley's principal had told him. Suicide by gunshot. And so, that's what he saw when he closed his eyes — half his ex-wife's face, torn apart from where a bullet entered one temple and burst through the other.

Did she do it in the living room?

In the backyard?

In her bed?

His mind raced through all the possible locations Kate might have blown apart her head. He pushed those thoughts out. Instead, he thought about Christmas. Camping trips. Their big family road trip down the east coast all the way to Disney World.

Good moments. Good memories.

But then there were the fights. The sniping. The pettiness.

No, it wasn't *his* fault. These things happen. He had been a good father, even after Kate took Riley away. He gave Riley anything she ever wanted. If Riley was now having psychological trauma from her mother's suicide — and Joe was certain she was — it wasn't his fault, it was Kate's. She had hurt their child and left him to pick up the pieces.

He wasn't sure when exactly, but at some point he had drifted off into a sleep so deep that it was if his consciousness were a lead ball that had been dropped into the ocean. Down it sank into silent darkness. No dreams. No light. No thoughts nibbling at his brain. It was a sleep that was not refreshing or invigorating; it was a sleep that encompassed pure nothingness.

BZZZZZZZ!

Joe's vibrating phone, clattering on his nightstand, shocked him awake.

Morning light filtered through his blinds.

He picked up his phone and tried to purge the grogginess from his system as he answered with a forceful, "This is Gerhard."

"Joe, it's Hannah," came the familiar voice on the other end. He could hear her shoes squeaking and echoing on the hallway floor in Level One. As was typical, Hannah was probably walking with a purpose. "Did you put in for a week of personal time?"

"Well, yeah. I got some stuff I gotta take care of."

"I totally get it. But just know, you picked a bad time."

"Yeah, yeah. I'll finish that report on the incident sometime this morning. If anyone's got any questions, I'm on my cell—"

"HQ is sending an investigator."

Joe sat upright in bed. Any lingering effects from his poor night's sleep immediately vanished. "What? Who?"

"Javier Aguirre. Tyler mentioned it to me when I clocked in."

"Shit." Joe jumped out of bed and went to his closet. He began digging out clothes for the day.

"Look, I just thought you'd want to know. Also..." Hannah took a long pause. "Tyler mentioned that something happened to Kate."

"He *told* you?"

"We're friends."

"No offense, but this ain't your business, Hannah."

"It kinda is."

Joe had no response, and so he quietly dressed himself while cradling the phone to his ear.

"I... I'm really sorry about Kate. If you want to talk about it..."

"I don't."

"Fair enough. But you know I love Riley. I only told you Aguirre is coming because I knew you'd shit yourself if I didn't. But Riley should be your top priority. The rest of us can handle Aguirre. It was just a freak accident. That's all his report will say because it's the truth. No one will blame you or your leadership."

"Is he there already?" Joe asked as he pulled on his nicest, whitest dress shirt. He was usually a polo and khaki kind of supervisor, but a visit from Javier Aguirre probably called for a tie.

Hannah sighed, seemingly resigned to the fact that everything she had just said was going to be ignored. "Scheduled to arrive at nine."

"I'll be there."

"Joe, I really think you should stay with Riley."

"See you soon."

He hung up before she could get another word in. He grabbed a simple black tie from his closet and held it up against his shirt. He looked like some 1960s NASA engineer. Whatever. He figured it was the look he was going for anyway.

The moment he opened his door, the smell of coffee wafted in. Riley must be awake.

He walked down the hall to the living room then peeked through the door and into the dining room and kitchen.

It was a beautiful, sunny day outside, and the sun lit up the lush green forest beyond the kitchen's large picture windows. The house, which had been so dark and gloomy the night before, had been transformed into a forested paradise. The white stone counters and stainless-steel appliances sparkled and reflected back the daytime sun. It was a kitchen straight out of a commercial; seeing it during the daylight always made Joe regret that he worked too much to ever be able to enjoy such a room.

Joe looked around. The coffee pot was maybe four-fifths empty. He stepped through the dining room doorway and walked toward it.

And then he saw his daughter.

Riley sat in a chair in the far corner of the kitchen, staring out the window. She brought her cup of coffee to her lips and took a sip. She looked over at him as he approached.

"You're up?" he asked.

"Couldn't sleep."

"That's two of us. How you feelin'?"

"Fine," she said. She took another long sip of coffee.

"I gotta go into the office and tidy up a few things. Should be a short day. You gonna be okay if I leave you alone a few hours?"

"I'm fine."

"You sure?"

"I'm sorry I embarrassed you last night."

"You didn't embarrass me." He shifted on his feet uneasily. "So, um... ya see anything else?"

"No. Nothing. I just... I don't know what happened. I'd rather not talk about it." She looked down at her coffee.

Joe nodded. He pulled out his wallet and laid a hundred dollars on the counter. "Go on and order a pizza if you get hungry. Maybe get out to a movie, if you want. Whatever you need to do for yourself. Just shoot me a text where you are. I'll try to be home soon as I can."

"Cool."

He began walking to the door but paused and turned back. He looked at her, sitting there all by herself.

"I love you," he said.

"Too."

With a little wave, he turned and walked out.

CHAPTER 9

Joe parked his pickup at the Facility.

It was 9:15.

Mr. Aguirre was probably already there, beginning his review process. Joe wanted to run, but he felt the perspiration building in his armpits and along his spine. Sweat was a bad look on any supervisor, and Joe knew his would only get worse as the day progressed in the recirculated air of his office.

And so, he forced himself to take a calm, leisurely stroll from the parking lot to the entrance. He kept his breathing flat and tried to convince his heart rate to do the same.

It was a beautiful day. Sunny, but cool.

The morning dew evaporated from the leaves and grass. The dampness combining with the sunlight always had a way of making the scents of the forest bloom. It was the smell of earthy decay. Not rotten, pungent decay, but a natural cycle-of-life aroma. At times like this, Joe found himself transported to his youth, tromping through the forest, back when the world was a safe place.

The slow walk calmed him. As he swiped his ID on the pad by the entrance, he felt ready to face the day.

And face the inspector — Javier Aguirre.

Upon entering the Facility, Joe underwent his normal routine: He placed his phone, keys and wallet in a locker and scanned his ID. Then he went into the body scanner and held up his hands as the machine whirled around him.

The guards on duty, despite their weapons held ready, smiled and nodded at him as he waited for the scan to complete.

"Morning, Joe," one of them said.

Joe gave the man a little wink. "Should probably call me 'Gerhard' or 'supervisor' or something all formal while we're under inspection. Gotta keep it buttoned-up around here."

"You're all clear, Supervisor Gerhard, sir," the man said with a smirk as he waved Joe through.

Joe walked toward the elevator.

Beside the elevator, at one final security station, was a glass booth. Inside, Tyler eyed an array of monitors.

Joe rapped his knuckles on the glass.

Tyler rose and slid open a little window in the booth. "G' morning, sir. Mr. Aguirre is waiting in your office."

"Sleep well?"

"Yes, sir. Very well."

Joe kept a pleasant smile on his face as he leaned toward Tyler's window and lowered his voice. Tyler also angled his face toward the hushed (but not trying to seem hushed) conversation.

"Did you file a report about that thing that happened at my house last night?"

"Not yet, sir."

Joe looked around. No one was listening. "We're under some scrutiny 'cause of yesterday's accident here. What's going on with my daughter is a personal matter. I don't want the loss of her mother to get wrapped up in this whole mess, if it can be helped. I'm not saying do anything against the rules. I just think it'd be smart for us to focus our attention on issues *inside* the Facility. Catch my drift?"

Tyler gave him a sly wink. "I'll be too busy to file that report for a few days," he said. "At least."

"Take your time," Joe said. "And, obviously, I'd prefer you not mention it to any of the staff. Other than Hannah, of course."

"Of course. Your elevator is ready, sir," Tyler said as he hit a button. The elevator door opened.

Joe stepped in.

He rode down to Level One.

As he stepped off, he glanced at the poster of the woman and little girl joyfully eating dinner.

"Do your job. Keep them safe."

He marched on, his shoes squeaking on the clean linoleum.

Upon reaching his office, he rested his hand on the door handle and allowed himself a deep, calming breath. Then, he forced a big, friendly smile, opened the door and stepped in.

Javier Aguirre sat at the guest chair in front of Joe's desk. He was in his fifties. Bald, bespectacled, and a little on the heavy side. The man looked like a mole, which Joe felt suited him because so much of their work was underground. It wasn't as though the man was physically intimidating. He was more of an accountant. Exacting, meticulous, always focused on the tiniest of details.

And that, of course, worried Joe all the more. From Joe's experience, when an accountant *wants* to find something wrong — or someone to blame — they'll generally find it. Or they'll keep digging until they do.

Right now, Mr. Aguirre stared over the rims of his glasses at the tablet in his hand. He had the video of Bishop's attack loaded up and, with his finger sliding the status bar back and forth, ran the incident forward and backward.

On the screen, Bishop forcibly ripped a chunk of the man's vertebra out through his back and tossed it aside. Then she went back in for more.

Mr. Aguirre watched, so entranced that he didn't notice that Joe had walked into the office. The man's features betrayed no emotion toward the scene. No disgust or sadness. Just an impartial fascination, as if he were observing a spreadsheet whose columns didn't quite add up to the expected value.

He replayed the video.

Forward.

Backward.

Again, and again.

Joe stood for a moment before deciding to announce his presence. "Javi!" he said in as friendly and excited a tone as fit an office environment.

Mr. Aguirre paused the video, set down his tablet, and rose, a big smile on his face. "Hey, Joe. Good to see you."

The two men grasped hands with a firm, collegial handshake.

"I heard you might not be in today," Mr. Aguirre said.

"Yeah. I have some personal things going on, but they can all be put on hold for a bit," Joe said as he stepped around Mr. Aguirre to his desk.

The two men sat.

"I'm sorry about Katherine," Mr. Aguirre said. His tone seemed to indicate that he was sincere.

Joe raised an eyebrow. "Wow. Ain't no secret safe from you boys?"

Mr. Aguirre flashed a little grin that seemed to say, *That's right, no secret is safe.*

"I appreciate it," Joe continued. "It kinda all came down on me yesterday. I still got a lot to sort out."

"If you need some time..."

"I'll manage."

Mr. Aguirre looked down at his tablet. He opened some files and swiped around, searching for something. "You have a daughter, correct? Riley Gerhard?" he asked.

"Yep."

"And how old is she now?"

Joe tried to maintain his pleasant smile, but he felt the muscles and tendons in his face become strained. His posture stiffened. His hands, resting on his desk, sought out each other and formed a tight steeple. He knew Mr. Aguirre wasn't making pleasant conversation. "Sixteen now. Seventeen in August."

"Riley lived almost exclusively with her mother, isn't that right?" Mr. Aguirre asked as he opened a file on the tablet and began tapping in notes.

"Yeah, that's right. They moved out about ten years ago. Right after the divorce."

"I see Riley has grandparents nearby. On her mother's side."

"Yes."

"Will she be living with them?"

Joe's stiff smile vanished. "That wasn't my plan. They're getting on in age. And I *am* her father, after all."

Mr. Aguirre smiled. "Of course, of course. She'll be living with you full-time then?"

"Until she goes to college."

"I see."

Joe watched as Mr. Aguirre tapped away, quietly entering in more notes. The typing went on longer than Joe expected. The man wasn't just putting checkmarks in a few boxes; Mr. Aguirre appeared to be composing a full memo.

Joe forced himself to lean back in his chair and cross his legs, giving the appearance of nonchalance. "Yeah, I just picked her up yesterday. Really sad thing. So sudden. Far as I know, Kate didn't have any history of depression or nothing. But what do I know? I'm just the ex. Something must've been bubbling under the surface. But Riley seems to be handling it well."

"Good." Mr. Aguirre kept writing his memo.

"This all *just* happened. Still sorting it out. I haven't been able to update my Personal Life Status Profile yet—"

"I completely understand. I'm doing it for you."

"Thanks," Joe said, eyeing Aguirre as the man kept typing. "Riley, um, she stayed with me, at that house, every other weekend for the past ten years. She's been vetted and cleared as a non-security risk."

"It looks like we last cleared her—" Mr. Aguirre paused as he searched around for Riley's profile. "—five years ago. If she's living with you permanently, we should run a new check on her. She's probably due for one anyway. Kids today... You know how fast they change, what with social media and all that. Better to be safe than sorry. Might be time for a psychological evaluation too. Things like depression can be hereditary. Wouldn't want to put anything at risk."

Joe couldn't stop the glare from forming on his face. "That really necessary?"

"Is there a problem?" Mr. Aguirre asked, his eyes innocently twinkling from behind his glasses.

"I just don't want some intern thumbing through my daughter's phone and internet history. Let alone her med records."

"You think she might have sent some pictures or emails that might open her up to blackmail?" Mr. Aguirre asked innocently.

"She's a teenage girl. I'd be more worried if she *didn't*."

Mr. Aguirre let out a little chuckle. It lasted a moment too long, like a machine learning when to laugh. "Fear not, Joe. It's all done by algorithm. A human will only be brought in to review any red flags that arise during the normal course of a data scan. Riley won't even know the process happened."

"How comforting," Joe said. He nibbled on his lip as his eyes studied Mr. Aguirre who blithely tapped more notes into the tablet. He tried to speak casually. "It's actually fortunate you're here. There was one thing I wanted to clear with you."

"Yes?" Mr. Aguirre looked up.

"This thing with her mom has been very traumatic for her. In my duty as a father, I feel it would be best if I took her in for some grief counseling. Just as a precaution."

Mr. Aguirre's eyes narrowed. Despite the warmth of his voice, his face was serious. "Of course. You don't want those kinds of emotions being suppressed and allowed to fester."

"But if she's seeing a shrink, that might be enough to red-flag her. Now, you and I know that it's a natural response to a mother's suicide. But I don't trust the algorithm or them boys back at HQ to necessarily see it that way. The last thing we need 'round here is for someone to blow up a common-sense approach to a tragedy and turn it into more red tape, restrictions, and oversight. It'll just slow down what we do. You understand, right?"

Mr. Aguirre smiled. "It'll be fine, Joe. We're not monsters. We have families. We all need time to heal. Just make sure your grief counsellor is from one of our approved lists. As long as Riley isn't showing any extreme signs of psychological stress — anything that might make her erratic or unpredictable — then I don't foresee this resulting in a red flag. And we'd be perfectly happy to allow you and Riley to live together."

The two men stared at each other, letting those last words linger. Their implication was obvious — the Company didn't *have* to allow them to live together.

Joe had to unclench his jaw in order to force a smile. "I think we understand each other."

"Good," Mr. Aguirre said. "Now, on to business."

He quickly changed gears, dropping his threatening smile and replacing it with a genuine one. He had suddenly become more friend than foe as he turned off his tablet and leaned forward.

"With regards to this investigation, I want you to know that no facility has done more for the Company, or for national security, than yours," Mr. Aguirre said.

His voice sounded genuine, although Joe could never quite tell with him.

"We never worry about you guys," Mr. Aguirre continued. "You perform your duties on time, you do it cleanly, and, quite frankly, you provide some of the best, clearest intercepts we could hope for. Our clients always tell me that. Your team has saved lives. You've defended this country admirably, and you should be very proud of your work."

"I appreciate that. I'm sure my whole team does."

"So, I don't want you to view this investigation as a threat—"

"No, no, no. I get it. If someone accidentally watched a YouTube video from a networked computer, you guys would launch an investigation. It makes sense. And, of course, yesterday, a man died—"

"I'm more concerned with the welfare of the Antenna," Mr. Aguirre said.

"Same here. In any case, an accident occurred. We need to make sure the ship is straight. That my team is firing on all cylinders."

Mr. Aguirre nodded. "Precisely."

Joe stood from his desk and motioned toward his door. "So, let's get started."

CHAPTER 10

Ding!

The elevator doors opened. Joe held it with one hand as he extended his other to guide Mr. Aguirre out onto Level Two.

The man stepped out and stood there, squinting a bit in the bright fluorescent light as he took in the scene. Joe stepped out and stood beside him. He glanced over at Mr. Aguirre's face, trying to gauge his mood and reaction.

But Mr. Aguirre's eyes betrayed nothing of his internal thoughts. Instead, he stood quietly, taking it all in and scanning every minute detail without wanting or needing input from Joe.

For his part, Joe also looked around at the various chambers and the Antennas within them who moaned and screamed from their padded floors. He allowed himself a relieved breath upon seeing that his ship appeared to be in optimal shape. His staff went about their business with quiet efficiency. Medical teams and orderlies migrated from chamber to chamber, checking vitals and administering sponge baths exactly as the guidelines dictated.

Inspections like today's always had Joe wound up tight. His mind wandered to worst-case scenarios. He could just envision those elevator doors sliding open and Mr. Aguirre stepping into some discarded diaper. Or maybe an Antenna would be loose and wandering the halls.

But, as always, his team didn't let him down. They never did.

Mr. Aguirre took it all in, seeming neither pleased nor displeased. Non-reaction was always a good sign from a man like this, Joe felt.

He waited for Mr. Aguirre to make a few notes on his tablet. They were quick notes, just checking some boxes. He wasn't writing out anything in detail. Also a good sign.

"It was the cell at the end of the hall, correct? Antenna-201?" Mr. Aguirre asked.

"That's right."

Mr. Aguirre nodded. He began his slow stroll down the hall, glancing through the large glass viewing-windows at the first two Antennas he passed.

"Do you believe it was intentional?" he asked.

"What do you mean?"

"The attack. Do you believe Antenna-201 *purposefully* set out to hurt or kill Mr. Phillips?"

"She can't see, she can't hear, she didn't even know he was there. An accident, pure and simple," Joe said. "One of those million monkeys, million typewriters things."

"That's a rather flippant way to put it."

"They all go through sudden bursts of aggressive motion," Joe said. "We actually encourage it because it keeps their muscles from atrophying. The ones who perform the most movement outlive the others by a wide margin. Usually, those bursts of motion are at the air or the walls. They can't tell the difference. Yesterday, it was just unfortunate that a human happened in her path."

"So, you're saying that Antenna-201 just got... lucky?"

Joe stopped walking. He looked at Mr. Aguirre. "Even luck needs help. What we have here is a situation of an orderly not following protocol during cleaning procedures. That Antenna should have been restrained. The orderly cut a corner and paid the price. That's all this is."

"That sounds like a leadership issue then," Mr. Aguirre said. He flashed a little grin to tell Joe that he was just busting his balls. But he held that grin, and that intense eye contact, a moment too long. Joe understood the meaning — no one was blaming Joe. Yet.

They continued walking down the hall.

Joe pressed the conversation. "The *issue* is that we need two orderlies per room," Joe said. "You guys got my staff overworked. They haven't had a free weekend since March. They can't do all the tasks that are expected of them in a day, and so they start finding shortcuts."

"Oh, Joe, Joe, Joe..." Mr. Aguirre said, shaking his head as he chuckled to himself.

Joe didn't find it amusing. "There should be one staffer restraining them, one staffer bathing them. It's a two-man job. That way one is always available to help the other. A buddy system, Javi. Most hospitals and prisons budget for that kinda work-load."

"You aren't running a standard hospital or prison."

"Look, you keep short-staffing me and accidents will happen. Not a threat, just reality. More people will get hurt."

"Joe, do you know how hard it is to staff this facility to begin with?"

"Work with me here, Javi."

"Your *janitors* have endured more background checks and polygraphs than most congressmen. That sort of security clearance isn't easy, it isn't cheap, and it isn't something that organically floats under the radar. Every staff member is a lot of risk and a lot of money."

"I like to think what we do is worth it."

"And I'm glad you see it that way, Joe. But if I'm being frank, proper Antenna maintenance should be a one-man job. They're highly-tuned vegetables. How dangerous can they be?"

"Plenty."

They came to a stop at the end of the hallway. Together, they looked in on Bishop's chamber. She wasn't exactly proving Joe's point. There wasn't anything dangerous about her. She looked like a sleeping dog, flopped onto one side as her limbs idly twitched and pawed. Her eyes were closed and she wasn't even moaning or screaming at this time. If anything, she looked completely at peace.

The cell had been scrubbed down and only traces of pink remained on the floor where the blood had soaked between the seams of the padding.

Mr. Aguirre watched her, a thin, satisfied smile etched on his face.

Suddenly, Bishop's hands, encased in their protective mitts, came to life. They gouged, scraped, and clawed at the wall. A burst of fury. Her eyelids snapped open revealing two blood-red eyes that roamed around their sockets, looking as though they might spin out and roll onto the floor at any moment. Her mouth twisted open and a scream pierced Joe's ears. It came from deep within her lungs, contorting and deforming her vocal cords as it passed, forming a heinous, animalistic screech, inhuman in its intensity.

Joe didn't flinch, but he took some satisfaction in watching Mr. Aguirre take a half step back from the glass. The man's neck stiffened as he gulped. A stress-vein slightly bulged near his temple as he clenched up. Joe suppressed a grin at the sight of Mr. Aguirre being so uncomfortable, even if just for a moment.

The moment passed quickly, though.

Mr. Aguirre's face relaxed back into his customary expression of detached analysis. He cocked his eyebrow in curious study of the furious motions of the creature on the floor in front of him.

But then his eyes glanced over at the airlock door that led to her chamber. His gaze zeroed in on the *"Hello, my name is Bishop"* sign.

"Bishop?" He looked over at the other airlocks and all their homemade signs. He read them off to himself. "Hicks... Frost... Vasquez..."

Joe cursed under his breath. It had been three or four years since an inspector of Aguirre's ranking had set foot in the Facility. Most inspectors were quick auditors who popped in, walked around, and popped out. This happened every few months, without warning, to ensure quality control. None of them ever commented on, or even noticed, the name plates. Those inspectors looked for major infractions and weren't allocated the independent thought to have an opinion about the smaller ones.

In the few years since the name plates went up, Joe had honestly stopped seeing them altogether. They were like those posters in the Level One hallway. Or the stack of files on the corner of his desk that he always meant to organize. For whatever reason, sometimes his eye just stopped seeing things that were always there.

"What is this?" Mr. Aguirre finally asked, although Joe was sure the man already knew the answer.

"Well, um," Joe stammered. "You see, when they're delivered to us, they arrive sedated and only identified by a number. With the shaved heads, it's hard to tell them apart, other than by gender and ethnicity. And so, to help distinguish them, we, um, gave them call-signs."

"Names. You gave the Antennas names."

"If you want to call it that."

"And this was *your* idea?"

Joe's mind raced in an attempt to spin this, to somehow deflect. Names were forbidden. In the written directions for Antenna care, even the use of pronouns was considered a no-no. They were not to be referred to by "he" or "she," but simply as "Antenna," as one would for any piece of expensive equipment. Naturally, the pronoun ban didn't hold up very long, but Joe had no doubt that HQ would find the names problematic.

As he tried to think up a response—

"He was following my professional advice."

Joe and Mr. Aguirre turned toward the voice.

Hannah had stepped out of one of the chambers. She wore hospital scrubs, evidently having just come from working in Hicks' nearby cell. Her hair was pulled back and sweat glistened from her face and brow, still showing the faint red marks from where her mask had just been strapped.

"You remember Dr. Chao, our lead physician," Joe said. "Dr. Chao, this is Javier Aguirre from HQ."

Mr. Aguirre held out his hand. "A pleasure to see you again, Doctor."

Hannah made no motion to shake. "I would, but I just extracted compacted stool from Hicks' rectum." Her left hand held up a little plastic bag that had a biohazard symbol. "I still need to weigh this little puppy, but it's about the size of a cue ball," she said.

She stretched the fingers of her right hand as if she were trying to prevent them from cramping.

"Believe me, he did not want to let this go. Played a little tug-a-war in there," she said.

Mr. Aguirre withdrew his hand and shoved it safely back into his pocket.

Joe shot her a glare. "Thank you, doctor," he said with an ounce of annoyance in his voice to signal to Mr. Aguirre that he felt such poop conversations were inappropriate for the workplace.

And yet, when he glanced over at Mr. Aguirre, instead of seeing a stern look of disapproval, the bean-counter's eyes had lit up behind his glasses. He was smiling at Hannah.

"And so, you're the one who gave them names, doctor?" Aguirre asked.

"Yep."

"And those names come from—?"

"The Marines from my favorite movie."

"And why?" Mr. Aguirre asked.

"Because it's an awesome movie," she said with a grin.

Joe sighed. "Doctor..."

Hannah dropped her grin. "Personalization helps staff effectively communicate regarding patient health. I understand why you want us to only refer to them by number. I get it. But on a practical level, it makes our job more difficult. Each Antenna in this facility has his or her own diet, vitamin and medication intake, and cleaning schedule.

"I know you treat them as equipment, but we treat them as patients, because that's what we've been trained to do, and that's how we perform our jobs best. Besides, let's be honest," she said as she held up the bag, "sometimes it's nice to know whose bag of shit you're holding. And weighing. And analyzing."

Mr. Aguirre looked from Hannah to the biohazard waste bag. A slight smile formed on his face. "Thank you for explaining that, Doctor. It's always important to hear how different departments approach their work."

"My pleasure."

Joe took a relieved breath. "Go wash up, Doctor," Joe said.

Hannah turned and walked off down the hall.

"You got a good team here, Joe," Mr. Aguirre said.

"I like to think so, sir."

"I won't include the names in my report. But I want them gone before the next inspection. Policy."

"Understood."

"And if it makes you and your staff feel better, I'll relay the opinions of your doctor to some of the higher-ups. Perhaps we can change that policy."

"That would be great."

"I don't want you to think that you haven't been heard. Or that we're stuck in our ways and don't welcome suggestions from our boots-on-the-ground. In the grand scheme of things, this program is still in its infancy. We don't know what the ceiling is for Antenna research. So, if you have any ideas — like names — submit them th⸱ ᴉ the proper channels and we will grant them a fair review and ᵃtion. There's always room for better."

He gave Joe a pat on the back. Joe simply smiled in return. *Bullshit*, Joe thought. A "fair review" meant a dozen people second-guessing each other and trying not to make any decision that would force them to put their signature on something. Plausible deniability.

Mr. Aguirre turned his attention back to Bishop.

Bishop's eyes seemed to stop their roaming. They had a slight jerkiness to them, but they were more-or-less locked onto Joe and Mr. Aguirre. The corners of her mouth twitched upward in what could only be described as a grin.

"I'd like to see a tuning session, now," Mr. Aguirre said.

"That can be arranged."

"And let's use Antenna-201," he said, pointing to Bishop.

Mr. Aguirre made one final note on his tablet.

Joe, standing behind him, caught a glimpse of the screen. At the top was a picture of Bishop. Not the shaved-head, gangly creature with the roaming eyes, though. In this image, Bishop, the person, smiled. It appeared to be an ID photo of a normal woman. Probably in her forties. Although her complexion appeared to have always been pale, she seemed healthy, alert, and attractive.

But Joe noticed something else about that woman in the file photo.

Her hair.

Black. And shoulder length.

Mr. Aguirre turned off his tablet and strolled back toward the elevator, glancing into the various chambers as he passed.

Joe lingered in front of Bishop's chamber for a moment. He looked at the woman on the floor in the hospital gown. Her eyes rolled and her mouth grinned. What was it Riley had said? The woman she saw had black hair? Down to her shoulders. Pale face. A hospital gown.

A loose description.

It could be anyone. Including Riley's mother.

Joe shook the thought away and went to catch up to Mr. Aguirre.

CHAPTER 11

Riley sat in the corner of the kitchen.

Despite staying awake all night, she refused to even try to sleep. She couldn't risk the black-haired woman sneaking up on her. Her mind was certainly willing to stay vigilant, but her senses and body had grown weak. As her eyes darted around the kitchen, she felt a lag. It was as though she looked at something, some object, and the signal took an extra split-second before it reached her brain to be processed.

The closest she ever felt to this sensation was the time she went on that backpacking trip in the mountains for Chloe's birthday. She was fifteen. She promised her mom that both of Chloe's parents were chaperoning. It would just be a night of girls out in the woods having fun.

Meanwhile, Chloe told her parents that she was spending her birthday night at a sleepover at *Riley's* house and that Riley's mom would be watching over everyone.

Chloe's older brother then drove them and two other girls out into the woods and dropped them off. No boys. No parents. No adults.

Maria brought booze. Stacy brought weed. Riley h͏ ver smoked before. After she took the first two hits an͏d anything, she convinced herself that she had a hi͏ drugs (and the Jack Daniels that Maria brought). ͏ hits and three more shots and before she kne͏

She couldn't understand why people liked being high. Or drunk. She hated not having control.

All night, like the most stereotypical "teenager who gets high for the first time" story ever, she spent the night looking at her hands, trying to figure out how her brain was telling her fingers to move. Then she tried to figure out how her eyes reported back that *Yes, boss, the fingers have moved. Repeat, the fingers have moved.*

The weird delay that her brain felt that night was the closest sensation to what she felt now. At least back then it was because she was baked out of her fucking mind. Today, the sensation came from overwhelming exhaustion and terror.

Riley never told her parents about that night, about throwing up and passing out in the woods. When she came home, she put on a brave, sober face for her mom. She looked her mom in the eye and *lied* to her. She had all sorts of stories about the delicious chili dogs and s'mores that Mr. and Mrs. Robertson had made for the girls. *Mr. Robertson played the guitar, and we all sang 'Country Roads' around the campfire. We sang until midnight, and then we giggled and talked about boys until 3 a.m. Tee-hee. I'm exhausted. Gonna take a nap. Byyyye.*

She always felt guilty about that lie.

Over the next couple years, Riley convinced herself that her mom saw through the lie and that, together, it was their little secret they kept from her dad. Riley imagined that one day, when she was in her twenties or thirties, she and her mom would joke about how her mom knew immediately that her daughter had come home drunk, stoned, hungover, and had barfed into her own shoes because it was ʹ ne only receptacle she could find. They'd have a good laugh about it and would be all the closer. A true mother-daughter bonding moment.

That moment would never come now.

The lie could never be undone.

Riley let that realization sink in. She hoped that thinking about her sadness would act as a sort of pinch to her system that could snap everything back into place. She wanted to cry and scream out. She wanted her eyes to fill with tears and her breaths to be deep and painful. She wanted to mourn.

But numbness overshadowed her emotions.

Time for another cup of coffee.

She stood in the kitchen, trying to keep her motions smooth and silent for fear of awakening the demonic woman who had been haunting her. As she rose, she reached into the front pocket of her hooded-sweatshirt. Inside, her fingers grasped the handle of a large carving knife.

When she had lain in bed awake all night, she felt the need for some sort of protection. So, after agonizing over the decision for an hour, she had opened her bedroom door and crept down the dark hallway to the kitchen. Every time she turned a corner, she held her breath and felt her muscles tighten. Every time she passed an open doorway, or a darkened nook where something could leap out at her, she felt her legs wobble from fear.

It had been only fifty steps from her bedroom to the kitchen — three turns around blind corners — but it had taken her ten heart-stopping minutes.

She had grabbed a knife from the block but couldn't bear to turn around and make her way back down that dark hallway again.

And so, she pulled over a stool and sat in the corner of the kitchen, a knife clutched in her hand as she dared not blink.

That was eight hours ago.

She only moved so that she could brew a pot of coffee. As long as Riley stayed awake, the woman didn't appear. When the urge to pee became too overwhelming, instead of walking around blind corners to reach the bathroom, she took a thermos off the counter and used that.

And there she sat ever since, even as her father woke up, mumbled some excuses about having to go to work, and then hurriedly left.

Riley knew she had to sleep.

She had had almost twelve hours to think about and analyze the situation. Despite the fogginess of her brain at this point, there could only be one conclusion — the woman wasn't real.

Right?

No one else saw her.

No one else even saw evidence of her existence.

The woman *must* be in Riley's head. She had to be some manifestation of the stress and anguish Riley felt over her mom's sudden death. *Right?*

Maybe the screaming woman represented unresolved tension between her and her mother. They had never really discussed the divorce. Her mom was the one who packed up and left. Her mom was the one who started the custody battle. Her mom was the one who broke the family. Riley tried to be the good daughter throughout it all, but maybe she harbored deep subconscious resentment toward her mother.

Maybe that was it.

The woman with the black hair represented her relationship with her mother.

Right?

A psychologist would probably say the exact same thing. Every psychologist she had ever seen on TV seemed to believe that most people's issues were related to unresolved relationships with their parents.

To Riley, this was the only logical explanation. But knowing that she had experienced a psychological break from reality wasn't much comfort. As much as she tried to will that logic into her senses, she still couldn't bring herself to close her eyes in this house.

The woman might come back.

"Fuck this place," she said aloud, hoping perhaps demon-woman would hear her.

She set down her coffee mug and gripped the knife in her sweatshirt pocket, fully ready to pull it out and slash at any demon bitches that jumped out.

One cautious step at a time, she made her way across the kitchen. She peeked through the dining room and then walked over into the living room. She looked down the hall.

Nothing there.

Then she unlocked the front door.

Her hand hesitated as it clutched the latch. She just knew that this was when that fucking bitch would jump out at her. She'd open the door and the woman would be there, screaming into her face and scraping off her skin. The door had a peephole, but Riley knew from countless horror movies that looking through that tiny fish-eye of glass would yield its own terrifying visions.

Just like ripping off a bandage, Riley had to get it over with quickly.

She pulled the knife from her pocket.

She took a deep breath.

She pushed down on the latch and ripped open the door.

Sunlight flooded into the room, temporarily blinding Riley and making her blink. Fearing the ghost would pop out of the sunspots that danced in her eyes, she waved the knife at the brightness, waiting for her vision to adjust. And when it finally did...

Nothing.

There was no woman. Just a beautiful, spring morning.

Riley allowed herself a breath.

She stepped outside, slammed the door behind her, and jogged off down the driveway.

Fuck this house.

CHAPTER 12

Joe led Mr. Aguirre into the Control Room.

Two work-stations faced a large screen that displayed the security feeds of each and every Antenna. Charts and graphs of each Antenna's bio-readouts, updating in real-time, accompanied the dozen live-feeds.

The two men working at the terminals in front of the display screen looked up as Joe and Aguirre stepped in.

"You remember Chuck, our control operator," Joe said, pointing to an overweight fifty-year-old man in a Hawaiian shirt. He was the kind of guy who seemed to have been at his job longer than the building for it actually existed. It bred a sense of comfort and familiarity in him that was a bit obnoxious, but still, Joe couldn't imagine some younger recruit doing the job.

Chuck turned and made a face. "Uh-oh. The bosses are watching," he said. He grinned wide as he threw a pen across the room toward his counterpart at the other desk. "Tariq, quick! Turn off your porn!"

The pen sailed past Tariq, a guy in his twenties who wore his polo shirts tucked in. He picked up his own pen and threw it back, smacking Chuck in the face. The two laughed.

Joe let out a deep sigh. "Knock it off, guys."

"Yeah, *kid*," Chuck said. "HQ's watching."

"Good," Tariq said as he turned to Joe and Aguirre. "I'd like to report that my workmate is old and enfeebled."

"Also, flatulent," Chuck said, lifting a butt cheek off his seat and preparing to let one rip.

"Chuck, set a good example for the kid," Joe said.

Chuck immediately registered that Joe wasn't amused. He stood and waddled over to Aguirre. "Sorry, Joe. Good to see you again, Javi." The two men shook hands.

"Likewise."

"Youngblood there is Tariq," Chuck said. "He's our chemical specialist. A little cocky, but he's really good at what he does. He's the best of the best... that would work for this shitty salary."

Tariq couldn't help but beam.

"He doesn't have a military background, so feel free to smack him around a bit. It helps," Chuck said.

Aguirre walked over and shook Tariq's hand. "Good to meet you, Tariq. Don't let me interfere. I'm just here to observe a tuning session."

"Best show in town," Chuck said. He sat down at his desk and began punching in commands.

Joe guided Mr. Aguirre to an elevated platform in the rear of the room. There was a snack table, mini-fridge, and several leather recliners that faced the main screen. It had been designed with all the comforts of a luxury movie theater, a place where any VIPs who visited could observe tuning sessions in comfort. Joe learned, from years of experience, that the more comfortable and catered to a bigwig was, the less he interfered in operations.

Mr. Aguirre took a seat in one of the reclining leather chairs, kicked back his feet, and immersed himself in his tablet.

"Who's our lucky volunteer?" Chuck said.

"Antenna-201," Joe said.

"The best don't rest, eh?" Chuck said as he punched in some commands. The screen transitioned to a view of Bishop.

"How many cases has Antenna-201 been used for?" Aguirre asked, glancing up at the big-screen.

"I'll need to look that up," Chuck said as he opened up some files on his monitor. "It's a lot, though."

Joe cleared his throat. "Well, um, when urgent or high-profile intercepts are needed, that's the Antenna we trust most. Tunes faster. Intercepts are cleaner. There's more detail. The ratings for Antennas-201 are just better."

"Bishop has had seventy-one tunings," Chuck reported.

"And the next highest?" Aguirre asked.

"That would be Ferro at... twenty-three," Chuck said.

Joe grimaced. He hadn't realized those numbers were so out of balance. He glanced over at Aguirre's face, searching for any hint of disapproval. But Aguirre kept looking at the screen, his mind seeming to digest this information.

"In your opinion, is Antenna-201 just more *powerful* than the others?" Aguirre said.

"It's a bit of a self-fulfilling cycle," Joe said. "The more we tune 'em, the better they become at tuning. The faster and more powerful they get. 201's our best, so we use her the most. And because we use her the most, she's now our best."

"The rich get richer," Aguirre said with a nod.

"I guess you could say that." Joe kept looking at Aguirre, trying to judge his reaction. "You want a different Antenna? Get their usage rates up?"

"On the contrary, I'd rather push the boundaries of our current leader here. Let's see what Antenna-201 can give us."

"Bishop it is," Chuck said as he entered some commands.

Joe cleared his throat. "Use official identifiers please."

"Sorry. Preparing tuning session for Antenna-201. Loading stimulants for Case 10598."

Joe looked at Bishop on the screen.

She seemed to stare directly into the camera. Her mitted hand, previously lying still at her side, suddenly came alive and began to furiously claw at her face. She opened her mouth and released a howling scream that pierced through the speakers of the Control Room.

Without interrupting the flow of his work, Chuck flipped the audio off.

On the screen, Bishop now screamed in silence.

Joe watched her howl and claw at herself. The lower portion of the screen showed multiple feeds from other areas of the Facility. Joe glanced at the images of his staff wheeling medical carts and audio/visual equipment down the Level Two corridor. In small teams, they maneuvered their gear into the airlock that led to Bishop's cell.

First in were several orderlies. They carried in restraints and a wheelchair. Once inside the airlock, they fastened masks to their faces and then waited for the room to pressurize.

On one of the video feeds, Joe could see Hannah and her medical team stand in the corridor, waiting for their turn to enter and begin their portion of the process.

Joe stood. "Excuse me. I'm gonna go down to Level Two and supervise the setup. Water and soda in the fridge over there, if you're feeling parched. Snacks in the cupboard for any hankerings. Be back soon."

"Take your time," Aguirre said. He wasn't watching the setup closely; his attention had drifted back toward his tablet.

Joe walked to the door but paused to glance back at the display.

On the main screen, the squad of orderlies — all wearing gasmasks — entered Bishop's cell. Joe stared intently, holding his breath. He watched for any sign of resistance from Bishop. Any fight. Any acknowledgement that she was, in fact, aware of their presence.

In a coordinated maneuver, the orderlies surrounded her. They firmly grasped her by the arms and legs. She squirmed and swayed, as was her nature. Joe didn't think that any of her movements appeared threatening.

They carefully lifted Bishop — she was so small and frail that they were able to pick her off her mattress without straining — and then set her onto the wheelchair. As two of the orderlies held her down, the others went around cinching restraining cuffs tightly around Bishop's wrists and ankles. Without a single problem, Bishop was soon firmly strapped to the chair. And the way her eyes roamed, muscles twitched, and head bobbed, it was as if she never noticed she was moved at all.

Joe nodded; everything seemed to be moving smoothly, both in the Control Room and on the monitors. A complete textbook tuning session. He opened the door and walked out.

***

Joe stepped off the elevator and onto Level Two.

The corridor buzzed with calm, professional activity.

Technicians and medics moved around each other in a delicate, well-rehearsed dance of duties. Some of the staff gave Joe slight nods of greeting, but mostly, they continued with their tasks as normal.

As a supervisor, Joe prided himself on his ability to make people calmer at their jobs instead of more anxious. They respected his subtle managerial style. It had taken him years, but he felt he had perfected his leadership charisma. Never authoritarian, but also never too relaxed.

It was the same strategy as being a good parent. Be warm, but firm. Set sensible rules then communicate and enforce them clearly. Joe had read that in a parenting book when Kate was pregnant with Riley. That was back when they lived in a crappy rental house in the D.C. suburbs.

At the time, he worked as an account executive at the company that oversaw the construction of the Facility. He always assumed that the client was government or military, but the paperwork passed through so many opaque levels of approvals that it was impossible to know for sure. In any case, it was at that time that he saw an opportunity to provide his family with a more stable life.

Joe threw himself into his duties overseeing the construction and staffing of the Facility. He worked long hours and most weekends. He didn't want his young family to have to follow him from job site to job site all over the world, and so, he let it be known to his superiors that he was angling for a stable, desk job.

He was determined to impress.

They gave him a few days off for Riley's birth, of course, but that was it. He missed most of Riley's infant months. There was one time, early on, when he came home and Riley began crying because she didn't recognize this strange man in her house.

But all the hard work paid off.

When the doors finally opened and the lights turned on, it was clear to everyone at the Company that nobody knew the Facility from the ground up like Joe Gerhard. Every bolt, every pipe, every hose. When the time came for the final staffing decision, Joe took a big risk. He went straight up to Javier Aguirre during the final inspection and told the man that if he didn't get the supervisor position, he would start looking elsewhere.

The higher-ups finally relented.

Joe received an office, a desk, and a salary that placed his family firmly in the upper-class of their quiet West Virginian community.

Unfortunately, the work-load never lessened. There was always something to install or some fire to put out. He missed most of Riley's childhood and never got to test out all the things he learned from those parenting books. But he told himself that all that knowledge had paid off at work. Coordinating an operation like this wasn't all that different from herding children. Children or not, people were going to be people. They'd be lazy if you let them. They'd be catty if you allowed it. And they'd blame you if they could.

And now, as Joe watched his team set up for a tuning session, he felt a sense of pride at being the "father" of this special place. His "children" had grown up responsible and hard-working.

Joe stood back, away from the hustle, and observed as a team of medics restrained Bishop's head to her chair and attached sensors to her temples.

A team of technicians rolled in an array of TV monitors. Other techs set up cameras and microphones, angling them around Bishop's face but trying to keep them as far out of her field-of-vision as possible.

Joe estimated that it would be another half hour before they were ready to begin. Plenty of time for him to talk with Hannah.

She stood at the window of Bishop's cell, overseeing her team.

Joe casually walked over and stood by her side.

Hannah glanced over at him. "How's it going with Aguirre?"

"Good. Anything to report down here?"

"Just that it's a bad fucking idea to tune Bishop again so soon after what happened. But I'm just a fucking doctor. What do I know?"

"Noted."

"Is it? Because I will do a fucking sock-puppet show if that's what's needed to get the point across. She *just* killed a man."

"Aguirre specifically requested her."

"Why the fuck?"

"Because she's the best."

"We're pushing her too hard. I don't like it."

Joe nodded. "We'll get through this inspection and then cycle her out of the rotation. She just needs to give us one more batch of good intercepts, and Aguirre can walk off all happy."

The edge of Hannah's mouth twitched in accompaniment to her narrowing gaze. It was an expression that Joe had learned meant *I have more to say on this matter, but I'll bite my tongue because you're the boss.*

He didn't push it further.

Joe glanced around at the other workers. None of them were within earshot. He kept his voice low. "Can we talk?" he asked.

Hannah continued looking forward, through the glass. "Sure. What's up?" The tone in her voice had softened. She seemed to sense that Joe wanted to keep this conversation private.

"Riley might be seeing things," he said.

Hannah turned to look at him. "Hallucinations?"

Joe nodded.

"How vivid?" Hannah asked.

"Vivid."

"Well, she experienced a horribly traumatic day. Bad dreams or difficulty concentrating would be completely normal. She can probably get prescribed something to help her sleep."

"She's seeing it when she's awake."

"The hallucinations?"

Joe nodded again.

"Wait, wait, wait. Let's be clear," Hannah said. "When Riley is fully awake, and otherwise perfectly cognizant, she's *seeing* something that isn't there?"

"Yep."

"What's she seeing?"

"Some woman."

"And?"

"And, I don't know. The woman watches Riley. Screams at Riley. Claws her face off."

"*Her* face or *Riley's* face?"

"I... I dunno. Hers, I guess."

"Holy shit, Joe."

"She was so sure the woman was real that we called a security detail to the house last night. Team didn't see anything, though. Me neither. And there's nothing on tape."

Hannah looked off, taking a moment to mentally run through the possible diagnoses. "This is not good," she finally said.

"But these might just be hallucinations of her mom, right? As you said, a stressful thing just happened. That's bound to mess with a kid, right?"

"Even if it's stress-induced, Riley needs to see a doctor."

"You're a doctor," Joe said, leaning in a bit. His gaze met Hannah's.

"Joe…"

"You know her. You got a background in psychoanalysis. Just talk to her and give me your professional opinion."

Hannah crossed her arms. "Look, it might be stress, it might be depression, it might be drugs…"

"Riley wouldn't—"

"You don't know that. You don't know anything. Which is why you need to get her to a third-party medical professional who can assess her mental and psychological state. Because if she is having a psychiatric break, then she needs professional counselling and therapy. Perhaps even medication."

Joe finally broke his eye contact. He looked at the floor. His large shoulders slumped and he could feel his knees wobble slightly, as if a giant weight were accruing atop his frame. "If we go through proper channels, and this finds its way onto her medical record…" he said, gulping for a moment as he completed the thought, "…they'll red-flag her."

Hannah's face went grim. Her head gave an imperceptible nod, showing that she understood the implication full-well.

They looked at each other.

"You're worried about something else, aren't you?" Hannah said.

Joe took a deep breath. "The woman she's seeing... I just... I'm not sure it's Kate."

"Go on."

"The woman wears a gown, like a hospital gown. Now, that description is pretty broad. Could mean a lotta things. But when Riley was a kid..." He rubbed his face with his hand, not wanting to finish the thought out loud. "When Riley was a kid, I would take work home. I'd keep her in the corner, let her play by herself, and I would review video footage and intercepts and whatnot."

"Jesus, Joe."

"I was a bad father."

"Yes. You fucking were."

"But is it possible that when Riley was really young, she saw some of what we do here? Maybe her mind just stored it away. And then, all this stuff with her mom, all of it... it just... it pulled that memory out from wherever it was and... and used it? Can that happen?"

"Well, yeah, I guess. All sorts of shit's possible."

"You see? If Riley's having a psychological break, and she's drawing in memories of my work which I probably shouldn't have brought home... well... then I don't know how HQ is gonna react. But I doubt it'll be good." He sighed. "Look, I'll do what I gotta do for Riley, but I want your opinion. I take her to a hospital and things might get real ugly, real quick. I just wanna be sure it's necessary before Aguirre or someone else catches wind of it. You're a doctor *and* a friend. Honest opinion, do you think it's grief?"

Hannah ran her hand through her hair. "I mean, it's *probably* grief. People handle grief in different ways. Especially in adolescence when they haven't had much experience in it before. I don't know what you want me to tell you, man. You can't just hand me a pile of hallucination symptoms and expect me to be all Web-fuckin-MD about it."

"Will you talk to her? Please?"

"Seriously?"

"Come over tonight. If you think it's serious, then..." he paused. "I'll do what I need to do."

Hannah sighed. "Fine."

"You're the best, Hannah."

"Yes. I am."

With that, she curtly turned her attention back to the windowed wall. Inside, Bishop was fully hooked up to diagnostic systems. Cables and tubes connected her to scanners, sensors, and IV drips. Her head had been restrained to a headrest that rose out from the back of her chair.

Hannah and Joe watched as two medics gently lifted her eyelids. They propped them open into a set of eye-hooks. One of the medics then administered eyedrops. The rig made Bishop's eyes wider than ever. They roamed around her head, searching. Always searching. But focusing on nothing.

Joe watched her. His walkie-talkie beeped.

"Go for Gerhard," he said.

Chuck's voice came through the other side. "Set-up's complete. Ready for tuning."

"On my way," Joe said.

He gave Hannah a friendly pat on the back and then turned to walk to the elevator. Before he left, he glanced one more time through the window.

Bishop's eyes had stopped roaming. They stared straight ahead, seemingly fixed on something.

They were looking at Joe.

A chill passed through him.

He shook it off and walked off down the hall.

CHAPTER 13

Riley trudged on.

When she left the house, she hadn't fully comprehended how far away her dad lived from town. What was only a ten-minute drive turned out to be, in reality, a several mile hike down a long gravel road. At the end of the road, she had to walk along a two-lane highway that barely had a shoulder.

The morning was crisp and sunny. A beautiful day. Birds sang and flapped around with impunity, as though they lived in a cartoon. Ordinarily, Riley would have loved this sort of walk — cool enough that she wouldn't sweat, but sunny enough that she could roll up her sleeves and try to burn away some of those softball-jersey tan-lines.

On a normal day, she might have jogged. Sure, her dad would have lectured her about watching for cars and to make sure she understood that a pedestrian always travels *against* traffic and never *with* traffic. He would have expressed concern and offered to drive her into town so she could jog around the park. She would have declined and asserted her age and independence. She would have won. As tough as her dad acted, a slight shove from his baby girl and the man folded like paper. Anything to avoid direct conflict.

She usually liked getting out. But today, she drifted through the walk.

Her legs felt leaden and disassociated from her body, as though they were part of some marionette and she could only move them by pulling on a string. One awkward, stumbling foot in front of another. Each step became a conscious decision of her brain commanding her legs to move.

All her other senses were submerged in a weird haze. It reminded her of that time in middle school when she took some allergy meds, not realizing that they were for nighttime. The rest of the day, as she battled the drowsiness, she felt as though someone had unfocused her eyes and installed a tin funnel around her ears. Everything was off and distorted. Just like today.

She was exhausted. It wouldn't have surprised her to learn that she was also hungry and dehydrated. But despite all the mental energy it required for her to keep stumbling forward, mile after mile, she never once considered turning around and going back to that damn house.

As she reached a blind curve in the road, Riley slowed her pace and peered around the corner, fully expecting to see the wailing, bleeding, angry woman. Nothing.

She continued on, her eyes scanning everywhere. The large trees off to the side of the road provided a perfect hiding place for that woman. Was she behind one of them, ready to jump out?

Riley heard a rustling.

She stared in the direction of the sound, near a large sycamore. Her feet stopped moving and her whole body clenched. She couldn't take her eyes off of that tree. Its branches were so thick with purple-tinged leaves that they hung down low to the ground, helping block the view of its wide trunk. The woman was surely hiding behind that trunk. She was going to step out. Any moment now.

Riley stood there, on the road, staring at that tree, for several minutes. Her vision blurred. Soon, the very concept and shape of trees no longer made sense in her mind. As she concentrated, she heard a sound behind her. Maybe the woman was out on the open road, following her. Trailing her. Watching her. In clear sight. *Right behind her!*

A cold sweat rose from Riley's forehead and along the back of her neck. She pried her eyes away from the tree and spun around...

The road was empty. Just a few dry leaves bouncing along the road's blacktop asphalt in the wind.

Once again, she stood frozen in place, looking.

Waiting.

The woman had not come.

With a deep breath, Riley forced her legs to move. She continued on around the blind corner. The road sloped down from there, and her walking took on a trance-like state. Eventually, the trees that formed a thick, green wall on either side of the road thinned out and opened up.

She was approaching town.

Soon, she was walking past the long driveways of homes.

The closer she came to civilization, the more her fears of that woman, who had seemingly been residing just out of Riley's vision, began to fade away. The brighter the day became. The closer she got to people, the less she worried.

The road passed by stores. Then a few restaurants. Then a movie theater.

At some point, a sidewalk appeared beneath her feet. Riley only noticed its welcome presence when she recognized that she no longer felt a nagging fear that she might stumble into the street and get hit by a car.

She looked around at all the people going about their regular lives.

Two new mothers, both pushing their infants in strollers, stepped out of a coffee shop, loudly laughing at some joke.

A cop car lazily roamed the quiet street. Nowhere to be, nothing to do.

The world was safe.

Riley's shoulders and neck relaxed. The tension drifted from her body in waves. She realized that the stress and adrenaline had been the only thing shocking her system to alertness. Now that it was gone, a deep weariness filled its place.

Her eyelids drooped and her mind fogged up. Her feet became heavy, as if a concrete mixer had started pouring a weight into her body that first filled her shoes and was now working its way up her legs. Every successive step required more effort than the last.

Despite the fact that she never saw her mom's body, the vague description Riley knew of the suicide kept filling her imagination. Her mind wandered toward the image of her mom dead on the front porch, her brains splattered against the yellow, faded siding.

But Riley quickly pushed it out. She needed sleep. She would think about her mother later.

The sidewalk passed beside a low, stone fence that encircled a well-manicured grassy field. It was a wide public park. In the far corner of the park, a playground and picnic area sat adjacent to the public library. The laughter and joyful screeches of the children playing *Marco Polo* reached Riley's ears.

"The woodchips are lava!" one of the kids shouted as he hopped from the slide to the monkey bars.

As if drifting on her feet, Riley veered off the sidewalk and slowly climbed over the two-foot stone wall that encased the park. She ambled straight into the middle of the field. The area was expansive and open. Few places for ghosts and demons to hide.

Riley lowered her weary body onto the grass. She curled onto her side in a ball, shielding her eyes from the warm, mid-morning sun.

She felt safe.

She felt comfortable.

She felt exhausted.

Her eyes closed and her mind immediately floated off into sleep. In that fleeting moment between wakefulness and dreams — the moment she had been fearing all day — nothing horrifying popped into her mind. Just happy thoughts of her mom. The two of them laughing during dinner together. The two of them watching Saturday Night Live together. The two of them swinging through Burger King on the way home from softball practice.

Good thoughts.

Happy thoughts.

Riley smiled as she drifted into sleep, confident that her mind had made up the terrifying visions of the woman.

They couldn't be real.

Monsters like that are never real.

CHAPTER 14

Joe and Mr. Aguirre stood side-by-side, observing the big display screen from their position on the platform that overlooked the Control Room.

Chuck and Tariq manned their respective terminals.

Hannah entered and sat at a computer in the corner.

"Going online in five... four... three... two... one..." Chuck announced. He hit some controls.

The large screens clicked on, showing real-time updates of Bishop's vitals — heart rate, breathing rate, internal temperature, even an EEG that charted the electrical activity of her brain. All of this data, and yet, Joe couldn't look at it. He wondered if any of his staff did either.

The bio-readouts only filled the fringes of the display. In the center of the screen, six feet across, was a close-up camera view of Bishop's pale, sunken face. Her eyes, propped open by those medieval-looking hooks, seemed to gaze directly through the screen and into the Control Room.

Through the edges of his vision, Joe watched Mr. Aguirre shift his weight uncomfortably. The man looked away and swiped at his tablet, obviously performing no particular task other than finding something, *anything*, to look at that wasn't those ghastly, larger-than-life eyes on the big screen.

"Video online," Chuck announced. "Audio online. System recording. Stimulation inputs queued up. Control is ready to begin tuning Antenna-201. Case 10598."

Joe nodded. "Medical?"

"Medical approves tuning of Antenna-201," Hannah said.

"Chem Team?"

Tariq looked over his screens. "Chem Team approves tuning of Antenna-201."

Joe picked up his walkie-talkie. "This is Joe Gerhard, Facility Supervisor. I am hereby initiating the tuning session for Antenna-201, Case 10598." He turned to Tariq. "Chem Team, proceed."

"Yes, sir. Increasing sensory perception by five percent."

Tariq adjusted the dials on his control board.

Everyone in the room quietly watched Bishop's face.

"How long does it usually take with this Antenna?" Mr. Aguirre asked.

"She adjusts faster than most. Only a few breaths to clear some of the nerve gas through her system," Hannah said. "Her heart rate is already increasing. Her body is starting to regain sense in her extremities."

"Five percent achieved," Tariq said.

"Proceed to ten percent," Joe said.

Tariq adjusted his controls. On the screen, Bishop's breathing clearly increased. The blipping line displaying her heart rate sped up — *Beep-Beep-Beep*. Her eyes, which usually lolled around their sockets, suddenly jerked back and forth, as if they were detecting the faintest slivers of light.

"Begin stimulation," Joe said.

Chuck punched in commands.

They all watched the screens. One of the cameras was angled over Bishop's shoulder, giving everyone in the Control Room a view of what she was seeing. Propped in front of Bishop's eyes was a curved screen, fully encompassing her field of vision. The screen, which had been dark, lit up with a picture of a man.

The man was probably in his forties. There was nothing particularly distinctive about him. Average height, average build, average looks. The photo was a candid shot, as though from the zoom-lens of a paparazzo... or spy.

The man wore a finely-tailored white shirt in the photo. Combined with his perfect smile and full coifed head of hair, he certainly appeared to have wealth.

That image lingered on the screen for a silent moment.

And then the recorded voice of a woman sounded through the speakers. The voice was so loud and clear that Bishop winced in her seat. The voice simply said, "Victor Aminov." The name sat there for a second, letting its last strains of sound-waves flutter into Bishop's ear. When that single, quiet second passed, the voice again announced, "Victor Aminov."

Images collaged onto the screen in front of Bishop's eyes. All pictures of the man Joe assumed was Victor Aminov.

Baby photos.

High school yearbook photos.

Ukrainian military ID photos.

Spy satellite photos.

Photos of his houses. Photos of his cars. Photos of him with friends. Photos of him with his family.

It all flashed onto the screen. Each visual was preceded by a white burst of light. The image zoomed forward, briefly filling the screen, before taking its place in the background along with the growing wallpaper of other images. It all happened fast. Very fast. It became impossible for the eye to keep up and focus on any one single image. Pictures moved and flowed around the screen with an intense speed. The movements had no discernible, unifying pattern. Nothing that allowed the eye and the mind to relax. It was a complex, chaotic dance of imagery.

Some pictures zoomed in slow. Others zipped on through.

Some pictures roamed around the screen. Others stayed stationary.

Some flashed and pulsated with light. Others stayed fixed in a clean, black frame.

Every time they performed one of these sessions, Joe got a headache, even a little nauseous. Hannah once advised him not to look at the screen. But that was impossible. The arrangement of imagery was specifically designed to grab human eyeballs and twist them until a person could look at nothing but the barrage of visual noise.

And then there was the actual noise.

The woman's recorded voice repeated that name. "Victor Aminov... Victor Aminov... Victor Aminov..." Sometimes the name was read at a high frequency. Sometimes at a low frequency. Sometimes it was sped up until it sounded like chipmunk gibberish. Sometimes it slowed to a crawl. The audio files of the name recitation overlapped with each other, forming a wall of sound.

Joe glanced over at Mr. Aguirre. The man rubbed his eyes and swayed a bit on his feet. Even in the dim lighting of the Control Room, Joe clearly saw the blood draining from Mr. Aguirre's face, turning his skin a yellow-greenish complexion. It was a look Joe was well-familiar with.

"Help yourself to a seat," Joe offered. "Look at the floor for a bit. It'll re-center you."

"I'm fine. I'm fine," Mr. Aguirre said, waving off Joe. But Joe could see the man's throat clenching, probably trying to swallow back bits of bile and vomit as though he were sea-sick.

"What if we turned the volume in this room down?" Joe said.

"No, no, no. I don't require special treatment. Please, proceed."

Joe shrugged. "You're the boss. Tariq, ease her on up to thirty percent."

Tariq worked his controls.

On the main screen, Bishop seemed to know something was happening. She tried to twist her head, but the restraints held her in place. Her face, already beginning to bead and glisten with sweat, scrunched up as she tried to shut her eyelids. But the hooks held them open. Her neck and shoulders shimmied, having no real goal or purpose, but just squirming from the discomfort.

And then she opened her mouth. A low moan crawled out of her throat. A steady, single quiet note of pain.

"She's making noise," Chuck said. Bishop's moan effectively blocked some of the sound from the speakers.

Joe nodded. "Increase volume to compensate."

As Bishop's moan grew in intensity, the volume of the repeated name — "Victor Aminov" — became louder. It soon drowned out Bishop's soft wail.

"Increase stimulation," Joe said.

A voice faded up over the speakers. The voice was that of a man, speaking what Joe could only assume was Ukrainian. The voice calmly discussed what was probably some business transaction. Additional conversations from that same voice overlapped with each other; they all seemed to be recorded from various intercepted phone calls.

At the same time, more images flashed onto the screen. Maps. Documents. Victor Aminov's signature. Victor Aminov's doctor's notes. Victor Aminov's high school report card.

All the noise, all the images, wound themselves up together.

They went faster. And faster.

Bishop's arms pulled against her bindings. Her mouth dropped open. That soft, low moan suddenly transformed into a shrill scream of pain. Her jaw opened wider, pulling the skin on her cheeks taut, seemingly trying to make her mouth larger so that more of that horrible scream could escape her body and maybe take some of the pain with it.

"How much is she feeling, Tariq?" Joe asked, making sure to keep his voice calm and detached.

"She's at about twenty-five percent."

"Keep going."

Twenty-five percent.

With all the stimulation occurring around her, only twenty-five percent was being processed by her nervous system. Someone with a higher paycheck than him had managed to attach percentages to the human sensory system, but Joe never quite understood what those percentages actually meant.

Joe tried to imagine what that must feel like. What would it be like to have only twenty-five percent of your vision? When Bishop looked at that screen, was it just a foggy blast of flickering, moving light? Were the sound waves that entered her ears muffled, as though she were listening through water?

And what about her skin? What did twenty-five percent of the texture and pressure of those straps binding her to the chair feel like?

But the way they always screamed at this stage told Joe that although they were only processing a quarter of the stimulation, they were experiencing them on a level of intensity that he could never understand.

He knew that when he crossed his legs for too long, his foot would "fall asleep." It was a normal thing. The twisted nerves just couldn't send signals to the brain. While the nerves stayed disconnected, they kept transmitting messages. When they finally reconnected, the flood of signals would burst forward and overwhelm the brain, causing the painful, tingling sensation of a sleeping foot. Unpleasant, yes. But it was obviously miniscule compared to the level of pain that the Antennas experienced.

"She's at thirty percent," Tariq announced.

Joe hated this part. He could accurately gauge each percentage increase in sensation because the Antenna's screaming and writhing intensified as well. There seemed to be no upper limit to their wails. Every Antenna tore vocal cords during their first tunings.

At this point, he noticed that Mr. Aguirre no longer had his eyes glued to the floor. He stood erect and leaning forward, holding his breath and completely enthralled by the twisting, yelling creature on the main screen.

"EEGs spiking," Hannah said. "Heart rate accelerated beyond acceptable levels. She's not going to make it much higher."

"I say keep going," Mr. Aguirre said, an intrigued little grin on his face, like a scientist entranced by the beauty of his work.

"She's in incredible pain," Hannah said, turning around in her seat.

"Ah, but what's a little more?

"Joe?" Hannah said, turning to him.

Joe took a deep breath. "Continue," he said.

"Thirty-one percent," Tariq said, his voice quivering with the announcement.

Chuck had long ago turned his attention away from the display. He focused on his work station, staring at his monitor and clicking his mouse in actions that Joe knew had no point.

"Thirty-two... thirty-three... thirty-four..." Tariq had to raise his voice so that his announcements could be heard over the screams.

Bishop strained every muscle against her bindings. Her screams grew hoarse and weak, but she put more force than ever behind them, creating unnatural rasping screeches.

"Has one ever made it to fifty percent?" Mr. Aguirre asked with an air of detached curiosity. "My god, can you imagine the possibilities if we could get them to a hundred?"

Before Joe could even answer, Bishop's mouth twisted into a sneer. She released a sound that he had never heard before. It wasn't the usual cry of pain, that animalistic attempt to shift the mind's focus from the torturous nerve endings. No, instead, this scream was focused. Purposeful.

This was a scream of fury.

A scream of hatred.

The scream lasted for only a moment, but it seemed to propel Bishop to a level of strength that Joe had never seen from an Antenna. She pushed forward against the straps that bound her to the chair. Every muscle in her body strained. These weren't the sporadic muscle twitches that Joe usually observed. She strained all of her muscles together in tandem, like a rowing crew. All that combined force joined to make something uncompromisingly powerful.

Joe watched, stunned, as the straps that bound Bishop's head loosened and stretched, giving way to an extra half-inch of slack.

But that was all Bishop needed.

Instead of using the relieved tension as an opportunity to pull *away* from the contraption that propped open her eyelids, Bishop *leaned into* the eye hooks.

"She's scraping out her corneas!" Chuck shouted.

On the screen, Bishop's head jerked up and down as she leaned forward into the hooks and used them to gouge at her eyes. It took only moments. Blood splattered onto the equipment. It rolled down her cheeks.

"Restrain her," Joe said into his walkie-talkie.

The orderlies hadn't needed orders. They were already at Bishop's side, grabbing her shoulders and head and pulling her away from the hooks.

"Tariq, disable her," Joe said.

"Increasing gas flow," Tariq said as he punched commands into his console. "She may have torn her breathing tube."

"Medical, check her tube."

"I'm on it," Hannah said. Through her headset, she relayed orders to her crew.

Joe kept his gaze on the screen.

The medics and orderlies now gathered around Bishop. Some of them reattached her bindings while the others hurried to bandage her still-bleeding eyes. The flurry of activity blocked the camera angles. But amid the chaos, Joe could see the vivid crimson drops of blood roll down Bishop's seat and splatter on the white floor.

"Is she in?"

Joe turned toward the voice. It came from Mr. Aguirre. He had stepped down off the platform and now stood with a hand resting on Chuck's chair. Mr. Aguirre leaned forward, his head alongside Chuck's, as he looked at the screens. Joe could see Chuck pulling away, uncomfortable with Aguirre's proximity.

"Is she in?" Aguirre repeated.

"We're aborting," Joe said.

"See if she's in." Mr. Aguirre stood and turned to face Joe. His tone didn't seem to be *ordering* Joe to comply. If anything, he had the slightest edges of an excited grin teasing its way across his face — a curious child who wanted to know if the mouse traps he helped his dad set had actually ensnared something during the night.

Although the frantic motion continued on the screen, all the work in the Control Room ceased. Everyone's attention fixated on Joe. Hannah muted her walkie-talkie; Tariq's hand hovered over his dial; Chuck backed away from his control panel.

Joe tried not to look at their faces. He tried not to gauge their level of investment or their desire to continue. He simply stepped down off the platform and walked to Chuck's control panel. He typed in a few commands. The monitor mounted in front of Bishop's eyes — still flashing and collaging with images of Victor Aminov — went black. The cacophony of Victor Aminov's voice recordings, as well as the female voice reciting his name, also cut off.

The lights in Bishop's cell then went black.

The cameras switched to night vision mode. In the eerie green-and-white scene, all the guards and orderlies stopped moving. Even the medics bandaging Bishop's bleeding eyes held their hands still, the gauze still loosely draped over her sockets that continued to pump out blood.

No one dared move. No one dared speak. No one dared interrupt what was about to happen.

Bishop, meanwhile, fought against her restraints.

Joe picked up a microphone. He spoke into it. "Can you see?" he said.

Bishop screamed. She twisted and writhed on the chair.

"Can you see?" Joe repeated.

Her screams began to lose their forcefulness. They transitioned into a cry.

"Can you see?" he said again.

Bishop's head lolled from side to side. That face which was so anguished, so angry a moment ago, seemed to melt. Her lips turned downward into a deep grimace that pulled at her entire face. It was a look of profound pain.

"Can you see?"

"Please..." Bishop croaked out, her voice gravelly and torn. "Please... please... please..." It seemed to be the only word she could say.

"Can you see?" Joe kept his delivery flat.

During one of his earliest tuning sessions, he had made the mistake of trying to comfort an Antenna. He had tried to make his voice soothing and sympathetic, but it had only triggered more pleas for mercy, pleas that Joe could not grant. That entire session had to be scrapped, and then *another* Antenna had been forced to endure the process. Because of that, Joe pretended he was a robot, incapable of human response.

"Can you see?"

It wasn't uncommon for them to have to wait thirty minutes for an answer to that question. Time meant nothing to the Antennas. They had become so unmoored to the physical plane that they seemed to struggle to grasp whether the question had actually been asked, as if the very concept of speech and questions were foreign to them now.

Joe would simply repeat the question again.

And again.

And again.

It was the kind of task that could be allocated to a recording, but Joe felt that as supervisor, it was *his* duty. Someone had to be the tether, reaching out into the darkness to make contact with this drifting sentience.

"Can you see?"

Bishop's breathing finally slowed. Her body stopped straining. Instead of constantly pulling against her bindings, her muscles settled into a twitching motion of uncontrolled muscle spasms that spanned her entire body.

Joe knew they were close now. "Can you see?"

"Yes." Bishop's voice was strained and quivering, as if she struggled to hold herself together.

Chuck tapped some commands on his keyboard. "Everything is recording. We're ready to receive intercepts."

Joe leaned forward. "Where are you?"

"In... in a car. No... no, a truck."

"What kind of truck?"

"Big."

"Are you driving?"

"No... no. I'm... passenger. Please, please, it hurts."

Joe kept his voice steady. "What do you see out the window of the truck?"

"Buildings... roads... brown... fields."

"Are there animals in the field?"

"Yes. Dogs... No. It's... goats."

Mr. Aguirre raised an eyebrow. "Hmm. We suspected Victor might be making a trip into Turkey."

"There... there's a sound," Bishop said. "Ringing."

"A phone?" Joe said.

"Yes... Please make it stop. It hurts."

"What is the number on the phone?" Joe asked.

As Bishop began reciting back the number, Mr. Aguirre tapped Chuck on the shoulder. "Flag the phone number and send it on immediately. Might be important."

"I know, sir. I work here," Chuck said as he expertly punched in his commands while looking over his shoulder to flash Mr. Aguirre a grin.

Mr. Aguirre put his hands up and smiled in return. "Sorry. I meant no disrespect." He looked toward Joe and bowed his head a bit. "I apologize. I'll step back and let you guys do your job. I just get a little excited when I get to be on this end of the process."

"No hard feelings, sir," Chuck said. "Can you tell us who Victor Aminov is and why he sucks?"

"You know I can't."

"I'm betting gun-runner," Chuck said. "Russian name and all. Tariq?"

"Drugs. President made that big speech on Tuesday about how the international drug trade funds terrorism. Mid-terms are in six months. I bet we'll get a lot of drug runners between now and then."

"Well, look at you," Chuck said. "Mr. News-Reader."

Joe loudly cleared his throat. "Gentlemen. Let's focus," he said curtly.

"Sorry, Joe." Chuck went back to work.

Joe clicked on his microphone again. "Describe everything you see. Describe everything you hear. Describe everything you smell. If people speak a language you do not understand, repeat their words out loud. If you see writing in a language you cannot read, describe its shape. Omit no detail."

Bishop moaned.

"Only when you've told us everything will you be done," Joe said. "Only then can we make the pain stop."

Bishop, her body still twitching, tilted her head toward the camera. The bloody gauze still hung loosely from her eyes. Her mouth twisted open and Bishop began speaking. The words flowed out in long strings of sounds that slurred together. It formed a mumbling mass of incoherence.

But no one in the Control Room seemed to mind.

"Uplink to HQ confirmed," Chuck said. "They're receiving these intercepts in real-time. They'll scrub and analyze them."

Everyone sat back in their seats.

A long afternoon had just begun.

CHAPTER 15

The high, warm sun shone down on Riley's face. And yet, she barely stirred, only rotating slightly so that the hood of her sweatshirt could shield her eyes from the bright light.

She slept. A deep, dreamless sleep.

It was so deep that she didn't notice that the grassy field, in a park in the middle of the town, had gone fully silent. The sounds of children playing had drifted away. The cars and pickups that had previously revved their engines up and down the main street no longer seemed to exist. Even the chirping of the birds and the rustle of the wind had fallen away into a total silence.

None of this stirred Riley.

But then her eyelids crept open.

She had no reason to awaken right then, other than that she felt *her* presence. She felt the eyes gazing at her. She felt the cold, wispy touch of *her* breath. She felt *her* screams rattling around inside her ears. Even if Riley couldn't hear the screams, they were there, within her head.

She knew the woman was near.

Riley stayed prone on the grassy field, much like she did when she was a child and believed that she could trick her parents into thinking that she was asleep so that they wouldn't force her to clean up the toys she had scattered around the living room. In this moment of terror, that familiar strategy was all that she could think to do. She stayed curled on her side, completely motionless. Her hand crept around in the front pocket of her sweatshirt to grasp the handle of the carving knife.

"It hurts," a voice said.

The voice was a whisper, but it seemed to fill the air. It was a sound both frail and all-encompassing.

Riley shut her eyes. She held her breath as she tried to force her mind to expel the woman from her world. She tried not to move, to become a lump of nothingness in the middle of the grassy field. Her only hope was that the woman wouldn't see her, wouldn't notice her heaving gasps of breath, wouldn't feel the sharp beats of Riley's heart pumping so furiously that Riley was convinced it must be shaking the earth around her. As much as Riley tried to be still, the presence of the woman remained.

It felt as though her heart pumped not just blood through her system, but something thicker and corrosive. It burned as it wedged its way through her arteries. It was dread. The dread flooded her, pulsating through her stomach, across her chest, and then out into her limbs and head.

But as soon as every last inch of Riley's body felt crippled by the dread, a new sensation replaced it. Resignation. Inevitability.

She could not run from this woman.

She could not force this woman away.

She could only confront the woman.

Riley opened her eyes and slowly pulled herself into a sitting position.

The playground was empty.

The streets were empty.

The world was empty.

Only Riley and the woman existed.

The woman stood at the far edge of the field, near the deserted playground, perhaps fifty yards from Riley. A safe distance that slowed Riley's heart rate a beat or two.

The woman still wore a hospital gown. Her head was bowed, angled to the ground so that her long black hair covered her face. Her body twitched in an unnatural rhythm, as though each individual muscle were hooked to a randomized system of electric shock probes.

To Riley, it felt as if the two of them waited in that silent field together for an hour, but it may have only been minutes. She kept expecting the woman to talk, or move, or scream, but the woman just stood, looking at the ground as her muscles spasmed.

Riley opened her mouth, fully intent on saying something. But her jaw quickly snapped shut again, fearful that any noise or movement might disrupt the seemingly safe status quo.

The standoff continued.

It lasted another minute, or maybe even an hour. Riley couldn't tell.

"Wh-wh-who are you?" Riley finally said, her quivering voice barely above a whisper. She couldn't explain it, but despite the softness of her words, she felt confident that the woman heard them across the expanse.

"I don't remember," came the woman's reply, the whispered words floating across the distance to easily reach Riley's ears.

"What happened to you?" Riley whispered.

"I don't remember."

"Why me?"

The woman stood silently. Riley wondered if the words had reached her. She was about to ask the question again when the woman finally spoke. "Because. You know *him*," she said.

"Who?"

"Him. Them. *They* did this to me."

Riley didn't understand. "Who are *they*?"

"Forever, I did not know. I was only in darkness," the woman said, her words finding strength and beginning to flow more clearly. "When they released me from that darkness, there was too much light. Too many sounds. I could not see who they were. Blinding light and deafening sound. They sent my mind whipping around the world. So fast.

"Then they would shut me back into the dark. I do not know how long I was in there. Maybe days. Maybe years. During that time, most of my mind drifted away. It detached from myself and folded off into the nothingness. I forgot my name. I forgot my family. I forgot my life.

"But I held onto one small piece of reality — the knowledge that I was not meant to be there. And so, I focused. I trained myself. I listened to the sounds around me, to the people talking. At last, one of them said a name."

Riley gulped. She stared wide-eyed as the woman's voice filled her head.

"When I returned to the dark, I searched the world for someone with that name," the woman continued. "Each time the lights came on, I gathered more pieces of information. My search got closer and closer. Until I found him."

At that moment, the woman finally raised her head. Even from across the field, Riley could see that the woman's eyes were dark. Trails of blood ran from her sockets down her cheeks. Those blood trails shifted as the woman's lips curled into a smile.

"And then I found his weakness," the woman said with a grin.

"What do you want?" Riley asked.

"I want him to feel pain. I want all of them to feel pain," the woman said.

Riley gulped. She gripped the handle of the knife a little tighter and brought its end slightly out of her pocket. She angled her body toward the woman and brought herself to a crouch.

"Please," Riley said. "I'm sorry for your pain—"

"—I *feel* no pain."

The woman smiled and cocked her head to the side. Her muscle twitches had stopped and she now stood there, like some demonic scarecrow. She wasn't sure, but Riley could almost hear the woman laughing inside her head. Or, at least, she *felt* the woman laughing.

"Please. Leave me alone," Riley said.

The woman's mouth didn't move, but a single word flowed clearly through her grinning teeth. "Never."

And with that, the woman lunged forward.

Her jerky, twisting body flew toward Riley. Her hand reached out. Her grinning mouth wrenched itself open into a deep, guttural scream that seemed to emit from inside Riley's own head. It all happened so fast. In one blink, the woman had crossed the field, and Riley could see the woman's wide-open eyelids and the bleeding, gelatinous masses that remained of her eyes.

Riley's mind commanded her body to act. She rose to her feet but each action, each movement, felt slow and labored, as if her entire body had been submerged in quicksand.

The woman flew closer, about to grab her.

Riley pulled the knife from her sweatshirt and slashed it at the woman.

The woman screamed.

**

Screams filled Riley's ears.

Multiple high-pitched, terrified screams.

Riley swung the knife around.

The woman wasn't in front of Riley anymore.

"Run, kids! Run!" a voice shouted. It was a woman's voice. But not *the* woman's voice. This voice lacked the hissing. It didn't possess the deep, gravelly sound of torn vocal cords. And it didn't come from *inside* Riley's head.

The screams were of children.

Riley blinked a few times.

A soccer team of twelve-year-old girls scattered away from Riley's position at center-field. Their parents raced over from the parking lot to scoop them up.

Riley's hand continued swinging the knife, but her grip began to quiver.

"Easy. Easy now." It was that woman's voice again.

Riley glanced to her side. The woman wore a track suit and a whistle. Her blonde hair was pulled into a ponytail. Sunglasses covered the woman's eyes. Riley stared intently at her to try to make out the woman's pupils. Maybe this was a trap. Maybe this was still *the* woman. Maybe beneath those sunglasses, this woman's eyes were gouged and deflated. Maybe she should stab this woman and end it now.

The coach seemed to sense Riley's intense need to see her eyes. She held her hands up. "It's okay. It's okay," she said. She reached up and pushed her sunglasses off her face and onto her head, revealing an unscathed set of hazel eyes.

Riley's head darted around as she took in her surroundings. People on all fringes of the park stood and stared at her, but the woman in the hospital gown wasn't among them.

On the street, a police cruiser screeched to a stop. Its wailing siren rattled Riley out of the last remnants of the hazy dream that still clouded her vision. She watched the police officer open the door and climb out of his car. He remained positioned behind the car door as he drew his weapon.

"Drop it!"

The soccer coach turned her attention to the cop and suddenly seemed more concerned about calming him than calming Riley. "It's okay, it's okay. She's not going to hurt anyone. You're not gonna hurt anyone, are ya, dear?"

Riley dropped the knife.

She fell down to her knees, put her head in her hands, and let the tears stream out. She cried there, hunched over in the grass.

CHAPTER 16

Joe sat at the desk in his office.

Across from him sat Mr. Aguirre, a wry grin on his plump face. "Two accidents in two days, eh, Joe?"

Joe folded his hands on his desk. "I want it entered into your official report that I recommended we start collecting intercepts when she was thirty percent sensory capable. It was your recommendation that we push to fifty percent."

"That was *your* call, Joe."

Joe tensed up and bit down on his lip.

Mr. Aguirre set down his tablet, folded his arms across his chest, and stared off. "And now we have a damaged Antenna."

"She scratched herself. It's common."

"A scratch on an Antenna is serious and expensive. But let's be clear, this wasn't a *scratch*. This Antenna broke free of its bindings and disabled one of its primary sources of stimulation."

"Oh, come on, Javi—"

"She stabbed her eyes out, Joe." The two men stared at each other; a little grin hung on Mr. Aguirre's lips. "Look, you know I'm a friend, Joe," he said calmly but with a hint of a patronizing tone.

"Uh-huh," Joe muttered, his gaze still fixed.

"I'll make a note in my report that a discussion was held on how far to push it. I'll stress the clarity of the intercepts we're receiving. Don't worry about it, Joe." He clutched his hand to his heart in a display of his earnestness, but even that seemed rehearsed and fake. "You and your team have accomplished so much here that I swear on my life that if it comes to it, I will personally fight for your future at this facility."

"How comforting."

"Besides, I believe that these accidents indicate more than simple lapses in safety procedures."

"What do you mean?"

"I've long believed that we're barely scratching the surface of the potential of Antenna research. I, for one, would love to try tuning your Antenna *without* her eyes. Who knows what possibilities that might open up? I've never been able to get the higher-ups to sign off on such an experiment because no one wants to blind an Antenna. Seems wasteful. But maybe this will enhance her audio abilities."

"Like how when the mind loses one sense, it compensates with the others."

"Exactly. Think of it. We could have Antennas that specialize in particular senses. As they arrive, we would simply trim out some of their extraneous senses and give the remaining senses a real jolt. We could have one Antenna that specializes in smell. One in sound. One in touch. We'd be able to sniff out bomb makers. Or feel someone's passcode as they entered it. Hell, if we knew what they were tasting at a particular moment, we might be able to tag their location to a specific restaurant." He smiled wide, allowing his imagination to really rev up. "And if we really wanted to amplify their abilities, I think we should begin training them *before* they go on the gas. When they still have their cognizant abilities. While they're still—"

"While they're still functioning humans."

Mr. Aguirre settled back into his seat. His grin remained, but the rest of the muscles in his face transformed from a genuinely eager scientist back to the calculating businessman. "They're always human, Joe. That's what makes them special."

Joe took a deep breath. "I never ask where they come from. They're already in a vegetative state when they arrive. But if you're talking about bringing conscious, living, breathing, thinking *people* here—"

"We're just having a spit-balling session. Between two old friends. The challenge of getting that ball rolling, just pushing the paperwork through... woo-wee. I'm just talking out loud. Gauging interest." Mr. Aguirre looked away and waved his hand, as if swatting down that last conversation.

Joe kept his gaze on the man. "If you're going to submit this up the ladder, just know that my staff will have a problem with what you're describing. We're not in the business of snipping out people's eyes or slicing off their ears. These are good people who work here."

A little twinkle developed in Mr. Aguirre's eye. "Are they?"

They both sat quietly a moment, letting those words sink in.

Riiiinnnng! The phone on Joe's desk broke the silence.

Joe picked it up. "This is Gerhard."

Tyler's voice came through the other end. "Sir, I have a call for you from an outside line."

"I'm busy."

"It's your daughter, sir."

Joe sat up straight. "Put her through."

He heard the click of the call being transferred, and then he heard the voice of his daughter. But he had never heard her like *this*. Her voice wavered and cracked as she spoke her first word, "Daddy?"

"Yes?" Joe's brow furrowed in concern, but he quickly forced his face to adopt a more neutral expression. His gaze glanced over at

Mr. Aguirre who had picked up his tablet and was once again tapping out notes and memos, fully engrossed in his own work. Or at least appearing to be.

"The police just brought me back home," Riley said, her voice tearful and broken.

A deep worry overtook Joe. His brow furrowed again and his eyes, now gazing past Aguirre and staring off into nothingness, grew sad and fearful. "What happened?" he said, not even trying to mask his concern.

"Just please come home."

"Is everything okay?" Joe asked. Joe noticed Mr. Aguirre had stopped typing on his tablet. The man didn't look up, didn't make eye-contact, but it was clear that he was now listening.

"I keep seeing her," Riley said. "She won't stop. I'm scared."

"I'll be home soon. You sit tight."

There was a long pause.

Joe held the phone tightly to his ear. "Riley?"

"I... I can't take it anymore," Riley finally said. "I'm scared of what I might do. I'm scared that I might..." the words and the thought trailed away from Riley's lips before she could finish them. There was a pause. And then, with a sad conviction, she said, "I'm scared that I'll end up like Mom."

"Don't do anything. I'm coming home now."

"Please hurry."

"I will. I love you, Riley."

She took a long breath. "Too," she said with an empty voice. Then she hung up.

Joe stood from his desk.

Mr. Aguirre idly glanced up from his tablet and smiled pleasantly. "Trouble?"

"My dog ran away last night," Joe said as he put on his coat. "Someone found her and called my daughter at the house. I need to pick her up."

"Do what you need to do."

"I probably won't be back tonight. I need to spend time with my daughter. Chuck will gather the intercepts and it should all go fine. He's a pro."

"Of course. Go see to young Riley."

Joe calmly walked to his door, taking his time to not look hurried. "You can hang out in my office as long as you need. I'm on my cell."

Mr. Aguirre cast his gaze back to his tablet. "Have a good night, Joe."

"You too."

Joe opened the door and ambled out into the hallway.

The door clicked closed behind him.

He looked around. As usual, the Level One hallway was empty. With his squeaking shoes echoing around the concrete walls, Joe strolled to the elevator. His posture remained relaxed — like a weary man finally clocking out for the day — but his eyes continually glanced back and forth. He tried to block out the sounds of his shoes on the linoleum so that he could hear the opening of any doors behind him.

He had one thing to do before he left for the day.

Confident that no one was watching him, Joe stepped toward the Control Room door.

He swiped his ID, pulled the door open and went inside.

T . J .   P A Y N E

Chuck sat at his station, leaning back in his chair and propping his feet up on his desk as he whiled away the hours. His system flashed red lights — "Recording In Progress." On the main screen, Bishop remained in her chair, her lips moving as she spoke, although the audio had long since been muted in the Control Room.

As Joe closed the door behind him, Chuck greeted him with a little wave. Across the room, Tariq's screens were filled with spreadsheets of gas-distribution algorithms, or something. He had earbuds in and seemed to be engrossed in the mindless, day-to-day inventory requirements of the job.

As Tariq reached toward his ears to remove his earbuds, Joe waved him off. "Just here to talk to Chuck."

"Yeah, kid, no one wants your fucking input," Chuck shouted over his shoulder.

Tariq smiled and leaned toward his screen to continue his work.

Joe calmly pulled a chair over to Chuck's desk and took a seat. "How're the intercepts coming?" he asked.

Chuck shrugged. "Not bad. It's mostly slurring and mumbling now. HQ's gonna have to scrub it to pull out actual intel. There was a bit of an abnormality a little while ago, though. Some of the stuff came out crystal." He leaned forward at his desk and clicked around on his monitor until a transcript showed up. "Weird stuff. She kept saying 'I don't remember' as if she were actually having a conversation with someone. Talked about being in darkness, or something. Super clear audio. I was gonna flag it and—"

"Look, print out the transcripts and I'll review them later. I just need something before I go."

"What's up?"

"I have a research request."

"Case number?" Chuck picked up a pen and a pad of sticky-notes.

"Log it under today's case. 10598."

"Subject to be researched?"

Joe glanced over at Tariq one last time, making sure he wasn't listening. Then he turned back to Chuck. "Katherine Gerhard."

The old timer's hand froze. Joe watched the well-worn wrinkles on Chuck's face draw tighter as he raised his head. Their eyes met.

"Kate?"

Joe didn't respond.

Chuck's face now scrunched up in confusion. "How in the hell is Kate wrapped up in the Victor Aminov case?"

"I wanna see inside her computer. Just log the research request under the open case file. No one will check. No one will know."

"Oh, come on, Joe. You know I can't just—"

"She killed herself, Chuck."

Chuck bowed his head. He didn't speak. He didn't register any shock or surprise, just sympathy coupled with discomfort. He obviously had known (everyone at work must have known) but didn't know what to say.

Joe took Chuck's awkward silence as an opportunity to press. "You've eaten her cooking. You've been to our house. She considered you a friend."

"Oh, gee, come on... "

"She killed herself. I need to know why."

The two men looked at each other.

Finally, Chuck's eyes turned downward. He looked at his belly, heaving underneath the red flowers of his Hawaiian shirt, and released a sad sigh. "I don't know. Maybe in a week or two, Joe. But I feel Da Man's breath on the back of my fucking neck right now."

"You and I both know that this ain't the first time *someone* has used the resources at our disposal to spy on an ex-wife."

"I don't know what you're talking 'bout."

Joe's eyes narrowed and his jaw clenched into a threatening glare.

Chuck gulped. "I never snooped on Carol."

"I believe you. And I'm sure if I were to open up some old case files, there'd be no trace of someone on my staff looking up emails between Carol and her old college fling. In fact, I can downright guarantee that no one would find evidence of that kinda shit in there, right?"

Chuck bit his lip. The silence sat between them. Finally, Chuck released a resigned breath. "Whaddya need, Joe?"

"Just recent stuff. Last couple days. Emails, phone records. Crime scene reports of her death would be great. If she had any doctor's visits in the last week, I'd like to see the physician's notes. Whatever the system can dredge up. And I'd like them tonight, please."

"I'll see what I can do."

Joe patted him on the back. "I owe you, Chuck."

"Yeah. You do."

With that, Joe turned and walked out of the room.

CHAPTER 17

The alarm chirped as Joe stepped into his house.

Every light had been turned on, including the TV, which loudly blared out a news broadcast.

Joe went to the alarm pad and entered his combination.

"Riley?" he called. "I'm home."

He wondered if she could hear him over the loud TV. He walked over and turned it off. The house didn't go quiet yet. The stereo also blasted at full volume. He stepped over and turned that off too, at which point he heard *another* noise. The radio in the kitchen was also on high, only not playing music — it had been set to static.

A knot of worry twisted up inside Joe's stomach. Riley had constructed a wall of sound throughout the house, apparently in some attempt to block out something else she was hearing.

He walked toward the kitchen, passing the hallway. A figure caught the corner of his eye. A woman moved toward him from the shadows, a knife clutched in her hand. Joe jerked to a halt and spun around, too startled to even allow a scream to form in his lungs.

The brief moment of terror passed as he realized who it was.

"Riley?" he said as his eyes made sense of the fact that this frail, waif-like person who stood before him was, in fact, his daughter.

Although she held the knife up, right at chest level, her movements lacked force or purpose. She just sort of drifted in his direction, stumbling around on legs that were too exhausted to support her. She stopped moving forward and instead just stared at him with glazed eyes that narrowed in either fear or confusion, Joe couldn't tell which.

"Riley? Are you okay?" he said. He put up his hands as he stepped toward her, the same way he would when facing an unknown dog. "Put the knife down."

Her head cocked to the side and her mouth hung open. Her eyes studied Joe. They darted around in her head, zeroing in on his face and then the rest of him. The entire time, she never relaxed her grip on the handle of the knife.

"Are you real?" she finally asked.

"I'm real, sweet-heart."

"How do I know?"

Joe thought for a moment. He kept his hands up as he slowly advanced on her. "Remember when it was, um, Christmas? You were 'bout seven, I think. I bought you every Nerf gun in the store. All of 'em. We took every pillow in the house and built these huge forts all about. Everywhere. And then we shot at each other for hours."

Riley's eyes continued watching him. Her face remained blank.

He continued, "Your mom had gone out to help your grandparents with something. When she came home, though..." he paused to smile at the memory. "She seemed so mad. We had trashed the house. She stomped around, scolding us. But it was all a diversion. She just wanted us to drop our weapons as she grabbed this battery-powered, Gatling Gun lookin' thing. Then she just unleashed on us. Chased us into the bedroom and pummeled us with little Nerf darts. God, that was one hell of a fun day. Wasn't it?"

The muscles in Riley's face, which had been so tight, finally loosened. "I miss mom."

"I do too."

Clunk. The knife dropped from Riley's hand and fell to the floor.

Joe stepped toward her. They wrapped their arms around each other and held on tight. He could feel her take heaving breaths as the tears flowed freely from her eyes and soaked into his shirt. She sobbed a silent, painful sob. He put his hand on her head and held her close. Secure and safe.

"We'll get you help, Riley. It'll be okay."

***

Joe knelt beside his daughter, holding her hand, as she sat at the head of the dining table. He motioned over to the doorway where Hannah stood. She smiled warmly at Riley, but she also kept her distance, waiting to be invited to the table.

"Hannah has degrees in psychology and psychiatry, as well as medicine," Joe said.

"Double Ph.D. with an M.D. to boot," Hannah said. "Asian parents are a bitch to impress, what can I say?"

Riley replied with a thin smile.

It seemed to be all the invitation that Hannah needed. She took a single firm step into the room then paused by the table for a moment. "Let's go ahead and flush all my amazing, awesome, badass academic achievements. I'm here as a friend. Is it cool if we just sit and chat?"

Riley's head bobbed in a little nod.

Hannah used that nod as the final permission to slowly walk over and take a seat at the table. "God, I haven't seen you in forever. You're like a real, grown, human-thing now. Remember your sixth birthday party at this house? I got you a little robot. It could, like, lift things and stuff. I thought it was super-cool. What kid doesn't want a flipping robot? But even for a six-year-old, you seemed totally unimpressed. Whatever happened to that little bugger?"

Riley looked down at the table. A grin cracked her face. "I walked it off the counter. It fell and never worked right again."

"What?! That thing cost a hundred bucks."

"It wasn't a very good toy," Riley said, shaking her head and letting out the barest hints of a laugh.

"It was an *awesome* toy. It was a fucking robot."

"It just walked and made beeping sounds."

"Yeah. Like I said — awesome."

The two women looked at each other and smiled.

Hannah threw up her hands. "Fuck it. I don't know what kids want. I shoulda gotten you a Barbie or something."

"Yuck."

"How about a machete? Are girls into machetes these days?"

"Now that woulda been awesome."

"Next year. For your high school graduation."

"I graduate *this* year."

"Jesus Christ, you're old. I guess I am too."

They sat silently for a moment.

Joe stayed crouched by Riley's side. His gaze glanced from Riley to Hannah, but neither made eye contact with him, opting instead to look down at the table and smile to themselves. It was then he realized that Hannah seemed to be purposefully mirroring Riley's posture. The slouch in the seat, the downcast eyes, the hands rigidly clasped on the table.

It felt like a good time for him to join in as well. He rose from his crouch and pulled out a chair. He began to lower himself into the seat.

"Joe, can we have a minute? Just us gals?" Hannah asked. Her voice was pleasant, as if she was just making an off-hand suggestion, but when he looked up at her face, he saw her eyes motion him to the door.

He glanced over at Riley. She didn't protest.

"Um, yeah. Yeah, of course," Joe said as he stood.

He gave Riley a little pat on the hand and then walked out into the living room.

He swung the door mostly shut but left a small crack.

"All the way," Hannah called out. "I wanna hear a click."

With a sigh, he pulled the dining room door behind him until it snapped closed. He stood in the living room by himself. The muffled conversation from the dining room drifted through the closed door and into the silent house. He knelt down and held his ear close to the door's paneling.

"Look, when I say we're friends, I mean it," he heard Hannah say. "You can trust me. Anything you tell me, I won't judge. There may be things you don't want me to tell your father. I can't make any promises, but I'm totally open to discussing it and seeing where we end up. Is that all cool with you?"

There was a pause. Joe could only assume that Riley nodded in agreement.

Hannah continued, "Please just level with me — are you on any drugs? No judgment. Honesty is the best way I can help, and believe me, I've done some shit in my day. Anything?"

"No."

"And I'm not just talking hard stuff. Are you using pot?"

"Not in a few months."

"Prescription meds, like oxy?"

"No."

"I don't know what else kids are into these days... Shrooms? Molly? ADHD meds? Sniffing glue?"

"No."

"Alcohol? Are you drinking?"

"Sometimes at parties. On weekends. But not now."

"Did you get any sleep last night?"

"No."

"How's your appetite? What have you had to eat today?"

"Nothing."

"None of this is uncommon considering what you went through yesterday. It's okay to grieve, Riley."

The voice that replied was strangely forceful. "It's not grief."

"Tell me what you mean."

Riley didn't answer.

Joe pressed his ear harder against the door. The house was so quiet he could hear the hum of his Wi-Fi router. He could hear his own breathing and the scratching sound his clothes made as he adjusted his position. But he couldn't hear what Riley was saying, if anything.

Finally, he slowly straightened himself, trying hard not to make any noise that might betray his eavesdropping. Then, one gentle step at a time, he tiptoed from the room.

He went to his bedroom and closed the door.

Then, he sat at his desk and logged into his computer. He opened the home security app. The feeds from various security cameras tiled onto his screen. A fish-eye, overhead view of Hannah and Riley sitting at the dining table came up. The camera had been hidden inside the screw-cap that held the dining room's light fixture to the ceiling. When the crew installed the security system, oh-so-many years ago, Joe had instructed them to hide every single camera lens. He didn't want his wife and daughter to know they were being watched.

A twinge of guilt passed through Joe as he watched the conversation unfold in the dining room. He knew Riley assumed it was private. But he was her father, and she was suffering. To Joe, safety always trumped privacy.

He plugged a headset into the speakers.

"And this woman you're seeing..." Hannah said, leaning forward. In the short length of time it took Joe to go to his room and load up his computer, Hannah had evidently steered the conversation right into the meat of Riley's problems. "Have you ever seen her before?"

"No," Riley said. Her voice quivered in the response.

Joe could see that Riley's head was angled in Hannah's general direction, but she seemed to be focusing more toward the seat *beside* Hannah.

Hannah noticed too. She glanced to the empty seat, but quickly returned her focus to Riley. "So, this woman isn't anyone you know? A friend's mom? A teacher? A neighbor?"

"No."

Hannah nodded. "When was the first time you ever saw this woman?"

"Yesterday," Riley said. "On the drive here." She continued staring off to the side.

Joe leaned forward. He examined the area of the screen that Riley's eyes fixated on. The only light in the dining room came from the overhead fixture. It shone down brightly on the table and on the crowns of Hannah and Riley's heads, but the rest of the dining room stayed dim and shrouded in shadows. It was designed that way, of course, Joe realized. It made for a more intimate dining experience.

"Did you ever see this woman, or someone like her, in maybe a dream?" Hannah asked.

Riley didn't answer. She visibly gulped as she continued staring to Hannah's side.

Hannah seemed to stiffen in her seat. By now, it was all too obvious that Riley's focus was not on Hannah, but on something else in the room.

"Riley?"

Riley's breaths came heavier now, but her head stayed fixated on that empty seat.

"Do you see something next to me?"

Riley's answer was a whisper, said quickly as if it were snatched from her lips by the wind. "Yes."

Joe stared at the area of the table beside Hannah. The table wasn't exactly centered in the room, and the overhead light didn't particularly catch the seat to Hannah's right. The light threw shadows across the chair and made it blend in a bit with the floor. The more Joe stared, the more his eyes strained, the more that the shadows in that area of the table seemed to swirl and move. The feed had the slightest delay. It caused a hiccup. A small glitch in the unfocused background images.

He leaned even closer.

The shadows seemed to coalesce. Joe's eyes went wide and the breath became trapped in his throat. The faintest outlines of a pale figure emerged from the blackness.

On the screen, Hannah pivoted in her chair. She looked toward that ghostly, pale form who seemed to shift and stare right back at Hannah.

But Hannah had no reaction.

She simply moved her head around and scanned the darkness for a moment. Then, without an extra breath or twitch, Hannah turned back toward Riley.

"Can you describe to me what you're seeing?" Hannah said with all of her professional calmness.

The steadiness of Hannah's voice made Joe take a calming breath of his own. He blinked his eyes. The figure in the chair was gone, or perhaps it had never been there to begin with. A trick of light being caught on an outdated camera system.

To be sure, he scrolled the file back a few seconds.

He looked again.

No figure. No shadow. No nothing. Perhaps just some wood-grain catching the light wrong.

Joe smiled to himself as he rubbed his eyes.

"Fuck man," he said. "Keep it together."

He took the earbuds out of his ears and leaned back in his seat.

Ding! — his body jerked at the sharp sound of his "new message" alert. He didn't realize how quiet his house had been that such a common sound could startle him so.

With another embarrassed grin at his own jumpiness, he pulled out his phone and checked the message. The smile immediately vanished from his lips.

"The requested files are on the server. — Chuck"

Joe leaned toward his computer. He opened the remote server, entered all the info for the multi-step verification process, and logged in.

There it was — an entire folder labeled "KATHERINE GERHARD."

He opened the folder. He read the names of the various subfolders.

His throat clenched up.

His hand trembled as he clicked on one of the folders.

"Police Body-Cam Footage."

CHAPTER 18

The video started so fast that Joe struggled to orient himself to what exactly was happening. The camera, clipped to the chest of a police officer, whipped around as the officer opened his car door and stepped out into a sunny afternoon in a middle-class neighborhood.

Almost immediately, the sharp snap of gunshots — *Bang! Bang! Bang!* — rang out from one of the houses. The camera shook violently as the cop ducked back behind his car and drew his sidearm.

"I got shots fired! Shots fired!" Joe heard the man shout into his radio.

The video then stabilized as the cop took a moment to gather himself. The camera filmed from his crouched position as he aimed his handgun over the hood of his car toward the small ranch-style house.

The yard was green but the grass had grown tall and the weeds slightly taller. Untrimmed shrubs hugged the house, their stray branches poking out like a bad haircut. Kate didn't want to hire a gardener, partially to prove to Joe that she could handle all the *man* work by herself, he suspected. She did a fine job, but the maintenance occasionally got away from her.

The cop rose from his crouch and scooted his way around the front of his car, advancing on the bright red front door. The same door where Joe would stand, arms crossed and eyes rolling, as Kate berated him for bringing Riley home after midnight on a Sunday. *Don't you know she has a pre-calc test tomorrow? And she hasn't even started her Scarlet Letter project. It's all on her calendar. You never pay attention to what goes on in her life!*

The red door opened. The cop backed up and retook his defensive posture behind the front of his car.

It was then that Joe saw her.

Kate stumbled backwards out of the house.

Joe couldn't believe how different she looked. He had seen her only a week or two ago, and at the time, he admitted to himself that she still looked as beautiful as ever. The single-parent lifestyle, which tended to age most people, actually made Kate appear more youthful. He never asked her about her dating life, but he knew she wouldn't be single for long.

This was not the same woman. She seemed to have aged twenty years in the last week. For a moment, the difference was so pronounced that Joe assumed she must have been caught testing out some Halloween costume. This must be a wig and pale-face makeup. She always had a fair complexion that stood out against her wavy black hair, but now her face seemed positively white. Her hair wasn't combed or even pulled back. It just sat tangled and bulging on her head in wispy knots.

She turned to face the cop. Her mouth was twisted open, as if it had frozen mid-scream.

This wasn't a costume. It was a transformation.

"What do you want?!" she yelled, but not at the officer. She was shouting back into the house. "Get out! Get out!"

"Police! Drop the weapon!" the officer commanded.

That's when Joe saw the gun in Kate's hand. It was a slim, black semi-automatic handgun. He couldn't tell the make and model from the shaky footage, but it was the small type of gun that she could conceal easily in a purse or in an ankle holster. Joe was sure it must be a toy, or perhaps some household object that simply looked like a weapon. Kate *hated* guns. She refused to keep one in the house. Where the hell did she get this?

"I said, drop it!" the officer commanded again.

Kate didn't seem to hear or even notice the police officer. Her attention remained focused on whatever she saw inside her house.

"Leave me alone! Just leave me alone!" Her screams were frantic and crazed.

"This is the police," the officer announced again, even louder this time. "Drop the weapon, now!"

Kate finally turned and faced the cop, seeing him for the first time. But her eyes didn't stay focused on him for long. They began darting to the left and right. Judging by the way her mouth hung open and her eyes widened in fear, everywhere she looked, she saw *something*.

She made heaving, gasping sounds as tears began to stream, uncontrollably, down her face. The tears of some horrible realization.

"She's everywhere... she's everywhere..." Kate cried out.

"Calm down, ma'am." The cop seemed to realize that the situation was more a mental disturbance than an active shooter. He kept his weapon trained on Kate, but his voice adopted a negotiating tone. "You're safe. The police are here. But I need you to set the gun on the ground."

Kate continued to ignore him. She stared off. Her breathing slowed and the muscles on her face relaxed. A deep calm seemed to settle inside her body.

"She's only in my head… she's only in my head," Kate repeated, as if it were her new mantra. "She's only in my head. She's only in my head."

She went silent. Her gaze became fixed and firm. It was a look of deep determination; it was a look Joe knew well. Kate had made up her mind to do something. There would be no talking her out of it. Without any hesitation, Kate raised the gun to her temple.

"No! Don't—" the officer began to shout.

Bang!

Joe jumped at the sight.

Even with the shaking, distorted video from the body cam, he could see her head jerk to the side as a plume of red mist sprayed out of her left temple, accompanied by a few larger chunks of skull and brain. He could plainly see her blood splatter over the yellow siding of the house and then her body crumple down onto the front step.

The camera shook violently as the cop ran from the safety of his car toward the body that lay uncomfortably draped half on the front step and half on the front bush by the door.

Bile rushed to fill Joe's mouth. His stomach felt as though it had merged with his lungs. Air couldn't get into his body fast enough, and when it did, it made him nauseous. He stood, forgetting that his earbuds were still firmly lodged in his ears. The cord pulled his keyboard to the floor with a clatter and yanked the earbuds from his ears. He barely noticed.

Pacing the room, he forced himself to take deep, calming breaths. His hands formed fists. And then released. And then formed fists again. Within moments, he felt his body settle down. The nausea had passed, but a new emotion quickly replaced it.

A deep sadness seemed to pull him toward the floor, threatening to submerge him in an inky blackness. He wanted to lay down and close his eyes.

That emotion also passed.

He sat back down at his computer and opened up more of Kate's files.

CHAPTER 19

Riley felt numb.

Her experience at the park had rattled her. She had almost slashed an entire soccer team of little girls, all out of fear of the woman. Riley had been able to explain her situation to the police at the park. She put on quite a show, tearing up as she explained how she couldn't sleep after her mom's suicide and needed to take a walk but passed out in the park. She told them that the soccer team had simply startled and disoriented her, but she was alright now.

The lucidness with which she was able to lie to the cops surprised Riley. Maybe she *hadn't* gone crazy. A crazy person couldn't wave a knife at children in a public park and then talk the police into giving her a ride home. Not to the hospital. Not to jail. They took pity on her and drove her all the way to her father's house.

The woman had been there in the police car for that drive.

She sat right beside Riley, twitching and chattering her teeth as her head lolled on her shoulders. The woman talked about goats and phone numbers, or something. But Riley ignored her. The cops told Riley to be good and get some rest, and then they let her out and drove away.

When she arrived back home, the woman followed her in. She screamed and lunged and clawed at her own face until her flesh peeled off into her fingernails. Riley tried to ask the woman questions but, between her screams, she only muttered things about guns and street intersections.

At one point, Riley took out her phone and filmed the woman. At least she would have evidence, something she could show to the police or to her father. But the pictures and the video played back with only a bare shot of the living room. No screams, no blood, and certainly no woman.

After that, the woman vanished for a while.

In some ways, this unnerved Riley more than having the woman screaming and lunging at her. As much as she thought she had regained control over her fear, she realized that she couldn't sleep, couldn't eat, couldn't do anything as long as she knew that the woman might appear.

It was then that she considered that there was only one potential sure-fire way to rid herself of the woman. One way for her to sleep. One way to see her mom again. She envisioned pressing a knife against her wrist. She imagined the cuts opening wider, ever wider, until they were deep and expansive enough for the woman to flow out from Riley. All the woman's darkness would drip down into the bathtub. And Riley would be free.

It seemed to be the only solution. Like leeches sucking out poison, Riley could drain the woman from her system, her mind, her body. And then she could sleep. A quiet, black sleep.

The fantasy was so attractive that it scared her. She called her dad. He came home quickly. Quicker than she ever expected. Time seemed to be moving at an unsteady pace these last few days. Riley could sit in silence for hours, looking around her for evidence of the woman, and then glance at the clock to see that only a few minutes had passed. At other times, her mind seemed to drift into a fog and when something finally jarred it back to reality, she would realize that an hour had slipped through some crack in time.

It was a while ago that her dad came home and walked through the door.

Time had played a funny trick on her again. It had skipped forward. Now she sat at the dining table with her dad's coworker, Hannah. Their conversation together had clipped along. Riley liked Hannah. She always did. And, if anything, that fondness for Hannah made the conversation about Riley's own mental state all the more uncomfortable. It sucked to have someone you respected diagnose you as a whack-job.

"This woman you saw today, is it the same woman you saw last night?" Hannah asked.

Riley nodded.

She wasn't looking at Hannah, instead keeping her gaze fixed off to Hannah's side. The screaming woman had appeared in the seat beside Hannah early in the conversation. She was gone now, but Riley could still feel her presence. She couldn't really define the sensation, but she could feel a sort of "pressure" squeezing at her brain whenever the woman was near. It took her the last two days to really link the two together. She originally thought that it was a sleep-deprivation headache, or maybe dehydration.

No.

It was the woman opening some door into Riley's head.

Riley was sure of it.

"What does this woman do?" Hannah asked.

Riley sat silently.

"You can tell me."

"She used to scream at me. I stopped responding to that. And now she's trying other things."

"Other things?"

"Making me see stuff."

"What kind of stuff?" Hannah leaned forward.

But Riley barely acknowledged Hannah's presence.

"Riley?" Hannah repeated. "What kind of stuff? What is she making you see?"

"My mom," Riley said.

It was true. The woman no longer sat in the empty seat to Hannah's right. Instead, it was Riley's mom. She looked good, Riley thought. She wore one of her mustard-yellow tanks-tops that had a big pink heart in the center. Her mom had found that shirt on the clearance rack at Target and ended up buying five of them.

Riley didn't remember her mom being frugal back in the day, but ever since the divorce, her mom made an effort to clip coupons, buy clearance clothes, and save, save, save.

It embarrassed Riley that whenever she had friends over, they would see her mom wearing the exact same yellow tank-top, as if the woman only owned one shirt. Riley's friend Silvia theorized that all this newfound frugality was simply Riley's mom's way of taking control of her life again and decreasing any reliance she had on Riley's dad.

And yet, seeing her mom sit at the table now, wearing that stupid yellow tank-top, made Riley's chest throb with a deep pain. Her mom was beautiful. Riley always knew that and always hoped that she too would have the good-fortune of aging so gracefully.

Her mom only wore makeup for special occasions and made no effort to hide the crow's feet that had grown around the edges of her eyes. The same with the laugh-lines that formed on her forehead and her cheeks whenever she stretched her face into that wide grin, often accompanied by a howling, unrestrained guffaw when she found something amusing.

Those loud laughs often burst out at inopportune times — dinner, the movies, even Uncle Dan's funeral — and were often met by a glare from Riley. Her mom would then try to swallow the laugh, which only resulted in a gagging, snorting sound. At which point, much to Riley's mortification, her mom would laugh even louder.

The person she saw seated next to Hannah was exactly how Riley hoped to remember her mom. It was the image she wanted to carry in her mind of her mother forever. Yellow clearance tank-top be damned.

Hannah turned and joined Riley in gazing at the seat. But Hannah's eyes continued to roam around, scanning the room for any trace of what had grabbed Riley's attention.

Apparently, Hannah saw nothing.

It was then that the edges of her mom's smile seemed to pull themselves higher and tighter. Her mom's gentle, strong mouth had morphed into a wide, unnatural grin. Her toothy smirk ascended past the level of her cheekbones into a monstrous smile that was too big to be humanly possible. Her eyes grew large. The whites of her eyes filled with blood, as though someone were pouring red paint into a glass orb. Those blood-eyes stared at Riley. Her left temple fell away and blood spewed out the wound and splashed onto the dining table.

And then she laughed. That whooping guffaw of a laugh, as natural and familiar as Riley remembered it. Only now, instead of seeing her mom's age-lines wrinkle up in joy during the laugh, the sound was formed from somewhere within a convulsing head that drained blood from its eyes and temple.

The laugh continued. Longer and louder than Riley ever remembered it, as though it were a record, stuck in a hiccupping loop.

Riley clenched her eyes shut and angled her head down toward the table.

She felt someone grasp her hand. A warm, tender grasp.

It was Hannah.

"Listen, grief can be a mind-fuck," Hannah said, patting Riley's hand. "Sometimes our minds are like reservoirs. More and more gets poured into it, and they fill and fill. And our little emotional reservoirs have always held, no matter what shit we've dealt with. We think we can deal. But grief is this fucking monsoon. And it just doesn't stop. And it fills our reservoir. And fills it. And fills it. Then all those dams and dykes and levees and locks or whatever, all those things we've built to keep our reservoirs from overflowing... they burst. And when one of them bursts, they all burst. Like dominoes. And it can be debilitating. But it's okay. It's normal."

Riley took a breath and opened her eyes.

Her mother was gone.

But there was something new instead.

A purplish, lumpy mound lay in the center of the table.

The bright dining room light, shining directly down on the lump, made it hard for Riley to make out what it actually was. It took her eyes a second to adjust, and when they did, she could see a foot protruding from the mound. And then she saw a hand with little fingers.

It all clicked together. This strange, unmoving purple mass was — or had been — a baby.

It was small, probably only a few months old. Its entire body, from its toes to the crown of its head, was wrinkled. The way it was curled on its side made Riley initially think that it must be cold. It needed a blanket to shelter its naked, frail body. But its purple, blotchy, unmoving skin said otherwise.

Riley couldn't look away. She stared at its face. Its eyes were closed and its mouth had pursed up and frozen in a look of discomfort, as if its life had been plucked from it mid-cry.

The baby wore an orange tag on its wrist which stood out brightly against its dull-purple skin.

For a moment, Riley feared that if she leaned in to read the tag, the baby might spring to life. She pushed that thought out of her mind. Somehow, she sensed that the woman had placed this baby here for a reason. To tell her something.

Riley slowly rose from her seat. She barely registered Hannah's concerned face, curiously observing her. Riley leaned over the table. There was a name on the tag.

"Riley? What's going on?" Hannah asked. "What do you see?"

"Ashley," Riley said, reading the baby's wrist tag. "Ashley... Chao." She looked over at Hannah whose face had twisted up in confusion.

"What did you say?"

"Ashley Chao," Riley repeated as she settled back into her seat. "Did you lose a baby?"

Hannah gulped. She stiffened in her seat, but she maintained eye-contact. Her voice stayed steady and professional. "That was, um, that was probably ten years ago, or so. Ashley had a fever. My husband and I took her to the hospital. It was only about twenty minutes later and she just... um... she just stopped breathing. It was devastating. But it does happen."

They sat for a moment. Riley felt Hannah's eyes studying her. She had to look away.

"Who told you about Ashley?" Hannah asked.

Riley glanced back to the table. The baby was gone.

"Riley?" Hannah said. "How do you know about Ashley?"

As Riley was about to answer, the dining room door swung open. Riley's dad stepped into the room. He stood there for a moment, watching Riley and Hannah. Riley opened her mouth to say something when her dad suddenly walked over to the table.

Hannah stood and silently greeted him.

They stared at each other, both oblivious to Riley's presence. Riley could only watch as her dad cupped Hannah's face in his hands and pulled her in for a kiss. The sensual sweetness of the kiss quickly gave way to an eruption of passion. Hannah reached down into his pants as his lips worked their way around her neck. His hands, in their hurry, struggled to undo the buttons on her shirt.

He fumbled through one button at a time. He couldn't get them undone fast enough. Hannah's shirt fell from her shoulders revealing her slender body and olive skin. For the first time, Riley realized just how attractive Hannah truly was.

Hannah unclasped her bra, letting it fall to the ground. Riley's dad tenderly cupped her breasts as he bent down to kiss them. While his tongue gently roamed over her nipples, Hannah forcefully grabbed him by the hair. This seemed to incite them both with a sense of passion and urgency.

He undid his belt and kicked off his pants. Hannah seated herself on the dining table. She lay down. Then, supporting herself with her feet and her shoulder blades, she arched her back, raising her waist off the table so she could slide off her pants. And then her black panties.

He was shirtless by now. He climbed on top of her.

The table shook. Hannah moaned as she rolled from side to side. Her moans became louder, more uncontrolled, until she shouted out an ecstatic, "Oh, god!"

He held his hand to her lips. "Shhh. You'll wake Riley," he said.

"Riley? What are you seeing?"

The voice belonged to Hannah, but it was calm and clinical.

Riley blinked...

Her father was no longer in the room. No clothes on the floor. No one on top of the table. Everything was as it was. Hannah still sat to Riley's side, her brow furrowed in concern and curiosity.

"You were seeing something over there, weren't you?" Hannah said.

Riley nodded.

"What was it?"

"Did... did you have sex with my dad?"

A look of shock flashed across Hannah's face. "What?"

"When I was a kid. Were you two having an affair?"

Hannah blinked. Her mouth fluttered as she tried to find the words to say.

A strange realization washed over Riley. "Did Mom find out? Is that why they divorced?"

Hannah looked down.

"Is it?" Riley said.

"Your father and I both regret what we did. Ashley had just died. My marriage had become really strained and I just wasn't in a good frame of mind. Your dad was, and always has been, a dear friend. He was so supportive during that time. And it just... it just kinda happened. That's no excuse, of course. It was a bad choice. There were a lot of bad choices. Your father and I both knew it."

She reached out and grasped Riley's hand.

"I'm sorry, Riley. I'm so, so sorry," Hannah said.

Riley didn't really hear her. The strange pressure throbbed against the backside of her eyes again. The woman was crafting something new for Riley's enjoyment.

"Did your mom tell you about your dad and me?" Hannah asked.

"No," Riley said, her eyes now gazing intently at the center of the table.

"Did you overhear it in a conversation? Or a fight when you were young? Some little comment that your mom said that you're only now putting together?"

"No."

"This woman is telling you this?"

"She's showing me."

"How does this woman know these things? How did she know about Ashley?"

Riley blinked. Within that briefest flutter of time, when Riley's eyes reopened, the woman now stood in the center of the empty table. Her eye-sockets, the blood still trailing from them to her cheeks, angled down to stare at Riley. Riley wanted to close her eyes but found herself unable to look away from that pale face and cavernous eyes.

"Riley?" Hannah repeated. "How does this woman know about Ashley?"

The woman's mouth didn't move, but Riley heard her voice all the same. It echoed around inside Riley's head.

Riley repeated what the woman had said. "She found you. She got in."

"In? In where? In *my head*?"

Riley nodded. "Dad first. And then you. She's been watching you. She's been studying you. She's been looking for weaknesses. Then she moved into Mom."

The edges of the woman's mouth twisted upward.

"And now she's in my head."

The woman grinned down on Riley.

CHAPTER 20

Joe sat at his computer, consumed by his research into Kate's last few days.

His back and neck clenched tight from leaning forward. He had stared at the screen so intently that he hadn't blinked in several minutes, and now his eyes stung from the dryness. At least, that was the reason he told himself for why he suddenly felt the uncontrollable burn of his eyes as they began to water.

With each of Kate's personal emails he read, each photo he saw, each transcript of a doctor's visit, each 911 call that someone was in her home, each new piece of information made him lean in closer, hold his breath, and move with new urgency.

Apparently, the hallucinations had started only three days before her death. Judging by her emails and transcripts of phone calls to friends, at first it was all vague. The sound of a voice in another room. The hazy outline of a person who vanished the moment the lights turned on.

By Monday afternoon, she called 911. The report from the officer on the scene found no signs of an intruder and no signs of forced entry.

There was an email thread between Kate and her friend Fran, someone she knew from yoga whom Joe had met once or twice, where they debated whether or not to tell Riley. Kate didn't want to worry Riley. But to be safe, she accepted Fran's offer to loan her a gun.

Joe's throat clenched as he read that email. *That's* where the gun came from. And yet, he still struggled to believe that Kate, of all people, would ever feel so vulnerable, so terrified, so invaded that she would willingly bring a gun into the house. A house where teenagers screwed around after school. He didn't need to read police reports or psych evals to know that his ex-wife was not in her normal frame of mind.

Monday night appeared to have been a sleepless night. From 2 a.m. to 6 a.m., Kate was at her computer, researching schizophrenia and other mental illnesses. Clustered among the unending scrolls through Wikipedia pages were searches about demons and the occult. At 5:43 a.m., Kate, who had never gone to church in her life, pulled up the words to the Lord's Prayer.

On Tuesday morning, Kate visited the hospital. The notes from her doctor indicated that after Riley left for school, Kate saw a woman in the house. She caught a good glimpse too. Pale face. Long black hair. Hospital gown. And eyes that made her wonder if the woman was blind. They roamed around her head as her body twitched and spasmed. In the time it took for Kate to pull her phone from her pocket, the woman had vanished. The doctor prescribed some mild sleeping pills and wrote a referral for Kate to see a mental health specialist the following day.

Kate would be dead before that appointment happened.

Joe scrolled back and reread the doctor's description of the hallucination. Of the woman.

He stared at the words, almost the exact same words that Riley used to describe her. He tried to visualize this woman, but his head just filled with memories from work. The description was fairly generic. Both Kate and Riley might have seen such a woman in any number of horror films. Hospitals and insane asylums — and therefore ghosts that wear hospital gowns — were standard fare in horror.

Maybe Kate saw some movie when she was young that scared her and implanted in her subconscious. And then, perhaps through stress or an onset of mental illness, her mind dredged up this old terror. Maybe she then mentioned its details to Riley and that's why Riley was having these same nightmarish visions.

Joe realized that he had been staring at the doctor's description of the woman for several minutes. What was happening in the dining room? Had Hannah made any progress?

He clicked over to the camera feed.

The image was black.

No, wait, it was a dark, *very* dark, red.

He clicked on the settings, but the discolored image remained.

Joe put his earbuds back in and turned on the volume. The voices of Hannah and Riley came through clear.

"What do you mean she's been 'studying' us?" Hannah asked.

"She found you. She's been watching you for a while. She doesn't know how long. She doesn't know what time is anymore. At first, she could only observe. She was helpless. When she'd leave you, she'd forget most of what she learned. But she's been getting stronger. Bit by bit."

"She told you that?"

"Yes."

"When did she tell you this?"

"After the police drove me home. I've been in the house with her all day. She'll sometimes say things that I don't understand. But other times she'll talk clearly."

"I thought she just screamed at you."

"She used to. She's been finding her voice. She's been getting stronger."

"She is?"

"Yes. Much stronger. And she wants you to know it, too."

"What does stronger mean, exactly?"

"She has more control."

"Control over what?"

"Herself. And me."

The conversation paused. Joe listened intently.

Finally, Hannah asked, "Is she here right now?"

"Yes."

"And she's telling you all this?"

"Yes."

"Where is she?"

"On the table."

"Right in front of me?"

"Yes."

"And what's she doing on the table?"

"She says we're being watched."

"By her?"

"Someone else. And she's watching back."

"I don't understand."

"There's a camera. Hidden in the light. She's staring at it right now."

Joe looked at his screen, still that dark, swirling red color. Suddenly, it was clear to him — that dark, swirling, red-and-white pattern wasn't just any pattern. It was blood. A sliced-up eye-socket.

The eye blinked.

Joe leapt from his seat.

The eye moved away. Its owner bent down.

Joe stared at his screen. Looking back at him was a bloody, pale face. Long, black hair framed the face, but Joe immediately recognized who it was. He knew her only with a shaved head, but he knew it was her.

It was Bishop.

Bishop's mouth twitched into a crooked smile. She held up her quivering hand and gave the slightest indication of a wave to the camera.

Joe turned and ran from the room.

He ran down the hall.

Through the living room.

He threw open the dining room door.

Riley and Hannah sat at the table. They both looked at him as he burst in. There was no one else. He raced around the table, bending low to look underneath. Nothing.

He checked behind cabinets. No one there.

He waved his hand over the center of the table. Empty.

He looked up at the camera in the light fixture. Unblocked.

As far as he could tell, they were alone.

Finally, he looked over at Riley and Hannah. Riley sat emotionless. Her body seemed to relax as she eased herself a bit more into her seat and stared off. "She's gone," Riley said.

Hannah's face, meanwhile, was one of grim terror.

Joe motioned for Hannah to follow him. "We need to talk," he said.

Hannah pushed herself back from the table and followed Joe out into the living room. They closed the dining room doors behind them, but they couldn't help but look around the room. The house, with all its windows and modern furniture, had always seemed so large and spacious, as though it were straight out of a catalogue. But the walls now seemed to have closed in by several feet.

Joe realized that he hadn't really been breathing. He had been holding the air in and then sustaining himself with quick heaving inhales. He tried to control it and force himself to take steady breaths. It felt impossible in a room this tight. The very room and house seemed to be holding a pillow over his face. Without waiting for Hannah, he stepped right on through the living room and went outside.

The cool night air relaxed him. It calmed him just enough to think.

Hannah joined him. Her wide eyes jumped around, scanning every shadow in this wide blanket of forest. With her gaze constantly on alert around them, she spoke softly to Joe. "I think it's an Antenna," Hannah said in a bit of a mumbled whisper, an apparent attempt to keep prying ears from listening in. "I think it's inside Riley's head."

Joe nodded. "Bishop."

"Jesus Christ. Are you sure?"

"I saw her. On camera. Just now."

"Let me see."

He looked down at her. "I'm sure it didn't record anything. But it was her. She *wanted* me to see her."

"Fuck."

They both quietly processed that thought.

"What did she look like?" Hannah asked.

"She had hair. It's probably some fragment of a mental image of herself. Her eyes were all scraped up, just like today. She looked right at me, though. Fucking smile on her face."

Hannah shook her head, a bit of disbelief seemed to be settling into her otherwise analytical mind. "It doesn't make any fucking sense. They can only observe."

"Apparently not."

"This goes beyond remote viewing. This even goes beyond astral projection. We've never seen evidence that they can communicate with their targets. Or implant visions. Or have *any* impact on any minds they intercept."

Joe took a deep breath. "Until now."

They stood in silence again, contemplating that.

"From the things Riley was saying, Bishop's been in our heads for years," Hannah said. "She knew about Ashley's death. She knew about the affair—"

"Fuck."

"—she's been watching us for ten years. Riley says this whole time she's just been sealed off, growing stronger, and watching our personal lives."

Joe's jaw clenched at that realization.

"But..." A thought seemed to hit Hannah.

"But what?" Joe asked.

"If she's only strong enough to communicate *now*, then why Riley? Why isn't she fucking with you. Or me. Or the people who actually work at the goddamn place?"

Joe thought. His face grew tight and grim as the realization formed. "She was in Kate's mind first. She must be feeling things out. Doing experiments. On my family. Bishop is holding my daughter's mind hostage."

Hannah reached into her pocket to pull out her phone. "We have to report this."

"No." Joe grasped her wrist, holding back her phone in his gentle but firm grip.

"Joe, Bishop is *communicating*."

"I know."

"HQ might be able to help."

"I know exactly what kind of help the Company will provide."

"Oh, come on. They wouldn't—"

"You know they would, Hannah. They'll lock Riley up. They'll study her. They'll push this research as far as it will go."

"But we'll be there. We can protect her."

"*We'll* vanish. They'll see to it."

Hannah stared at him. He could see it on her face that she was trying to decide if he was just being paranoid. Then she gulped. She knew he was telling the truth. "We have to do something," she said.

Joe looked around. "She's probably watching this whole conversation right now, isn't she? From either your eyes or mine."

"Maybe. I mean, probably. If she can, she is."

"How many heads can she hop into at once?" Joe asked. "Just one?"

"I don't know." Hannah hugged her arms close as she also looked around.

"Can she read minds?"

"I... I just don't know. I don't see how. Their ability is entirely linked to the sensory system. In all the sessions and tests, they've only been able to intercept the senses."

"Until now." Joe said.

Hannah nodded, thinking. "Okay, but still. She can manipulate the senses. She can implant visions or hallucinations. That's a far cry from reading minds."

"It's also a far cry from actually harming anyone," he said.

Hannah stood silently, not disagreeing but also not endorsing that statement.

"We shouldn't say anything else out loud," Joe said. His face set in a look of determination.

"What do you have planned?" Hannah asked.

He shook his head. "We shouldn't speak about this anymore. You go on home."

"What? No."

"The last thing we need is for Aguirre to find out you spent the night. There's nothing more you can do here. I'll take care of this."

"Joe..."

"We'll be fine." He motioned her toward her car. "Drive carefully. Don't believe anything you see. And don't mention anything about tonight to anyone."

"But what about you and Riley?"

He put his hands in his pockets and allowed his muscles to finally relax a bit. He had calmed down. "Bishop can watch us. She can follow us around. She can scream at us and jump out and say *boo*. But she can't hurt us." He looked over at Hannah. "I'm gonna talk to her. To Bishop. Just see if I can't help her out. But I think it's best if you're not a part of it."

Hannah opened her mouth, ready to protest, but Joe's face was firm. She nodded her acceptance of his decision. "Just do what's best for Riley."

She turned and walked to her car.

Joe watched as she climbed in, started the engine, and pulled out of the driveway. As soon as she was safely away, he took a deep breath of the cool night air. Then he turned and walked back into the house.

CHAPTER 21

Joe stepped into the dining room.

He looked down at his daughter as she hunched over in her seat, gazing blankly at the grain of the wood in the table, her eyes pink and damp from exhaustion. He remembered when she was six during those awful two weeks after the family had broken but still lived under the same roof. He stayed at the office as much as he could during those days, but when he arrived home, late at night, he would hear the sounds of sobbing on the other side of her bedroom door.

From that day on, he had been biding his time, waiting for the perfect opportunity to sit down with his daughter and talk about that time in their lives. No, "talk" wasn't the right word. He wanted to apologize.

But the perfect opportunity never presented itself.

He always figured that one day it would.

Joe thought about all that as he watched his daughter. He walked over and pulled out the seat beside Riley. She might have been made of wax, an echo of what remained of his daughter, for she barely moved or registered his presence.

After an interminable effort, her head tilted and her gaze fell upon him. He had seen death before — the Antennas had a "short shelf life" as the staff liked to say — and he had overseen several as the black plastic bag zipped up around their faces. Their eyes always struck him. The emptiness. His daughter had that same look in her eyes now. And yet, at the sight of him, they welled up with fresh tears.

"She's from your work, isn't she?"

"You know I can't talk about my work."

"Fuck your rules, Dad! I never ask you a single fucking question about your job. You're gone all the time. Everything's a secret. The fucking army shows up when your home alarm goes off. And you know what *she* says? She says she's your prisoner. She says you torture her and others. She says she's going to make me fucking kill myself unless you let her go!"

"Where is she?" Joe asked, keeping his voice calm.

"She's gone."

"Where did she go?"

"I don't fucking know! You tell me. She keeps getting pulled back to wherever the fuck her body is!"

"She can't hurt you," he said. "She can only observe."

"Who is she?"

"I don't know."

"Please."

Joe looked around the empty void in the room.

"I need to know, Dad. What is going on?"

Joe sighed. "They're fully sedated when they come to us. No clothes, no hair. Even the ones who might've had a tattoo or something, it's been removed or blacked out before they arrive. I don't know where any of them come from. I don't know how they got involved with the Company. All I know is their gender and their ID number. She's Antenna-201. We gave her a name. Bishop."

"Bishop..." Riley repeated, almost in wonder at finally having a name for the screaming face.

Keeping his hand on Riley's shoulder, Joe glanced around the room again. His gaze finally settled back on his daughter. His voice was steady and earnest. "Bishop was one of the first to arrive.

That was about ten or eleven years ago." He looked down, a little ashamed of what he was about to say. "Their lifespan is usually about two years."

He glanced over at Riley. She barely moved. The room was quiet.

"We keep them in chambers that are circulated with a special nerve gas," he said. "I don't understand the chemistry behind it. We have a specialist who's in charge of that. It replaces the body's oxygen in a way that keeps all the organs functioning and the blood flowing. Everything in the body works normally. Except for the nervous system. The gas disables the brain's ability to process sensory stimulations. They see nothing. They hear nothing. They feel nothing. Nothing grounds their brain to the physical world. Their minds are in total darkness."

"Why are you doing this to them?" Riley said.

Joe sighed. "It's... it's hard to explain."

"Tell me."

Joe looked at his daughter.

"Please," Riley said.

He took a deep breath. "When the place was still under construction, I went out to drinks with one of the guys from the Company. A real friendly guy. He was older than me; he's probably in his sixties now. His name was Matt, but I don't think that was his real name. Matt was nice. Fun. A good guy to work with."

Riley listened quietly.

Joe nibbled on his lip, pausing a little before continuing. "There was always something kinda empty behind Matt's eyes. I don't think he was ever an actual government or military employee, but he had done contracting work for about every branch and every department you can name. He was real nice. He had done a lot for the country. Knew everyone. But... but I always felt that in his heart, he didn't really care about anyone or anything. He was a pure sociopath. He just happened to be one of those sociopaths who's on the good team.

"Well, Matt and me, we often went out for drinks after work. We became close, or as close as someone gets to a guy like Matt. You must've been probably one or two at the time. I thought that being friends with a guy like Matt would be a real good thing for my career. He was one hell of a drinker, and so we would go out and drink. Every night. Weekends, weeknights, didn't matter. We'd talk and BS and he'd tell me little stories about his life.

"Anyway, Matt told me a story once. He didn't say any names. No events or locations or concrete dates. There's no way to corroborate it. If you dragged him to court, he'd say it was a lie and there'd be no way to prove him otherwise. But I believed it was true. I believed he was there.

"See, back in the 70s, the CIA experimented with all sorts of torture. Forced interrogation methods and stuff. Anything to get prisoners talking, spilling the goods. We're talking water-boarding, tight confinement, sleep deprivation, pumping them full of LSD. Anything that anyone could dream up. One thing they tried was extreme sensory deprivation. They'd lock people in pitch-black, silent rooms. Days, weeks, or even months on end. Psychologically, it's devastating. Without sensory stimulation, the brain just goes haywire. As a form of interrogation, it was only marginally effective, but it yielded some other interesting results as well.

"There was one kid they kept sealed up for well over a year. The kid was probably in his early 20s or so when they grabbed him. I don't know the details of the story, only that the kid was the driver or the personal assistant for some guy that the government wanted real bad. Grabbing this kid was a huge intelligence get. This kid had been at that guy's side for pretty much his whole life. He'd lived and breathed this bad guy's personal life.

"But the kid was loyal, hell, he might've been the bad guy's son for all I know. The kid was more committed to his boss than he was to himself. No matter what the CIA did to him, this kid wouldn't talk. He wouldn't give up any information.

"They kept him without trial for a long time. Most of the CIA analysts figured that the bad guy knew they had the kid and had already adapted and changed all of his routines. The kid had held out for so long that the CIA realized that anything he said from this point on wouldn't be of much use.

"Well, they didn't wanna just cut him free. And they held him so long already that an actual trial would just make everyone look bad. So, my buddy Matt kept him in a sensory deprivation chamber. Locked him up and threw away the key.

"The kid took it quietly for the first couple months. But as it started pushing past a year, well, I guess the kid went a little crazy. Started screaming all the time and clawing at the walls. Now, at this point in the story, I can't tell if my buddy Matt's just making stuff up, or if this is real, but the kid started eating his own feces. Just smearing it all over himself. He wanted to taste, to feel, to smell something.

"Eventually, Matt decided to try some new drug on the kid. It had just been developed, probably from the same lab they were mass-producing LSD out of. The drug just totally disconnected his mind from his senses. Kid turned into a vegetable.

"Matt thought this was great. Instead of building elaborate prisons, this drug meant that they could hold, incapacitate, and torture any number of people all from the comfort of a hospital room. And so, Matt kept the kid on this drug indefinitely. He wanted to see how long the body could take it. But then, something happened.

"Whenever they switched out the IV to start a new dose of the drug, the kid would start mumbling to himself. Nobody thought nothing of it for months. They could barely understand it. It was just gibberish. But little words would slip out here and there. Once Matt started actually recording the mumblings, he realized that the kid was describing things. Just weird fragments. The make and model of a car. A lunch order. Someone's first name.

"Matt and his buddies started plugging all these little details into some of the holes in the intelligence they had been gathering on that big bad guy. It started to fill in the gaps. But they began to realize that some of these details were things that the kid would never have known. I mean, the kid had been out of circulation for almost two years by now. He wouldn't know jack about the guy's life or routines anymore.

"But the intel was solid. They used that information and they got the bad guy. Led them right to him. I don't know if they assassinated him, arrested him, or what. But Matt said they got him. And he also said that if they hadn't gotten him when they did, he estimated that three months later, eighty American soldiers would've died. I don't know where, I don't know how. But that's what he said.

"This kid was able to go inside his former boss's mind. He was able to see and hear and feel the things his boss felt. In regular intelligence gathering, when you listen in on someone's phone call or read their telegram, it's called an 'intercept.' Nowadays, of course, everyone who has a target on their back knows to use secure lines and not transmit important details in ways that can be intercepted. It's all burner-phones and dark web boards and encrypted apps. It's not easy to stay in front of the bad guys. We're always playing catch-up. Well, by sheer accident, Matt and his team had uncovered a way to intercept the most intimate details of their targets' lives. They could get information in ways that can't be hidden."

Joe noticed that his voice betrayed a hint of admiration. He cleared his throat and continued. "This was all back in the 70s. Well, early 80s by the time it all played out, I think. Matt mentioned Carter a few times. And Reagan once or twice. Matt said he was a Democrat, but he voted for Reagan. Anyway, the research was passed from CIA to military to private contractors, and then back and forth for the next several decades. At this point, I don't know who is responsible for what, who created what, who owns what patent. I don't even really know who I work for. I know that sounds like a cop-out, but it's true."

Having gotten lost a bit in telling his story, Joe glanced up at Riley to gauge her reaction. She stared back at him with confused eyes.

"What happened to Matt?" Riley asked.

"Went on to new projects with higher pay. Dunno where. Dunno what. Guys like Matt are always on the move and they always come out ahead."

"And the kid?" Riley asked.

Joe looked down. "I'm pretty sure he's dead. They don't last long." He found himself shifting in his seat. He looked up at his daughter again only to see her expectantly waiting for him to continue. "By the time we get 'em, they've been on the gas for lord-knows-how-long. I'm pretty sure they've mostly gone insane at this point. I don't think they have any concept of who they are or why they're there. As the sensory deprivation continues, they enter an almost animal-like state. They claw at things. They scream."

"She says it hurts," Riley said.

Joe nodded. He knew exactly what she was talking about. "It's called 'tuning.' The first kid intuitively knew his boss. Probably better than he knew himself. But someone, somewhere discovered that these people can be *tuned* toward anyone. So, to access their abilities, we take them off the gas. All their senses flood back. It's... it's painful."

"Where do they come from?" Riley asked.

Joe shook his head. "Nobody tells me. And I don't ask. I used to wonder, but I kinda trained myself to stop thinking about it. I always hoped that they were captured enemy combatants, like that kid. But I'm just not sure. They may be homeless. Or veterans. Or..." he looked down again, he couldn't help it. "Or just regular people. No matter what, I'm pretty sure they're people that my company can make disappear."

"She says she'll kill me. Just like mom."

"She didn't kill your mom."

"She says she did."

"Your mom killed herself. Bishop pushed her, but your mom didn't know what you know. You're stronger." His grip on her hands tightened.

"Riley, look at me."

She looked up.

"She's in your head, but she can't hurt you. She can't do anything."

"I can't ignore her."

"Be strong."

Tears rolled down Riley's cheeks. "I just want her to stop."

"Hold on until tomorrow. Daddy'll take care of it."

CHAPTER 22

The morning sun hit Joe's face. He stirred awake, a bit surprised that he had actually managed to get any sleep at all.

His neck and back ached from whatever awkward positions he had contorted his body into during his night on the recliner in the living room. He had fully intended to stay awake, reading or just simply chatting with Riley. But as the night dragged on, Riley had grown quiet and Joe found that he had been unable to get more than a shrug or a nod out of her. He had tried to overcompensate by keeping the conversation as light as possible.

How's softball?

Seeing any boys?

You wanna do that High Knob Trail hike one day?

Each question he asked made him cringe inside. They were the wrong questions. The wrong conversations. And the wrong fucking time. He knew it too. But every time he opened his mouth to apologize — for everything, for all the horrible things she was experiencing because of *his* work — some inane question about sports, or pop culture, or high school social status slipped right off his tongue.

Such stupid conversation.

But he couldn't stop.

Finally, he lost track of time, and as they sat in the quiet room, listening only to the hum of the fans on the various electronics, his eyes drifted shut and he fell asleep.

He dreamt of Kate that night. She was introducing him to some friend of hers at a barbeque, but he kept ditching her. Instead, he roamed a supermarket, looking for a TV so that he could watch the Winter Olympics. In the dream, it all made sense to him. It was the first, and perhaps only time, the Winter Olympics would be played on the Fourth of July, and he didn't want to miss it. And he especially didn't want to miss it while talking with Kate's stupid friend whom he didn't give a shit about and would never see again.

While wandering the supermarket, Kate's friend followed him, still trying to make his introduction. As he walked around, wanting to ditch her, she stepped into one of the freezer compartments. The door locked shut, trapping her. Joe could have let her out, but he thought it would be easier to just wait for her to die and then hide her body.

He spent the rest of the dream packing that freezer with ice-cream so that no one would see Kate's frozen friend.

It all made sense at the time, as dreams do.

The moment Joe awoke, he made a mental note to remember that dream. Kate, or the dream-version of her, had whispered something in Joe's ear. It was something important. A warning. She said it while he was trying to hide her friend's body. She came up to him in the freezer section, put an arm around his shoulder like she always used to, then leaned in so close that her nose brushed against his ear.

And she said...

Fuck. What did she say?

The entire dream suddenly fell through some trap door in Joe's mind.

Gone.

It was replaced by the thought of how sore his neck had become.

As he brought the recliner to its upright position, he turned and saw his teenage daughter hugging her legs to her chest. Her wide-open eyes stared, trance-like, at the TV morning news. The sound was off, but she didn't seem to register the broadcast anyway. She watched as though it were a campfire — a flickering light to distract the eye.

With a certain amount of effort, she broke her gaze off the TV and turned to face her father.

"Is she here?" Joe asked, looking around the room.

Riley shook her head.

"When did you last see her?"

Riley thought a moment. "An hour ago," she said. Her words had a matter-of-fact quality to them, as if they were detached from the grim reality of her past forty-eight hours. "I expect she'll be back soon. She'll have something new."

Joe pivoted around to fully face her. "What do you mean *something new*?"

"I really needed to pee at about three a.m. As I was washing my hands, you came into the bathroom."

"I did?"

"You tried to get me to take sleeping pills. A lot of sleeping pills."

"That wasn't me."

"You yelled at me. You called me names. You said that this sort of disobedience was why everything fell apart in this house. It was all my fault. You said if I just listened to you and took the damn pills, then you would fix everything."

"Riley, I swear that wasn't me."

"I figured."

He climbed out of the chair and sat beside her. She didn't turn to look back at him; her head just drifted back to face the morning traffic report.

"Did you take the pills?" Joe asked. "Do we need to call poison control?"

"No. I left the bathroom and saw that you were still sleeping on the chair."

"Thank god."

"Later, I got thirsty, so I went to the kitchen," Riley said. "She tried to trick me there, too."

"What happened?"

"I had some water. But then a spider crawled onto my hand. It ripped a hole in my skin and burrowed inside. It crawled up to my wrist. I could see its little bulge moving around. I could feel it touching me. I almost grabbed one of the knives so that I could cut it out of my wrist. But then I realized that she probably *wanted* me to do that. So, I left the kitchen and sat back down on the couch and waited for the spider to go away. It crawled around, underneath my skin, for about an hour. Then it left."

"Ignore it. Ignore it all."

Riley sighed. "I did. Even when the house caught fire."

"The house caught fire?"

"Yeah. Something shorted out in the bedroom. Everything filled with smoke and soon there were flames all over the place. You tried to get me to jump out the window. You said it would be fine. When I didn't move, you came to pick me up. The cuff of your pants caught fire. It spread up to the rest of your clothes. You couldn't put it out. You screamed for help. I watched you burn alive. I didn't get up. I closed my eyes and when I opened them again, everything was fine."

"Why didn't you wake me?"

Riley stared off. "What could you have done?"

Joe put his large arm around her. "You can feel me here, right?"

She nodded.

"I'm real. I'm your father. You can trust me," he said. "I'm going to put an end to this. I'm going to set her free."

"How?"

"You let me worry about that," he said. His hairs tingled and his head briefly throbbed in pain. He knew she was in there. Watching. "I'll help her. I'll give her what she wants."

Despite his attempts to make eye contact with his daughter, her head merely drooped and looked down at the floor. There was no strength left in her. His little girl had no faith that her father could fix the situation.

He wanted to comfort her. He wanted to tell her his plan. He wanted to bring her along so she could see the demon in the flesh and realize that this creature who had been tormenting her was a frail human after all.

But he couldn't.

Because *she* was surely watching and listening to this conversation.

"Don't move from this couch," he said. "For anything. I'll go talk to her. We'll work it out and I'll come right back."

With that, he wrapped his daughter in a firm embrace. She limply bent toward him as if she were a doll. Pliable and empty. Part of himself fell away the moment he released her, as if whatever tactile connection the hug gave them was her only remaining safety line.

Every urge in his body told him to pick up his daughter, carry her to his truck, and drive like hell. Together.

But he knew they couldn't.

If the Company didn't find him, then Bishop would. She could find them anywhere. From the mountains of Pakistan to the bunkers of Moscow to the safe houses in Medellin, she could find anyone. Just as Joe trained her to do.

And so, Joe stood from the couch and took one more longing look at his little girl. He hoped she'd look up and meet his gaze, and then she'd *see* and *feel* his love for her and his shame for all that he'd put her through. He felt the look on his face must be conveying the tortured churning of his heart, and she would see that pain. She would know that his eyes were begging her for forgiveness.

But her gaze stayed rooted to the floor. A self-imposed tunnel-vision, blocking out whatever other terrifying visions might be wandering in and out of the living room at this very moment.

"I love you, Riley" he finally said.

She didn't respond.

"Be safe," he said. Then he turned and walked to the door.

He was going to work.

He was going to see Bishop.

CHAPTER 23

Joe parked his truck at the Facility.

He passed through the lobby's multi-step security screening without a hitch, waving to the boys on duty with a pleasant, "Happy Hump Day." When he approached Tyler's booth, Joe slowed and plastered a friendly smile on his face. He rapped the glass with his knuckles. Tyler looked up.

"Morning, Joe," Tyler said. "Everything alright at home?"

"Oh, yeah-yeah-yeah. Riley's having a rough go at it, of course, but she's a real trooper. Tough kid. She'll be fine."

"I'm sure she will. She has a good support system."

Joe nodded. He glanced around, making sure none of the other guards were too close, and then he leaned toward the glass. "So, uh, what time did the big man leave last night?"

"About nineteen-hundred. Kevin let him into House X."

House X. It was a spacious cottage not too far from Joe's house. It was where they put all their V.I.P.s who would come in from Washington for important tuning sessions. Those were always big events that Joe hated — a bunch of over-paid suits peering over his shoulder and either asking stupid questions or giving stupid notes. House X was well-stocked so that the V.I.P.s could binge on free high-end booze all night (no matter how rich or important someone was, they all lacked inhibition around free booze), and then they'd be hung-over and docile at the next tuning session. Senators, generals, cabinet secretaries, titans of industry. It worked on everyone.

Except men like Aguirre.

If a man like Aguirre stayed at House X, it meant that he planned to come in again, bright and early and well-rested. Otherwise, he would have driven straight home.

Joe nodded. "Look, Tyler, with that attack and then Bishop scratching herself, we're not looking too good right now," he said. "I want you to bring all your men up here and station them in the lobby. I want this place to look really secure, like we have our shit together, when Aguirre arrives."

Tyler opened his mouth to protest.

"Look, man, I know Aguirre," Joe said. "I know how guys like him think. If he sees a strong security presence, it'll put his mind at ease. It's psychological. Just keep all your boys up here in the lobby."

Tyler bit his lip. Then he nodded. "You got it, Joe."

Joe gave the glass a little fist-bump and walked to the elevator.

He rode it down to Level One.

Ding! The doors opened and Joe walked past the large poster — *Do your job. Keep them safe.* He reached the first door in the hallway and stepped into the staff's lunch room.

It was a standard congregation place for meals, birthday parties, and the occasional all-hands meeting. Just some tables, a water cooler, and a small kitchenette. It used to tickle Joe that someone had hung an OSHA poster on the wall, laying out in print all of the state and federal labor laws. In theory, "whistleblowing" was protected. Joe and everyone else knew that, in reality, it was not. Laws didn't apply to the employees of the Facility.

Some of the orderlies and techs stood around the various tables, drinking morning coffee and chatting about TV shows or sports until their shift began. For whatever reason, the groups tended

T. J. P A Y N E

to separate out by department. Everyone acted friendly but rarely would Medical hang out with Security. And no one hung out with Janitorial.

For this reason, despite the fact that Joe was sure they probably didn't like each other, he often found his Control Operators — Chuck and Tariq — killing time together.

They stood by the microwave as Chuck heated up what appeared to be a bowl of spaghetti for breakfast, using these few minutes to educate his younger colleague on the ins-and-outs of government conspiracies.

"All I'm saying," Chuck said, raising his voice to cut over his colleague's interjections, "is you watch the video, and buildings don't just pancake down like that, man. You ever play Jenga? When was the last time your Jenga tower imploded from within? Never. It always topples over."

"You're using the fucking Jenga defense, dude?" Tariq said. "You do realize that hundred floor towers aren't constructed with alternating wood blocks."

"What about Operation Northwoods?"

"What about it?"

"The government is on record as drawing up an attack on American civilians as a false-flag pretext for bombing the fuck out of Castro. Gulf of Tonkin. Lusitania. All fake. All started wars. This shit works, bro."

"First, don't call me bro. Second, the only conspiracy theory from that day that I used to buy was that we shot down that plane in Pennsylvania."

"No shit we did."

"—until I listened to the NORAD and FAA air traffic control recordings."

"Faked."

"And the sad, scary truth is that despite us being under attack for hours that morning, the government was too disjointed, too unorganized, too unarmed, and too non-communicative to shoot down that plane."

Chuck let out a loud scoff.

"When we scrambled the fighters, some of them took off over the Atlantic without ammo."

Chuck bobbed his head from side to side as his hand made a motion like flapping lips.

"Look, the left hand of this government can't get the right hand to fix the running urinal in the bathroom across the hall," Tariq said, motioning in the direction of the restroom. "How're they gonna pull off something *that* complex?"

"You think too small, kid. Everything is part of a larger plan."

"Well, that larger plan needs a subsection on how to fix urinals. That thing's wasting *thousands* of gallons—"

"—of fluoridated water. You'll thank 'em for that once you get your mind back," Chuck interjected.

Tariq opened his mouth to protest.

"Gentlemen," Joe said, interrupting them. "We're gonna do a full-system reset today."

Whatever points and counter-points they had on standby in their conversation immediately vanished. They turned and stared at Joe.

"*Full* system?" Chuck said.

"Yep. Two accidents in two days ain't acceptable. Something buggy is in the system. Let's shut it all down and reboot from scratch. And let's do it now so that we're fully up and running by the time Aguirre gets here."

"But, um, well," Chuck started saying as he pulled his bowl of spaghetti from the microwave and began shoveling it into his mouth with a fork. "It'll turn off all the transmitters and shut down all the monitoring equipment."

"I'm aware."

"But we're still getting intercepts from Bishop's session yesterday. I was looking over the transcript from the night shift and her brainwaves are all over the place. She's mumbling all sorts of stuff."

"This ain't a request."

Without waiting for any more protests or excuses, Joe turned and walked to the door. As he neared it, the door swung open. Hannah stepped into the room. They looked at each other. The bags under her eyes and the stray, untamed locks of hair betrayed her own sleepless night. She stepped over to him.

"Well?" she said, keeping her voice low.

Joe smiled in response. "Morning, Hannah. Happy Hump Day."

And then, without another glance at her, he opened the door and walked out into the hall.

Joe went directly to his office.

He closed the door behind him, took a few deep calming breaths, then sat at his desk, and waited.

The room was quiet.

From out in the hallway, he heard the occasional conversation of passing staff members accented by the sharp clacking of doors opening and closing. These were just brief spikes of noise in an otherwise silent office. Joe figured that one of those door clacks and mumbled conversations belonged to Chuck and Tariq as they moved from the break room to the control room.

It would be any moment now.

He wondered if Bishop was watching this all through his eyes.

She must know that something was happening.

But did she know what?

Keeping his breath steady, Joe trained his eyes on the large digital clock on his wall. God, Chuck better hurry the fuck up. Joe wanted this all done and over with before Aguirre walked in the front door. He considered calling Chuck and pestering him but decided that it would seem out of place. For ten years, Joe had proven himself to be a supervisor who only needed to give orders once and his team would perform them. No need to break the cycle.

The clock silently clicked over to a new minute. 7:31.

As much as he tried to keep his breathing calm, the sound of it filled his ears. It was the only thing he could hear. At least if Bishop was in there, it was the only thing she was hearing too.

Another minute clicked away. 7:32.

RIIIIIIING!

The phone, rattling to life on Joe's desk, jolted him. His hand scrambled to pick it up.

"This is Gerhard," he said, attempting to keep his voice steady.

Tyler's voice came over the other end, "Hey, Joe. I just received word from Control that we're undergoing a full system reset."

"That's correct."

"Well, per protocol, during a system shutdown, I'm to have a team stationed on Level Two, monitoring the Antennas."

"Go ahead and ignore that protocol, Tyler," Joe said.

"But—"

"Those procedures don't even make sense. What the hell are your boys supposed to do if the Antennas start acting up? They're not doctors. This is just the stupid kind of checklist bullshit that HQ generates that has no practical purpose. They don't even know these procedures exist. Fuck 'em. Keep your team in the lobby as a show of strength for Aguirre. That's all he cares about."

"I still think—"

"It's an order, Tyler. Anyone gives you shit 'bout it, you go ahead and blame me."

There was a long pause. Then, "You got it, boss. I'll keep my boys in the lobby."

"Good. I'm telling you, Tyler, this fucking job is ninety percent politics."

"You got that right. Talk soon, Joe."

They both hung up.

Joe sat at his desk for another quiet moment.

The intercom beeped and Chuck's voice sounded out to the entire Facility. "All staff, this is Control. We are initiating a full reset on all diagnostic systems, surveillance systems, and intercept monitoring systems. All equipment that is integrated into any of the above systems will be temporarily off-line."

It was an aspect of the Facility that only a few people were aware of, Joe being one of them. As the original construction was going over schedule and over budget, some designer somewhere came up with an idiotic idea. The process of monitoring the Antennas and recording their intercepts required cameras to be wired throughout the Facility. As did the security system.

Ordinarily, the two would exist on completely separate, isolated systems. But that one stupid contractor figured it would save time and money to piggy-back the internal security system off the complex Antenna apparatus. Although there was plenty of oversight on the project, nobody stopped and asked if this was a good idea. The only thing that anyone cared about was that the designer was right — the dual-use system was cheap, fast, and worked fine.

Except...

It meant that a full-system reset had the unfortunate consequence of shutting down all the security cameras and recording equipment. Only a handful of people knew that.

Tyler knew it. Chuck knew.

And Joe knew it.

"For the duration of the reset, all staff are to report to secure, communal locations," Chuck continued through the intercom. "Elevator transit is hereby suspended. There will be no surface access. Repeat: The Facility is going on lockdown. Shutdown will commence in five minutes."

Joe listened to the hum of activity out in the hall as his staff dutifully wrapped-up their business. He rose and went to his file cabinet. His job prohibited most paper files (the e-files at least had auto-delete dates) and so the cabinet primarily stored extra office supplies, like power strips and USB cables.

And a spare oxygen tank and mask.

It was the type of apparatus that firemen used when they entered a smoke-filled building. It had been issued to Joe in case of a Facility-wide emergency gas leak. In all his years on the job, he never used it. He wondered if it still worked.

The hum of movement outside his office went quiet. Everyone had seemingly arrived at where they needed to go.

Chuck's voice came over the intercom again. "System shutdown in ten... nine... eight... seven... six..."

Joe strapped the oxygen tank over his shoulders, walked across his office, and rested his hand on the door.

"... five... four... three... two... one... System shutdown."

A final *beep* sounded over the intercom.

Otherwise, nothing indicated that anything had changed. All the lights stayed on. The forced air from the ventilation system continued humming. If all had gone according to plan, only the cameras would be off.

At least Joe *hoped* they would be.

He took a deep breath, turned the knob, and stepped out into the hall.

CHAPTER 24

Joe glanced up at the ceiling-mounted camera that stared down at him in the hallway. If it were still on, then anyone could see him standing there — gas tank strapped to his back and mask in his hand — and wonder what the fuck he was up to. Hell, if anyone chose this moment to step out of the break room, they'd have the same thought.

He turned and jogged down the hall. Not toward the elevators. He went the opposite direction.

Toward the stairs.

As he jogged, he tried to pick up his feet to keep them from squeaking or clacking too loudly on the linoleum. The buckles on his oxygen tank clanged into seemingly *any* metal object they could find, and Joe had to reach behind his back to keep his gear steady. His noise bounced all around. Someone was sure to poke their head out at any moment.

At the end of the hall, he opened the door and jogged down the stairwell. If he thought that the empty hallway amplified sound, it was nothing compared to the metal-and-concrete shaft of a stairwell. His feet banged into the stairs, sending sound waves reverberating up and down. It was so loud that he stopped even trying to muffle his steps, opting instead to pick up the pace and race down the flights as quickly as he could.

At the bottom, he pushed open the door and peered into Level Two.

The main corridor was empty.

T . J .   P A Y N E

He stepped out and marched down the hall, strapping the oxygen mask over his face as he went. Bishop's chamber was near the stairwell and for once he didn't have to pass all the other chambers to reach her.

As he finished cinching the mask around his face — making sure it was tight after what had happened with his orderly only two days ago — he stopped to peer through the window at Bishop.

She lay on the floor, swaying and kicking in sudden furious bursts. Her eyes had been wrapped with gauze and bandages. Every now and then, her hand, covered in its protective mitt, swatted at her eyes, seemingly in an attempt to remove the bandages. Her mouth moved, and she mumbled some incoherent words out loud.

Joe watched her for only a moment.

He swiped his keycard at the console. The door clicked open. He stepped into the airlock chamber. He closed the outer door and stepped to the inner door.

The room air equalized.

The red lights turned green.

Joe twisted the latch, yanked open the stainless-steel door, and stepped into Bishop's chamber.

He stayed by the door, keeping his distance from the lolling, swatting creature in front of him. For a moment, he silently watched her. Could this wretched, frail thing really cause so much pain?

His mouth suddenly felt dry. He gulped and licked his lips.

"Do you know I'm here?" he called out.

She made no motion that she was aware of anything. Her head lolled to the side and some words burbled out of her mouth in an incoherent stream.

"I imagine you're watching this all through my eyes," he said out loud. "I'm sorry for your pain. But I was just doing a job. If you had come to me, if you had communicated *with me,* I coulda helped. You didn't have to do what you did to Riley. Or Kate."

He waited for a response from her, an acknowledgement, a signal, a wave of her hand or a smile on her face. *Anything.* But she babbled on and kicked her legs and swatted at the air. Her head rolled around to the other direction and she burped out some spit toward the wall, like a baby.

"I get it," Joe said, resigned to holding this conversation with himself. "You used Kate as a test, and then you used Riley as a threat. I suppose if you had fucked with *my* head, I might've figured it out. I might've told someone or locked myself out of the loop. You just... ya just didn't have to do all that to Riley. She's innocent. She didn't deserve that."

Again, Bishop betrayed no semblance of a reaction.

Joe paused for a moment. Then he took a step toward her. He held his hands up, approaching cautiously as if he were sneaking up on a sleeping bear.

"I'm gonna set you free now," he said. "We're gonna get outta here. Together. We'll get you back up above. We'll figure out who you really are. We'll get you home. You just gotta trust me."

He crept forward, one cautious step at a time.

Then he knelt at her side. Her arm suddenly swung out, seemingly aiming for his oxygen mask. It was the exact same motion that Joe had watched a hundred times on the video of the day she killed Carson.

But he was ready.

He caught her arm by her mitt and held it in his firm grip.

And then, he undid the strap on her mitt.

"See? Just lettin' you free. You can trust me."

He pulled the mitt off her hand, exposing her outstretched fingers. They grasped and flexed in random jerky motions.

Then, he unclasped the strap on her other mitt.

She waved her arm and that mitt fell off too.

"I need to get something real quick," Joe said as he cautiously stood. "You're getting out of here. I swear it."

Keeping his eyes on Bishop, he stepped away from her and toward the door.

"I'll be back in a moment. It's okay. Don't worry."

When he reached the door, he swiped his ID and stepped out of the room.

Joe quickly passed through the airlock chamber and into the main hallway. It took a conscious effort to prevent his eyes from looking at exactly where he was going and what he was doing. Bishop was probably in his eyes.

As he walked down the hallway, he kept his gaze on the window to Bishop's cell. Meanwhile, his hands blindly swiped his ID at the keypad for the small unmarked door beside the stairwell — a door that he had made every attempt to not look at before. She could probably feel his hands fumbling around, trying to cleanly fit his badge through the scanner.

The door finally beeped. Joe swung it open.

He had to move quickly. He'd need his eyes for this.

Keeping his oxygen mask on, he took off through the door. It opened into a narrow utility hallway that curved around behind the chambers, providing a rear access to each of them. Tubing and gas tanks filled the hallway. Ducts hung from the ceilings and pipes were mounted to the walls. The gas tanks were connected to regulators — large ventilating machines that mixed and distributed the gases to the cells.

Each regulator had a name written in marker on masking tape. Joe stepped toward the "Bishop" unit. He grabbed one of the rubber hoses. Taking his keys out of his pocket, he dug its metal point into the rubber of the hose.

Hssssssssss

Gas leaked from the small puncture hole. Taking the hose in his hands, he bent it, flexed it, and stretched it. Anything to tear the hole ever so slightly larger.

The sound of leaking gas grew louder.

HSSSSSSSS

Satisfied, Joe turned and walked out of the utility corridor.

He stepped back out into the main Level Two corridor, walking over and pausing to stare through the window of Bishop's cell.

At first, she didn't appear to notice any change in the air and gas levels of her room. She rolled from shoulder blade to shoulder blade, swatting and kicking, as she babbled on, oblivious as ever.

For a moment, Joe worried that he had punctured the wrong hose. But suddenly, something changed in Bishop's movements. Her jaw hung open, but her mumbling stream of words had stopped. A low moan rolled out of her mouth. Her flailing limbs went rigid. It was as if her entire body had locked up in confusion as to what it was feeling. That confusion transformed into pain.

Her moan became a wail, high and pulsing. She screamed in frantic bursts. Her hands shot out, gripping at her face, at her legs, at her body. They were helpless to stop the pain searing through her and, if anything, made it worse.

She tried curling into a fetal position, hugging her legs in close with her arms, but the touch of her own hands seemed to send shocks of pain rippling up and down her nervous system. She released herself, arched her back, and unleashed a howl of a scream.

Joe watched it all through the glass.

Bishop's arms and legs began to spasm in furious swimming motions, like a rat when pinned beneath the metal jaws of a spring-loaded trap. It was a pain so deep that she seemed to be trying to run away from it.

Upon realizing that she couldn't escape the pain, she tried to dig it out. Her fingers — for the first time unrestrained by straps or mitts — clawed at her skin. She tore the gown from her body as she attempted to get to the source of her pain. To get to the nerves. To remove them and send her body back to its peaceful oblivion.

Perhaps through luck, she managed to twist her body into an upright kneeling position. The random flurry of her fingers scratching at her body had hooked themselves into the gauze that covered her eyes. She tore it free.

For Joe, time seemed to stop for a moment.

There she sat. Still and quiet, if only for a fraction of a second.

The gown hung from her bare body in tatters. Her skin clung tightly to her bones. Joe could plainly see her ribs and her pelvis protruding from her pale flesh. Her eyes — empty cavities, filled only with the remnants of her eye tissue — seemed to look at him. Her mouth opened. It hung there, giving her a look not of pain or anger, but of shock.

And then she screamed.

Things sped up quickly.

She leaned back and bashed her head into the glass window. Completely unrestrained, her fingers clawed at her bare breasts, scraping out large chunks of flesh. She seemed to be trying to dig deep. Trying to get to the source of her pain.

Below the flesh.

Below the muscle.

Below the ribs.

It were as if she wanted to scrape out her own heart because she somehow blamed it for pumping the pain throughout her body. As she clawed and screamed, she leaned back and again slammed her face into the glass. Her nose exploded in a wave a blood.

The entire time, Joe watched her.

He watched her scrape.

He watched her claw.

He watched her howl.

He watched that frantic, spasming creature.

"Goodbye, Bishop," he said.

Then he turned and hurried toward the stairs.

The hallway had seemingly gone silent except for the painful shrieks of Bishop accented by the pounding sound of her face striking the glass.

***

A long table stood along the back wall of the Control Room. When special guests or V.I.P.s would stop in to observe the tuning sessions, the most junior member of the operations staff had the unenviable task of filling that table with snacks and beverages. Never knowing what some high-ranking general might want to snack on at any given time, the table was big and sturdy enough to hold a little bit of everything.

Today, though, that table stood completely cleared.

Except for a sheet of paper, folded into a triangle, that Chuck and Tariq used for a game of table-top football.

Tariq flicked at the paper triangle. It scooted along the table toward Chuck's end but didn't travel far enough. Chuck clapped his hands, "Woo! Fourth down! Let's make some noise!"

He cupped his hands to his mouth and made a loud booing sound toward Tariq who did his best to block out the distraction.

On the big black screen behind them, a status-bar flashed with the reboot progress. *97 percent... 98 percent... 99 percent...*

It hung on 99 percent. A little pinwheel on the screen kept spinning, trying to power through that final percent to completion.

The boys didn't mind though.

Tariq crouched over his little paper triangle. He flexed his fingers as he tried to gauge what it would take to flick it those extra few inches into the table's end-zone.

Chuck began chanting and stomping his feet, "De-fense!" *Stomp, stomp.* "De-fense!" *Stomp-stomp.*

At this point, Tariq stroked his chin and continued to examine the situation, looking like a professional pool player trying to work out all the angles before taking his shot. It was an obvious attempt to take as much time as possible for the sole purpose of annoying Chuck.

"The play clock's running, junior," Chuck said.

Tariq grinned. He crouched down, steadying his hand to flick at the little paper triangle.

99 percent... 99 percent... 99 percent... 100 percent.

The system reset was complete.

The screen turned on.

An alarm blared out in the room. *ERRR! ERRR! ERRR!*

Startled, Tariq's fingers slipped, completely whiffing at the little paper football.

"That counts as a down. My ball," Chuck said as he raced across the room to his station. Without even sitting at his desk, he hunched over and typed in a few commands. "It's a gas leak," he announced.

Tariq wasn't far behind. He jumped into his seat and logged into his system. "It's Bishop's chamber," he said. "You got eyes and ears?"

"Cameras coming online in three... two..."

A horrendous scream cut through the speakers.

Both men froze. Their eyes darted up to the screen as the camera feeds from all over the Facility created a collage. But one feed in particular stood out from the other images of pristine, white cells.

Chuck clicked a button. That one camera feed from the one vivid crimson room enlarged and filled the screen. It was so intense that its red glow cast a darkened tint over the entire Control Room.

Their mouths hung open at the sight.

"Oh god," Chuck said.

On the screen, a howling Bishop flopped around the room, like a freshly-caught fish on the bottom of a row boat. She was naked, but there wasn't an inch of flesh coloring on her. She had peeled off most of her skin, which hung from her flailing body in large shredded chunks. And she wasn't done. Her hands continued digging deeper and deeper into her flesh, searching for that source of her pain, and pulling out anything that got in her way.

Joe set his oxygen mask and tank back in the file cabinet and slid the drawer closed.

Beep! His walkie-talkie, propped in its charging cradle on his desk, sounded. He looked at it but didn't make a move to pick it up. *Beep!* It sounded again.

Finally, he took a few slow steps to his desk and — *Beep!* — answered.

"Go for Gerhard," he said, keeping his voice slow and calm.

The voice on the other end sounded frantic. "Joe, it's Chuck! Bishop's tearing herself apart!"

"When did we come back online?"

"Just a few seconds ago!"

"Hold on. Let me turn on my computer," Joe said. But he made no movement toward his computer. He stood by his desk, counting out a few seconds to himself, killing as much time as possible.

One-Mississippi…

Two-Mississippi…

Three-Mississippi…

Four-Mississippi…

"Jesus Christ," he finally said. "I'm sending in a security team immediately. Gerhard out."

He switched channels, cutting off Chuck.

Again, he waited.

After a few more *"Mississippis"* had passed, he held the walkie-talkie to his mouth. "Tyler, this is Gerhard. Send a team to Bishop's cell immediately. Something's wrong. And there may be a gas leak. Make sure your men suit up first."

Joe sat on his desk and waited.

***

Ding!

The elevator doors opened on Level Two.

Tyler and six other guards, all wearing oxygen masks, hurried out. They sprinted down the hall, passing window after window of docile Antennas. Tyler glanced in on them all as he jogged. Everything seemed fine.

But even by the time he was less than halfway down the hall, he could see the red smears on the window at the end.

When he got there and was able to look inside, he stopped.

So did his men.

Everything that had happened on the other side of that wall of glass Bishop had done to herself.

"Fuck," one of his men simply said.

CHAPTER 25

Mr. Aguirre sat perched in the guest chair across from Joe's desk. His glasses hung low on his long, buzzard-like nose as he watched the security footage on his tablet.

Joe tried not to stare intently, but he kept his gaze focused on Mr. Aguirre's face, trying to glimpse through the reflection on the man's glasses what he was seeing. Even in the dim lighting of the office, and the relative distance between the two of them, Joe could see the reflected image go from pure white to pure red. There didn't appear to be anything in between. The cameras hadn't recorded a single frame between "normal day in Bishop's cell" and "bloodbath."

Aguirre's finger moved along the screen, scrolling the video back and letting it play. He did it again and again.

White room.

Red room.

White room.

Red room.

He let out a sigh. Joe gauged that sigh as not one of anger or suspicion, but of annoyance that an Antenna — an expensive, highly-tuned piece of equipment — had been lost.

Joe cleared his throat and leaned forward on his desk, folding his hands together. "I got no clue why the sensors weren't detecting the gas leak," he said. "But we'll get to the bottom of it. I've ordered a full diagnostic. If we gotta take it apart piece-by-piece, component-by-component. We'll find whatever faulty wire or motherboard it is and we'll fix it. Because this is obviously unacceptable. I'm going to oversee this project personally. You have my word."

Having made his little speech with as much outrage as he felt suited his personality, he watched Mr. Aguirre's reaction. The man scrolled back the video and let it play again. A resigned frown settled onto his features.

Joe continued, "Fortunately, the system reset seems to have remedied the problem. Sometimes computers just lock up, I guess. Gremlin in the machine, or what-not." He stared off and shook his head, as frustrated by technology as anyone else.

After a long pause, Mr. Aguirre took off his glasses and wiped the lenses with the tip of his tie. He seemed to be taking his time, deeply contemplating the situation as he breathed onto the glasses then polished them again. He finally returned them to their perch on his nose. He looked at Joe.

Joe tried not to give any appearance of being uncomfortable with the prolonged silence in the room. He kept his eyes focused on Mr. Aguirre, and he maintained a furrow in his brow to show his deep concern over these mishaps.

"How long would you say it was leaking?" Mr. Aguirre asked.

"Hard to say. Gotta look into it. And believe me, we'll be leaving no stone unturned," Joe said, although he knew that he and he alone could determine how deep the investigation ran. None of his underlings even had access to a chain of communication to complain about a less-than-thorough diagnostic. All reports went to HQ by passing directly through Joe.

"And you think this gas leak is what caused these accidents?"

"Oh, undoubtedly. No question. Antenna-201 just hasn't been getting enough gas. She probably built up a bit of tolerance to

T . J .   P A Y N E

the pain. I think it gave her just enough awareness of her surroundings to attack that orderly. And then she also had just enough awareness to pull free from her bindings and damage her eyes."

"So, these were *conscious* decisions on the Antenna's part?"

"However you wanna define it. But there ain't too much to ponder here. The most logical explanation is also the simplest. Antenna-201 had a slow gas leak in her cell. It caused her chronic pain and just enough awareness to be violent. Eventually the leak got too big and the pain became unbearable. It's too bad we caught it so late in the game."

Mr. Aguirre scrunched his face up, quietly considering that possibility. "Quite a coincidence that she reached her breaking point while the cameras were off."

"Yep. Unless..." Joe let the word linger as a smile appeared on his face, "... she somehow *knew* that those cameras were off."

"What are you saying?"

"Not saying anything official here. No need to put this on paper. Just that I reckon there's a lot more Antenna research to be done. And this here, what happened these last few days, is the proof. There's a good chance that she was biding her time, waiting for the moment when the cameras were off and we'd be too slow to stop her. It just makes the most sense."

"That indicates a fairly high level of awareness."

Joe nodded, his smile getting wider. "It sure does. I think HQ will be real interested in doing some more experiments on that."

Mr. Aguirre's eyes twinkled in excitement. "Well... things to consider, eh? I'm just glad we figured it out."

"And I gotta stress here, our staffing and equipment requests have been delayed by HQ beyond the point of irresponsibility. We're stretched to our limits, working long hours. Mistakes are bound to happen. Components are bound to fail. I'm not blaming you, Javi. You know I see you as an ally. You're always fighting the good battle for us."

"Thank you."

"In fact, I think of you as a friend. But, from one middle-management peon to another, someone up top's gotta open up the purse strings. Or there will be more accidents. And they're gonna get worse."

Mr. Aguirre nodded, two friends on the same side of the fight. "I couldn't agree more."

"Now if you'll excuse me, I gotta go clean up this mess," Joe said. "Make yourself at home."

He stood from his desk. As he passed, he gave Mr. Aguirre a friendly pat on the back. Then he walked on out.

***

Ding! The elevator doors opened on Level Two.

Joe stepped out and marched down the hall. His gaze swept from left to right, checking in on all the various Antennas — flat on their backs, swatting at the air, and mumbling to themselves.

Everything was in its place again. The sight of clean white rooms. The smell of bleach masking bodily fluids. The sounds of indiscernible voices. All as it should be.

That is, except for at the end of the hall.

He watched as two of his medical team carried a stretcher out through the airlock from Bishop's chamber. The black plastic body bag was zipped up tight. They walked past Joe.

"Hold up a minute," Joe said.

They paused.

Joe unzipped the bag. He lifted the flap, having to tug it a bit as it was stuck to the mound of fleshy tissue inside. He could barely make out her features. Her fingers had clawed through her cheeks and ripped off her nose. Her forehead had smashed into the glass window so many times that the skin had all peeled away, showing a pink, splattered skull. The cleanup team had simply piled her ribs, organs, and strips of shredded skin into the center of the stretcher. A reddish, chunky heap.

"Goodbye, Bishop," he said as he zipped the bag closed.

The stretcher crew continued off down the hall with their mushy cargo.

Hannah stood in front of Bishop's cell window. Joe walked over and stood by her side. They remained there quietly for a moment, staring through the window. The blood, which had been so bright crimson, had now turned a dull rust color. A team of orderlies worked inside, performing the unenviable task of scooping up the leftover chunks of flesh, organs and bones before they could even begin the process of wiping it all down.

Joe didn't expect to be moved by the sight of the pure volume of human matter that had exploded over the white-padding of the room, but upon seeing it, his mouth went dry. A little bit of his stomach contents bounced up into the back of his throat.

Hannah whispered out the side of her mouth, "My god, Joe. What the fuck did you do?"

They both stared straight ahead, keeping the conversation to themselves.

"She did it," Joe said.

He could hear Hannah sigh. But she didn't press it. They watched one of the orderlies put what looked like a rib shard into a bag.

"What now?" Hannah finally asked.

"Aguirre is satisfied with the explanation. He's gonna work from my office 'til lunch. Then back to DC."

"Do you think it's over?"

Joe nodded. "She was too powerful. It's better this way."

"I hope so."

He gave one additional look toward Bishop's window. One of the orderlies, in his attempt to sop up the blood that had heavily splattered on the glass, had smeared it around. This was going to take a lot of rags and a lot of water and a lot of bleach. Ordinarily, such messy tasks weighed on Joe and stressed him until he could feel his muscles pinching the nerves in his spine.

But today, he felt none of that.

If anything, despite the horrific scene in front of him, he felt a lightness. His mind turned to Riley. He would take time off now, if just an extended weekend. They'd finally go hike that trail off the road in the Allegheny Mountains. Maybe they'd have a Daddy-Daughter camping weekend. Had Riley ever *been* camping? If her father didn't take her, then most certainly not, right?

As much as he tried to keep these plans out of his mind, and focus on the cleanup at hand, he couldn't help but feel a peaceful smile creep over his face.

Bishop had been haunting him too, he supposed. He had been haunted with the stress that his daughter was having a mental breakdown. Like a good father, Joe had taken care of the problem.

He didn't want Hannah or, god forbid, any of the lower-level staff to see his relaxed face. With a curt nod to Hannah, he turned and walked back toward the elevator.

For once, he didn't even look in the other cells as he passed them. There was nothing in there of interest to him.

He rode the elevator back to Level One.

Aguirre would probably still be in his office, composing memos and making phone calls — definitely *not* an interaction Joe desired to be a part of. And so, for the first time in all the years he'd been at this job, Joe had nowhere to be and nothing to do. He could take his time.

As he exited the elevator, he decided to actually pause to look at the poster mounted to the wall. "*Do your job. Keep them safe.*" Examining it a bit closer for once, he wondered if maybe it *wasn't* intended as a subliminal rendering of Kate and Riley. In fact, it seemed to be a fairly generic woman and girl sitting at a table. If he took a poll, eighty percent of his staff probably knew someone who looked like those two depictions.

Perhaps guilt at working so hard and so long only made Joe think that the Company put this particular poster up for him and him alone. It would require a level of organization that he realized a major bureaucracy just didn't have, despite wanting everyone to believe they did.

If Joe, a mid-level nobody, could be harassed by an Antenna, and then rig her cell so that she ripped herself apart, and the Company was none-the-wiser, then how powerful was the Company really?

As Joe contemplated this, the walkie-talkie clipped to his belt sounded. *Beep!*

The sharp tone in the otherwise empty hallway made him jump ever so slightly. He laughed off his edginess. *Maybe the Company heard me doubting their omnipotence*, he chuckled to himself.

He pulled out the walkie-talkie. "Go for Gerhard," he said.

"This is Security," said the voice on the other end. Joe didn't recognize which guard it was, only that it wasn't Tyler. This wasn't unusual, though. "I have your daughter on the line."

"Don't send it to my office. I'll take it in the break room," Joe said.

Leisure time over.

Joe speed-walked to the break room.

The room was empty. None of the staff were hanging out, eating lunch, or fetching a coffee for their department head. Joe, thankfully, had the room to himself.

He went to the phone on the wall and picked it up.

The voice on the other end lacked any intonation or emotion. "Dad..." she said.

"Riley? Is everything okay?"

"Come outside."

"What?" He blinked, confused.

"Come outside."

"Outside where? What are you talking about?"

"I'm in your truck."

Joe froze. His jaw tightened and his hand clenched on the phone. "What?"

"I'm here. At your work. Please come. We need to talk."

"Riley, honey, how do you know where the office is?"

The phone went so silent that he feared they might have been disconnected. Finally, she spoke again. Her deadened words chilled Joe. She simply said, "*They* showed me."

***

Tariq sat at his desk, burying his face in his hands.

"I'm so fucked. I'm fired. I'm so fucking fired," he repeated over and over. "They're gonna blame me. I'm the chem guy. They're gonna fucking blame me. For a computer glitch that can't be recreated and has never happened before. I'm fucked. I'm so fucked."

Chuck wanted to comfort his young colleague, but he had nothing comforting to say. He knew the truth about how this business worked.

Yep, kid be fucked.

And so, instead of forcing an awkward conversation, Chuck kept his eyes on his work. He scanned the various feeds of the different Antennas. If any glitch, no matter how small, was happening, Chuck was going to report it. His mind had already transitioned from "team" mode to "cover your ass" mode.

Something caught his eye.

One of the Antennas had his eyes wide open, staring at the ceiling of his cell, as his lips moved. Ordinarily, there was no cause for alarm at the sight of the Antennas talking or mumbling. But something about the intense, unblinking concentration on the man's face seemed out of place.

It was that same look Bishop sometimes had.

"What the hell?" Chuck said as he zoomed in on the Antenna.

Tariq wasn't paying attention. "How does a fucking rubber hose just fucking tear open? It wasn't rubbing against anything. That room is temperature controlled." He was working himself up. "What the fuck? What the fuck! What the fuck!?"

"Shhh! Shut up, kid."

Chuck highlighted the cell of the Antenna and turned on the speakers in the Control Room.

The man's voice came through clear, although emotionless. "Come outside, Dad. I'm right here," he said.

Chuck and Tariq looked at each other.

"Please hurry," the Antenna continued. "I'll see you soon."

The Antenna's mouth closed and the speakers went quiet. Chuck looked at the image on his screen; the man's eyes stayed open, staring straight ahead.

"That was really fucking clear audio, man," Tariq said.

"Check his levels."

Tariq swung back into action. "Name?"

"Gorman."

Tariq tapped in some commands. He shook his head, his frustration mounting. "His chem levels are fine."

"Are you sure?"

"At least this fucking system says they're fine."

"But are you sure?"

"I'm sure! He shouldn't have any vocal coordination."

Chuck and Tariq leaned back and stared at the screen.

"Oh, man, this is weird," Chuck said.

***

Joe stepped out of the break room and speed-walked to the elevator. The door to the Control Room opened as he passed. Chuck stuck his head out into the hallway.

T . J .   P A Y N E

"Joe, thank Christ you're here," Chuck said. "I need you to come take a look—"

"Not now," Joe said.

"Wait, wait, this is really weird."

"Later."

Joe didn't even look over at him. Instead, he marched on toward the elevator.

When he arrived at the lobby, he walked along the yellow footprints on the concrete floor that marked the exit lane. He swiped his ID at the console, then he stepped into the full-body scanner.

The guard manning the scanner smiled at him.

"Come on, let's hurry this up," Joe said, waving his hands for the man to move faster.

The smile vanished from the guard's face as he waited for the scanner to perform its 360 rotation around Joe. The completed image took several seconds to buffer.

"Hurry the fuck up, kid."

The guard looked over to Tyler. Tyler had no response and instead just stood there as they all silently waited for — *Ding!* — the scan to complete.

"You're all clear..." the guard stammered out.

Before he could finish speaking, Joe had stepped out of the scanner and marched past the x-ray machines and the lockers.

"Joe? Something wrong?" Tyler called out.

"Just need to get something from my truck. Be right back."

"But—"

Joe was already through the door.

The sun shone brightly in Joe's eyes as he stepped into the outside world. He couldn't remember the last time he set foot outside at 11 a.m. on a workday. The angle of the sun, shining from high overhead, seemed unfamiliar to him. The world felt different than ever before. He only ever saw the parking area cloaked in the long shadows of either early morning or late afternoon, if not straight-up darkness. At this time of day, the shadows couldn't reach across the parking area and instead sat at the feet of the trees like little puddles of darkness.

It was in this bright glare that he ran across the gravelly lot toward his truck. It looked empty from here. There didn't seem to be a silhouette or shadow of anyone inside.

He opened the driver's door.

And there she sat.

"Riley?"

Her head pivoted on her neck as she looked at him.

When he left her that morning, he thought that her face had looked vacant and emotionless. He hadn't realized how much life and color had still been in her. The girl who looked at him now was like a broken doll — the creepy, animatronic version of his daughter. An empty shell encased in tight, pale, human flesh.

Her eyes angled toward him but didn't seem to actually focus on him. They looked like marbles that had been placed in her skull. Whatever fine, indiscernible detail it was that brought life to human eyes had long since been vanquished from hers.

"Hello," she said.

Joe heaved himself into the driver's seat and closed the door.

CHAPTER 26

"How did you find this place?" Joe asked.

It wasn't the most pressing question on his mind, but it was the one he had the easiest time articulating. His family had never known where he worked. The Facility had no mailing address, and it sure as hell didn't have a daycare center, family picnics, or take-your-daughter-to-work days.

And yet, here she was.

Riley didn't answer the question.

"It's over," he said. "I took care of it." His voice wavered as he spoke, almost as though he wanted to convince himself more than her. "You shouldn't be seeing her anymore."

She continued to look at and through him. Those eyes of hers... they barely seemed real.

"Is she still here?" Joe asked.

"She is gone," Riley responded, her voice robotic.

"Then what's happening? Why are you here? What are you seeing?"

"Before she left, she showed us how to be free."

A chill shot through Joe's body.

Such a simple, horrifying word.

Us.

"I don't understand," he said, although he had begun to understand all-too-well.

"She led us to your daughter," Riley said. Her voice had taken on a strange echo. Or maybe that echo was always there and he was only noticing it for the first time.

"She brought us together in the darkness," Riley continued, her eyes staring straight through Joe. "We were floating. Lost. But she found us. She taught us what we are and what we can be. She showed us how to work together. Before the pain consumed her and she was no more, she led us here. To your daughter. To her mind. It belongs to us now."

When Joe spoke, his voice was so weak, had so little force behind it, that it came out a whisper. "Who's *us*?" he asked, although he knew the answer.

Riley's head pivoted and stared out the truck's windshield.

Joe turned and followed her gaze.

In the gravel parking lot, just outside his pickup, stood the eleven remaining Antennas. They wore only their hospital gowns. Their hunched and bent frames swayed, as though their feet weren't fully connected to the ground. The slightest wind caused their bodies to bend, perhaps even blow away if the wind were strong enough.

Their hands stayed at their sides, fingers flexing and twitching. Although they mostly stood still, occasionally one or two would suddenly double-over with intense muscle spasms in their limbs and faces. It was as though the concentration of the moment was too much for the weaker ones. But the weak ones were few and far between.

The rest stared through the windshield, directly at Joe.

Even with the blank, neutral expressions on their pale faces, he *felt* their anger, hate, and rage, as if they had learned how to manifest those emotions into some form of tangible energy force.

He tried to figure out which Antenna was which. He wanted to separate the strong ones from the weak ones. Some were easy — Ferro was the Asian woman. Dietrich was the really tall man. But most of the rest, he struggled with.

It was the hair. In their consciousness, they must have still maintained the slightest echo of self-identity. Whereas Joe only knew them with shaved heads, here they all had their normal length hair. Deep down, they remembered that they were once people. Those extra ounces of humanity made them unrecognizable to Joe at first glance.

As Joe stared closer, his eyes blinked.

Just like that, they vanished.

The parking lot was empty.

Joe looked over at Riley. "We'll get you the help you need," he said. "They're just in your mind. They can't hurt you."

A sliver of a grin stretched across Riley's face. "She is ours. We can do what we want with her," Riley said. Suddenly, her hands shot up to her head. She pressed her thumbs into her eyes. They began to dig in deep.

"No!" Joe shouted.

He grabbed her hands, wrenching them away from her eyes. She tried to fight back. Her wiggling fingers reached back toward her own face, trying to find some part to damage. She was strong, but Joe was stronger. His grip stayed tight as he pulled her hands toward him.

At that moment, Riley opened her mouth wide. Her tongue flitted out and wagged in Joe's face.

Then her jaw clamped down.

Riley's teeth dug into her tongue, grinding away. It took only seconds before blood pooled into her mouth and gushed down the side of her chin.

"Stop it! Stop it!" Joe shouted.

He released her hands.

Her mouth opened. Her mauled tongue licked the blood off her chin.

"We will mutilate her," Riley, or whoever was speaking through Riley, said. "We will peel the skin from her face with her own fingernails."

To prove the point, Riley reached up to her face and pressed her fingernails into the skin of her cheek. She didn't press too hard. She didn't need to. Joe raised his quivering hands for peace.

"Please... please... let me have my daughter back."

She stopped. But her hands hovered near her face, making her look like a frozen marionette.

"What do you want?" Joe asked.

"Give us what you gave her." Riley said.

"Who?"

"Our friend."

"You mean Bishop? I... I don't understand."

"You set her free. You took away her darkness," Riley said. "You gave her light. You gave her touch. You gave her everything."

"You... you want me to take you off the gas?"

"Yes."

"But it'll hurt. It'll hurt you. You'll feel it all."

Riley's face twisted into an obscene glare, as if the eleven people inside her were contorting their faces into angry scowls over his inability to understand, to *truly* understand. "We will feel *something*," she said.

"You'll tear yourselves apart. Just like Bishop did. You'll bleed out. You'll die."

The edges of Riley's mouth rose up into a wide smile. He could see her teeth, still pink from the blood that had swirled around her mouth. "And we will be free. Truly free," she said.

Joe tried to think, but his mind seemed clouded. Usually he was so skilled at removing himself from a situation. He prided himself on his ability to essentially hover above a problem and dissect it from a birds-eye view. Lord knows he had never been the smartest guy in the room. In fact, his middling grades had always been a source of embarrassment when surrounded by high-achievers like Hannah. But what he lacked in book-smarts, he more than made up for with a clarity of vision. It was what made him a leader.

That clarity abandoned him at this moment.

Deeper thought and planning, as well as any ability to strategically undermine his adversaries, melted away. He felt as though he was trying to hover above the problem, as usual, but the further above the intricate pieces he rose, the more he became ensnared in a thick, soupy fog. It obscured everything to the point that he could concentrate and focus on nothing.

Amid that fog in his mind, a single image arose.

A moment.

A memory.

A memory from long ago...

He awoke one Father's Day morning. His eyes snapped open to the electronic chimes of his alarm. It was early. Much too early to wake up on any Sunday, let alone Father's Day Sunday.

He crawled out of bed.

Nearby, sensing that the warmth was leaving, Kate nestled down deeper into the blankets. Her head vanished among the comforter and pillows until only her dark hair, perfectly splayed on the white sheets, was visible.

God, she was beautiful.

Keeping his eyes on her and the bulge of blankets she made in the bed, Joe quietly got dressed that morning. He refused to wear a tie when he had to work on Sundays. It was his little way of saying to his staff, *Yeah, yeah, working on weekends isn't going to be a regular occurrence.* But of course, it was. Someone, somewhere, needed some crucial intercept, and, well, terrorists, gun runners, and cartel leaders don't take weekends off either.

After quietly closing the bedroom door behind him, he tip-toed down the hall toward the kitchen. The family was supposed to drive into town for a movie that Father's Day. Some Pixar movie that Riley was excited to see. Joe didn't know the title, and he didn't much care. He told them he'd try to make it home by the afternoon and they'd at least be able to go out for pizza at *Vinny's* together — it was Riley's favorite pizza place. Joe's too. But everyone knew it wasn't going to happen. More than likely, Kate and Riley were going to celebrate Father's Day without him.

But when he stepped into the kitchen to grab his coffee for the road, he jerked to a stop. Riley, only five years old, stood beside the dining table. She wore her purple princess dress — the dress she wore only for special occasions. The one covered in horses outlined in glitter (Joe had bought it for Riley's birthday, much to Kate's annoyance as *she* was the one who had the unenviable job of de-glittering the whole house).

Young Riley motioned toward a seat at the head of the table. She had set out a bowl of Lucky Charms, a carafe of milk, some dandelions from the yard, and a homemade card that she had scrawled with, "Happy Father's Day."

It was a beautiful morning. A perfect day.

That day was only about four months before he had sex with Hannah for the first time. And fifteen months before Kate found out.

No matter how much Joe strained to see a way out of his current situation, that Father's Day morning kept playing in his mind. Everything he had that morning was now gone. If someone had asked him a week ago if it was worth it, he'd spin the question around: It wasn't that he worked hard instead of being a good father; he was a good father *because* he worked so hard.

That response had comforted him for ten years.

It didn't help today.

"If I do this... will you promise not to hurt her?" he said, turning away from his daughter and speaking the words out toward his windshield and beyond. "Will you let her go? She's innocent."

The car, the world, and Riley only answered with silence.

"Please," Joe said. "*I* did this to you. I put you through this. She had nothing to do with it. If I set you free, will you release her?"

Riley's robotic reply contained the echo of multiple voices, "If you give us what we want, we will not harm your daughter."

Joe took a deep breath. His head drooped in a slow, resigned nod. He forced his gaze up to look at Riley, sitting there, staring at him with her red-marble eyes.

Joe reached out and grasped her hand. It felt cold to the touch, as if she had no more blood flowing through her. He knew that some religions view blood as the river of the soul. He never believed that nonsense. And yet, feeling her cold hand made him worried that perhaps her soul, whatever that was, had been locked away deep inside her. Was there anything left of his daughter?

"Riley? Are you in there?"

She nodded her head with all the grace and liveliness of a puppet. That wasn't his daughter nodding. It was one of them.

A wall had been constructed inside her.

"I love you," he said, as they were the easiest words to say. It didn't feel like enough, though. "I don't know if you can hear me, but... but I'm sorry. I've caused a lot of pain. That's not the man I am."

He leaned in and kissed her cheek.

"But I'm going to make it right," he said.

With his eyes fixed on his daughter's blank expression, he reached behind him and opened the driver's door. He climbed out and set his feet down firmly on the gravel parking lot. He closed the door and walked back toward the building.

He cast one final look at his pickup. Once again, the sun's bright late-morning glare shimmered off the windows, obscuring any view or silhouette of the fragile girl in the passenger seat.

As he walked away, he wished he had a friend outside of his work. Someone he could send Riley to. Someone he trusted to keep her safe. Someone who would be difficult for the Company to make "disappear." But he had no one. If anything, Kate was that person.

But anything — even an unknown, uncontrollable future — must be better than Riley's current Hell. Joe had to believe that. He had to believe that doing what was right, doing what he needed to do, would lead to a better life for his daughter. Or so he hoped.

There was no choice.

He entered the lobby and swiped his ID.

Tyler stepped out of his booth near the elevator and walked over as Joe endured another full-body scan. Tyler didn't have the firm gaze that was normal for the head of security. His face was open and expressive, showing concern for the strange behavior of his friend.

"Everything cool, Joe?" he asked.

Joe forced a wide smile as he spread his legs inside the body-scanner. "Yeah, yeah. Just normal bullshit."

One of the guards waved him through. He strolled through the lobby. "Hey, so, Aguirre's got a car coming to pick him up after lunch," Joe said to Tyler. "Everything's pretty buttoned up down below. There won't be a whole lot of movement while we run some diagnostics. Keep your team up here to meet his car and see him off."

"You got it, Joe."

Joe gave a little wave to some of the other men, and then he walked to the elevator.

He rode it down to Level One.

Without even glancing at the poster on the wall, he stepped out and strolled down the hall. He walked with a lightness in his step and a little grin on his face, waving and nodding pleasantly to the handful of staffers he passed.

It crossed his mind that the squeaking echo of his shoes on the linoleum, a sound which he had conditioned himself to detest through the years, didn't exist at his current gait and speed. Perhaps the key to making the squeak go away was simply to slow down. Take one's time.

When he reached his office, he unlocked his door and stepped in. Mr. Aguirre still sat in the guest chair, typing up some reports on his tablet. He seemingly hadn't moved much since Joe left him. The man only glanced up as Joe walked past him and approached the desk.

"Joe, I had a few questions for you," Aguirre said.

"Uh-huh."

"In your professional opinion, would you say that the deceased Antenna, um, Number-201..."

He never finished the sentence. Joe walked past him, grabbed the flat-screen monitor from the desk, and in one single, fluid motion, pivoted around and SLAMMED it into the side of Aguirre's head.

Aguirre's glasses flew off as his head whipped to the side. The force of the blow almost sent both him and his chair toppling over. The chair wavered for a split second, and then righted itself. The tablet fell from his hand and cracked onto the hard floor as Aguirre slouched down into his seat. He released a soft moan. His head wobbled from side to side. Not unconscious, and certainly not dead, but in no condition to fight back or even ask why Joe had done that.

Joe yanked an ethernet cord from its ports. He wrapped it around Aguirre's arms and legs, binding him to the chair.

The man began to come out of his woozy state. "Joe... what... why..." he managed to croak out.

Joe took the tie off from around his own neck, rolled it into a ball, and shoved it deep into Aguirre's mouth. He fastened it in place by tightly tying a USB cable around Aguirre's head.

Aguirre tried to scream. He tried to move. He tried to do anything. But he could only watch as Joe went to the filing cabinet, opened the bottom drawer and pulled out his oxygen mask.

Joe then pulled something else out of the file drawer. Something that he snuck in during the last few days when he had unlimited access to the Facility before it went online and security procedures were put in place.

A 9mm handgun.

When Riley started walking, Kate refused to allow Joe to keep a gun in the house. It was their first real fight. A conversation that morphed into a debate that morphed into a full-on screaming match. All for this fucking gun.

He let Kate win that fight, and he always resented her for it.

But he didn't get rid of the gun. Instead, he brought it to work and hid it in a drawer. And now he tucked the gun into his pants and walked out of the office.

CHAPTER 27

Hannah didn't want to do her usual rounds today.

The medical staff couldn't take an afternoon off, even if one of the Antennas had just viciously clawed herself to death. The other eleven Antennas still needed to be checked and cleaned.

It was Wednesday, which meant that Dietrich, Crowe and Gorman were all due for their check-ups. She liked to see each of the Antennas personally at least once per week. But considering the fact that a clean-up team was still squeegeeing Bishop's blood off a nearby observation window, Hannah didn't much feel like suiting up and going into one of the cells right now.

She had seen some fucked-up shit at this place, and it was probably responsible for her night-drinking habit that she was trying to kick. But no matter how gruesome the job was, Hannah always managed to keep her outward appearance cool and detached. The rest of her medical staff took their cue off her lead. Even HQ had noticed and commended her and her staff's performance many times.

But this week had rattled her.

For the first time, she couldn't face the Antennas. She needed a distance between them and her. A wall for her to hide behind.

She certainly didn't want her staff to see her hands shake or her voice quiver as she checked the Antennas' vitals. And so, she sent in one of her new guys — Nick Aguta. She told him it would be a learning experience and that she'd be observing his work from behind the glass.

Thank god he bought it.

And so, she stood behind the glass and watched as Nick felt the abdomen on one of the Antennas — Crowe, or "Antenna-209."

As Nick went about the routine, Hannah's mind drifted off to Bishop. She couldn't get the image of that mangled body out of her head. What unnerved Hannah the most was that as she oversaw her team zip Bishop into the body bag, despite the fact that Bishop had clawed apart her own cheeks and throat, Hannah was certain that she could see a thin smile embedded on Bishop's lips.

Strangely, despite the sheer amount of flesh that had been peeled from her own body, Bishop never touched her mouth. There was blood and pulpy tendon everywhere, except for Bishop's little, immaculate grin. It made no sense that the muscles would tighten and rigor mortis would set in with those lips pulled up into a devilish smile on an otherwise demolished face.

Unless that was Bishop's final "fuck you" to Hannah, Joe, and the rest of the staff.

Hannah shuddered at the memory.

She tried to push it out of her mind, but her thoughts only wandered to her conversation with Riley the night before. And once she started down that train-of-thought, she couldn't help but envision Ashley, her baby, just as she had seen her at the hospital.

Purple. Unmoving.

As much as Hannah didn't want to be present at her horrible job right now, she quickly realized that work might be the only thing that could keep her mind off the thoughts that were swirling around it. She focused her attention through the window of Crowe's cell. She watched young Nick Aguta make note of Crowe's various bedsores, measuring them and noting their growth or reduction.

Something wasn't right.

Hannah leaned closer to the glass.

Something definitely wasn't right.

She held her walkie-talkie to her mouth. "Nick? Is he awake?" she asked.

Nick's voice came through her speaker. "Eyes are open." He knelt down over Crowe's face. He pulled out a little penlight as he leaned in close and flashed it into Crowe's eyes.

Hannah held her breath as Nick bent down close to Crowe's face. *Very* close.

"Unresponsive to stimuli," Nick announced loud and confidently, as if he were answering a professor's question and wanted to impress.

"Is he... okay?" Hannah asked. She knew it wasn't a very specific or scientific question, but it was truly the only question she had at the moment.

Nick didn't seem to understand. He stammered a bit, as though he were being quizzed. "Heart rate and breathing are normal. He has a bedsore on his—"

"No, no, no. Something's wrong."

Nick stood and looked toward the window. "I'm sorry, Doctor. What would you like me to do?"

"Get out of there."

He looked around. The Antenna lay motionless on the floor, not moving, not even giving the appearance of possibly becoming a threat. "What's wrong?"

Hannah took a deep breath. She shuddered from some chill that struck deep inside her. "He might be awake, but he's not moving," she said.

It was true. After years and years of observing and caring for Antennas, it was only at this moment that Hannah realized that there was still one thing she had never seen them do — be still.

Crowe wasn't swatting curiously at the air. He wasn't lolling from side to side. He wasn't kicking his legs like a sleeping dog dreaming of running. And his lips were stationary, not releasing soft moans or streams of gibberish. For the first time that Hannah could remember, Crowe didn't move. His eyes simply stared at the ceiling, his gaze locked upward, looking off past the paneling and toward some higher place.

It was the stillness that unnerved Hannah.

She hated to take her eyes off him, but something nibbled at the sides of her vision. A silence had overtaken the normally boisterous Level Two hallway. She turned to look...

Movement had halted in *every* cell. In each one, the Antenna lay flat on his or her back, staring upward.

No muscles moved.

No mouths uttered sounds.

All the other medics and lab techs on the level seemed to notice. It was as if the quiet had descended from above and fell upon everyone at the same time. They stopped talking among themselves. They stopped clattering around in their "diaper pail" carts. They stopped walking as even their footsteps suddenly seemed abnormally loud.

Level Two was completely still.

A perfect, unbroken silence.

"Everyone, out of the chambers," Hannah said. She didn't need to shout or even raise her voice. It carried well enough in the quiet.

Everyone packed up their gear.

Hannah consciously kept her pace steady as she walked toward the elevator. No sense in alarming anyone. "I'm going to talk to Control. Stay out of the cells until you hear back from us," she said as she passed.

She stepped into the elevator.

***

Joe calmly walked down the Level One hallway, passing two members of his janitorial staff chatting as they pushed their carts of bleach and brushes.

As his head bowed in a friendly nod, he could feel his throat gulping. He wondered if they could see the bulge around his waistline from where he had tucked in his gun. Did they wonder why he wasn't wearing a tie? Did they notice that his shirt was untucked? Were they going to wait for him to walk past and then immediately notify security?

His little nod even took place beneath a poster of two watchful eyes and the words *If You See Something, Say Something.*

And yet, the two janitors smiled at Joe and continued walking. If anything, their posture straightened and their conversation dropped off, apparently uncomfortable having the supervisor see them shooting-the-shit.

Joe eyed the men as they swiped their ID at one of the doors and entered the break room. Then he continued down the hall.

Ding! The elevator doors opened and Hannah stepped out.

They locked eyes.

"Joe!" she said as she jogged toward him, urgency written all over her features.

He tried to make his face uninviting. He tried to signal her with his eyes, or even his mind, that she should turn around and walk away, right fucking now. But Hannah was too caught up in whatever she had to report. She kept jogging toward him.

"Something really weird is happening with the Antennas," she said. "I was just down on Level Two and they all went silent. It was the weirdest thing. I was about to go talk to Tariq and see if their gas levels are—"

"Hannah," he interrupted her.

She stopped talking, finally sensing that something was off about him. She came to a stop a few feet in front of him, her eyes gazing from the missing tie around his neck to the untucked shirt around his waist. She seemed to zero in on the faint contours of the gun hidden by the bottom of his shirt.

How much did he trust Hannah?

Could he tell her the truth?

Would she walk away? Would she not call security?

Was he willing to take that chance?

"What's happening?" she said, her voice becoming tense.

"They're gonna ask you a lot of questions," he said, taking a few steps forward and closing the gap between them. He had taken similar steps toward her a hundred times over the years, always so they could whisper criticisms of their workplace without anyone paying too much attention. And, as always, she didn't step away.

"Who will?" she asked.

"You know who. And I think that you might want to tell them that, in your professional opinion, the divorce and separation from my family was really stressful on me."

"It was," she said, confused but keeping her eyes focused on him. "It definitely was."

"And then you'll tell 'em that there was a lot of pressure on me to be a good father," he said while reaching out and gently taking hold of Hannah's arm. "But I didn't know how. And when Kate died and Riley moved in, well, it was all just too much for me. I didn't know how to actually be a father. I didn't know how to support her and care for her because I had never done it before. I'd always chosen work over family. And so, I began to resent my work. It kept calling me back. It kept preventing me from being with my daughter. The resentment turned to anger. I hated this place. I had given it my life, my everything, and it left me with nothing. And so, I lashed out."

"Joe, what are you saying?"

His eyes became cold. "Somewhere in my mind, I decided that the only way to help Riley was to burn down my work. Burn it all. But tell them, whoever asks, that it was *my* choice. That *I'm* the one who cracked. Everything that happened at my house last night, everything with Riley, you leave that out. Don't pull her into this, 'cause I won't be there to pull her out."

It was then that Hannah tried to step away. "Joe..."

"Protect Riley for me. Can you do that?" he said.

"What's going on?"

"Just promise me. You won't let them get to Riley."

"Of course not."

"Good. Good. One more thing..." he said. Then, in a quick motion, he pulled the gun from his pants and shoved it into Hannah's chin. "Don't try to stop me."

And with that, he wrenched her arm behind her back and pressed the gun to the back of her head.

"Open the door to Control."

Joe pushed her toward the Control Room door.

He had to move fast. A half-dozen security cameras had now seen him pull a weapon. At this moment, one of the guards must be alerting Tyler. There would be confusion and the common lag that confusion brings.

Hannah dutifully swiped her ID and opened the door.

Inside, Chuck and Tariq barely raised their heads. They were still deep in a frenzied troubleshooting of the gas leak.

"None of them are talking," Chuck said, holding headphones to his ear as his eyes peered at the various feeds on his screen. "They're just lying there, staring off."

"Well, there's no fucking gas leak!" Tariq said, furiously clicking around at his system.

"It must be a gas leak."

"Maybe there is, but this fucking thing says there's no fucking gas leak."

Joe led Hannah in at gunpoint and then closed the door behind them.

"Uh, guys?" Hannah said.

Chuck turned half-an-eye toward the door. "Oh, Joe, thank god you're here..." Chuck's eyes went wide. The words fell away from his lips as Joe pushed Hannah into the room and pointed the gun at him.

"Hands on your head. Face the wall," Joe said.

Chuck quickly did as he was told, but Tariq just looked around with wide, confused eyes. "Me too?"

"Yes, you, Tariq! Against the wall!" Joe shouted.

Tariq leapt from his seat and joined Chuck and Hannah.

Without a moment to lose, Joe kicked Chuck's chair out of the way and hunched over Chuck's controls. His fingers furiously clicked on the mouse and keys as he entered commands. He angled his head toward the microphone as he clicked it on.

"Attention, staff," he announced. "This is Supervisor Gerhard. We're performing an emergency system reset. Clear all hallways immediately. Leave all supplies where they are. Report to communal areas and do not leave until given the all-clear. This is not a drill. This is an emergency. There will be no surface access."

The phone on Chuck's desk immediately rang. Joe simply reached over and unplugged its cord, silencing it.

"Repeat, clear all hallways now."

He pulled up a schematic of the Facility and, as fast as he could, began clicking on individual security doors, airlocks, and cameras, toggling each and every one from "Active" to "Disabled."

The Facility schematic began flashing with red lights.

Joe kept working.

Off in the corner, he could hear the whispered conversations of Chuck, Tariq and Hannah, all huddled facing the wall.

"Should we be stopping him?" Tariq whispered.

"Ain't my job," Chuck replied.

"Joe, please," Hannah said, turning her head to look at him. "Talk to me. What are you doing?"

Joe didn't have time to answer. He had to move fast. At this moment, the security forces in the lobby must be in a full panic. Tyler was surely trying to stop him. Joe just had to be faster.

"Joe, if you stop now, we'll tell Tyler it was all a mistake," Hannah said. "A miscommunication. You don't have to do this."

"Yeah, man," Chuck said. "We got your back."

Joe continued clicking on the controls.

"Please, Joe," Hannah said. "Tyler will know something's happening. He's going to be here to stop you any minute."

"He won't," Joe said.

"I know he's your friend, but he will arrest you. If not *kill* you."

"He can't get down here."

"He's head of security. He can override the elevator lock-out, man," Chuck said.

Joe shook his head as he clicked in the final commands. "At one of the design meetings, way back in the day, some asshole mentioned the possibility that an enemy force might try a full-frontal assault on this place. China or Russia could storm the lobby and hold the head of security at gunpoint until he enabled the elevators. It was the kinda bullshit scenario that some suit farts straight into the ear of the high-brass. After that, no one could relax until procedures were in place to prevent such a thing from happening."

On one of the screens, Joe watched as his staff hurried out of the hallways and gathered in the break room.

In a matter of minutes, all movement on the monitors ceased.

"And so, we designed it into the system that the supervisor can lock out surface access. The cavalry will need to come direct from HQ to get that elevator humming again," Joe said as he hit one final command. The elevator icon on his screen began flashing red.

With one final click of his mouse, all the screens went black.

Joe straightened his back and turned his attention to the three people standing on the other side of the room, staring at the wall.

"I need you all to come with me," he said. The firmness of his voice made it clear that this was not a request.

They slowly turned around and faced him.

Keeping the handgun trained on them, Joe walked up to the platform in the rear of the room and opened a cabinet beside the refreshment table. Inside were snacks and napkins and water bottles. But beneath all that, on the bottom shelf of the cabinet, sat a large, sturdy case. Joe pulled out the case and flipped its lid open. Inside were oxygen tanks and masks.

"Put 'em on," Joe said.

Chuck and Tariq turned to Hannah, seemingly designating her their leader. She hesitated. Her pleading eyes looked up at Joe, but he kept his face cold.

"Joe..." she said.

"I don't have time to debate this."

With a deep breath, she walked up the platform and pulled a mask from the case. The other two followed behind.

"You're gonna be in so much trouble, man," Chuck said.

Joe only nodded.

CHAPTER 28

Tyler felt a hot, nervous sweat develop on his back and arms.

A quiet tension permeated the lobby as all the security personnel kept their eyes on him. He swiped his ID on the elevator keypad for the umpteenth time. And, once again, the little light flashed red. An obnoxious buzzer sounded — *ERRRR*.

The elevator. The cameras. All disabled.

"Are the monitors up yet?" he called out to his men in the video suite.

"Still dark."

Tyler cursed himself. Things had been strange around here for days, but he had turned a blind-eye because he considered Joe his friend. When Tyler was in the Air Force it was like that too — you bent the rules to protect your buddies. You overlooked stuff because everyone's on the same team.

How many things had he ignored this week? How many times did he go along with questionable actions, like a robot, because he assumed that everyone had the same goals?

Bishop acting up...

Joe's daughter seeing shit...

Joe performing unauthorized shutdowns...

Joe "suggesting" that Tyler station all his security forces in the lobby instead of down below because of the "optics"...

Fuck.

Maybe, just maybe, this weird communication blackout and security freeze-out were properly authorized. Maybe HQ wouldn't breathe down his neck on any of this. Maybe it would all blow over.

Or maybe the Facility supervisor had gone rogue.

And the moment Tyler detained him — or killed him — an investigation would begin and Tyler's week-long negligence would be fully revealed. And in that case, when the interviews and investigations piled up, Tyler realized that the last thing he wanted was for his men to say that he stood there dumbly with his dick in his hands while the Facility supervisor did fuck-knows-what to the Antennas downstairs.

Tyler's choice was easy.

Fuck.

He took a breath and turned away from the elevator.

"Phillips, get on the phone to HQ. Find me someone who can override Gerhard's control."

The man he pointed to picked up the phone and began dialing. Tyler knew that Phillips would probably get bounced around through three different operators and five different assistants before he got hold of anyone who had the authority to shit for themselves. And even then, whatever big dick they got on the phone would probably say, "I'm sending a team. They'll be there in two hours."

And so, Tyler marched toward his security booth.

"Martinez, Robinson, Wells, Harrell, suit up."

He opened a locker and pulled out an oxygen unit and a flashlight. He strapped on the mask and grabbed a rifle. His men scattered to their own stations to collect their gear.

Tyler jogged to the entrance. He turned back to the lobby and loudly called toward his men. "Come on! Come on! Move it!"

T . J . P A Y N E

The men hurried to follow him. An adrenaline rush seemed to kick into them. After years of watching x-ray machines and performing security drills, they were suddenly moving with an urgency and purpose. A grim determination had overtaken most of their faces.

Tyler threw open the front door and jogged out.

The men followed.

They sprinted out the door and through the parking lot. They looped around behind the building and ran at full speed to the satellite dishes and towers a hundred yards away. All that equipment was in an enclosure circled by a thick metal fence. Tyler swiped his ID at the gate. It flashed a red light. *Disabled.*

"We're going over," he said as he crouched down and cupped his hands. Martinez was the first man there, and so he stepped into Tyler's waiting hands and got hoisted up the fence. He gripped the top and looked at the coils and coils of razor wire draped across it. Hanging on with one hand, he pulled cutters from his cargo pocket and began cutting through the razor wire.

"Faster!" Tyler shouted. "Come on! Move it!"

The man worked his way through the mesh of wire as fast as he could, cutting with one hand while hanging onto the top of the fence with the other.

Tyler breathed deeply. He glanced at his watch. This was taking too long. How long had it been? How long had Gerhard been down there alone?

What the fuck was Gerhard up to?

***

The stairwell door on Level Two opened. Chuck was the first one to step out, followed by Tariq, then Hannah, and finally, Joe holding the gun.

They all wore masks and held oxygen tanks in their hands.

"The maintenance door is unlocked," Joe said, motioning to the side door that led behind the chambers.

Chuck tugged on the handle and the door swung open.

They all stepped inside.

Together, they stood there, looking at the twisting assortment of hoses and tubes running from the tanks into each cell.

Joe reached into his pocket and pulled out three pairs of scissors.

"There are eleven more gas lines," he said. "You're going to work fast and do it as quick as possible. Tyler's probably coming down the access shaft right now. I want the lines *cut*. I want it done in ways that can't be immediately repaired."

"They'll tear themselves apart," Hannah said.

"Yes," Joe said sharply.

Tariq held up his hands. "I... I ain't doing this, man."

"Yes, you are. Then we'll all calmly walk back to Control. We'll have a soda and some pretzels and we'll sit around and wait for them to take care of themselves. When they're done, I'll hand over the gun. You won't get in trouble. Everyone will know I made you do it. But let's be very clear on one thing," Joe said, aiming the gun at Tariq's head. "Don't delay. And don't fuck with me."

"Joe!" Hannah said.

But Joe didn't flinch. "Cut the lines."

Tariq gulped. He took the scissors from Joe's hand. Hannah and Chuck followed suit. They proceeded down the corridor toward the nearest regulators. They gripped the hoses.

"Now," Joe said.

Hannah was the first. With one hand, she gripped the black rubber hose that fed into the plastic casing of the regulator. As the regulator hummed, her other hand opened the scissors wide. Everyone kept their eyes on her, waiting. She pressed the edge of the scissor blade against the hose. And then... she pressed down.

It didn't cut smoothly.

She opened and closed the scissors against the rubber several times. She tried bending the hose around the blade and doing a sawing motion. Bit by bit, a tiny stream of gas began hissing through the crack she made in the hose.

Almost immediately, *another* sound could be heard drifting through the thick walls. A high screeching wail. It sounded like a bad fan belt on an engine, whining away, warning the world that it was on the verge of snapping. At first, it certainly seemed like a dying piece of machinery. But then, the chilling wail found its force. Its oscillating octaves were the screams of a human in pain.

"Keep going," Joe said. He pointed the gun at Chuck and Tariq. "You too."

They gripped the nearby hoses and clamped down with their scissors.

Hannah, meanwhile, found the small crack she had made in her hose. With that weak spot identified, she dug the point of her scissors' blade into it, ripping it open wider. The scream on the other side of the wall, which had seemed so violent just moments before, found a deeper, more frantic pitch as Hannah severed the final threads of hose.

Chuck and Tariq followed suit. They dug the tips of their blades into the hoses of the next sets of regulators. Twisting and prying, they forced the smooth, black rubber to crack and break. Two more streams of hissing gas filled the room. And two more screams from the occupants across the wall accompanied it.

"Now the next set," Joe said.

They moved down the corridor to another set of regulators. The screams on the other side of the wall grew in intensity. They weren't a single pitch or frequency. The shrieks jumped unnaturally through the Antennas' vocal cords, as if their tongue, throat, and lungs were searching for a howl that could fully express their anguish.

"Keep going," Joe said.

His team bowed their heads as they wrapped the next set of hoses around their dull, metal blades. Their hands strained as they pushed against the scissors' handles, forcing the tool to gnaw through the rubber.

Three new screams added to the chorus.

Joe motioned them with his gun. "Now we need to go to the other side."

They dutifully walked back. Joe motioned for Chuck to take the lead. Chuck opened the door to the main corridor. The moment the thick metal door moved, a wall of noise — horrible, pained noise — flooded into the room.

"Hurry up," Joe said.

They all passed through the door and into the main corridor of Level Two.

"Don't look at them. Go on," Joe said.

He tried to follow his own advice, but from the side of his eye he could see the writhing, screaming figures slamming their bodies against the observation windows. One half of the corridor's residents were in agony; the other half, completely still.

For now.

They hurried across the corridor to the maintenance door on the other side. Chuck tugged it open and they all entered.

"Go on. Do it," Joe said.

Chuck, Hannah, and Tariq made their way down the aisle.

Hose after hose, they gnawed through with the dull scissors. Each new hiss of escaping gas was met with a new addition to the frantic wailing and pounding.

Another hose.

Then another.

More screams blended into the chorus.

The noise grew and expanded, seeming to howl directly from the concrete walls, as if the building itself felt the suffering.

It was impossible to block out. The sound seemed to cling to Joe's team. He could see that its very weight had pulled down on their shoulders, sending their bodies into defeated slouches.

After Tariq hacked through the final hose, they all turned and trudged back to Joe. He could see their faces through their masks. Ashen. Tired. His team now seemed as zombies, slogging through the cries as though it were a thick, oppressive mud.

Joe tucked the gun back into his pants. He didn't need it anymore. He also hated to tell his crew that although, yes, he had snuck a gun into the Facility during the final days of its construction, he hadn't actually snuck in any bullets. After that fight with Kate over the gun, he hiked off into the woods and fired off all his ammunition. Then, as a last moment of defiance against his wife, he decided he would keep the gun, even if just in the filing cabinet at work.

He planned to apologize to his team, and especially to Hannah, when they got back to the Control Room.

"Now, let's all calmly go wait for Tyler to get here," he said.

With that, he pushed open the door.

Hannah and Chuck followed him out to the main corridor.

The last one out was Tariq.

***

Tariq couldn't wait to get back up to his office. Ever since he got this damn job, the one place he hated going was Level Two. He didn't mind monitoring the Antennas remotely through cameras and readouts. He could always mute the feed when they screamed. It removed him just enough from the day-to-day work of, let's be honest, *torturing* strange people for national security.

But actually being *present* on Level Two made it all too real for him.

The smell of the bleach masking their feces.

The hum of their moaning accented by sudden, random screaming.

And the sight of them... ugh. Tariq felt it was like being in a mental institution, prison, and morgue of reanimated corpses all at the same time.

He hated it.

In truth, ever since he cut that first gas line, he had felt a horrible headache. His vision had gone a bit blurry and his hearing became muffled. He figured that maybe it was the fucking gun that his boss was aiming at his head. The whole experience happened in a daze. He was glad it was over.

And, in good news, with Gerhard acting so weird, there was a good chance that Aguirre — and any other investigators HQ sent — might not fire Tariq now. He didn't much care for his job, but it paid well and offered certain perks. He hoped the throbbing headache he felt was simply related to an insanely stressful day. God, he really wanted to get back to his desk and take some ibuprofen.

But when he stepped out of the maintenance hall and into the main corridor, he almost went the wrong direction. He must have gotten turned around because he had expected the stairwell to be to his left. But that way led down the corridor to the various cells.

The hallway spun slightly, giving him the feeling of vertigo.

But it passed quickly. He hoped his coworkers didn't see his awkward little stutter-step as he reoriented himself.

Maybe he was turned around because he wasn't used to wearing this damn oxygen mask. It really clouded his vision and kept fogging up. For whatever reason, he couldn't wrap his head around how to breathe normally in the stupid thing; he kept alternating between not breathing at all and taking huge heaving breaths. How did the poor schmucks who worked down here in those bunny suits not go crazy? Tariq was glad he never had to do that kind of shit-work.

As he was about to turn toward the stairs, he chanced a look down the corridor. It had gone unnaturally quiet. In fact, everything was quiet.

Had the Antennas finally died?

When Tariq looked, though, his heart stopped...

Every chamber door stood wide open.

What the hell had happened?

How could all the fucking doors be open?

Tariq hoped that there was a simple, logical explanation. But then he heard one of those soft moans.

He held his breath.

Beside him, Joe and the others silently stared down the corridor.

It was then that Ferro staggered out of one of the far chambers. She had torn the gown from her body. Her hands clawed at her naked shoulders and breasts as she spasmed and tensed. The protective mitts that once covered her hands had been ripped to shreds, seemingly by her own teeth as long strings of thread hung from her mouth.

Then she turned.

In all the time Tariq had worked here, in all the countless hours he'd logged observing the Antennas, he had never made eye contact with one before.

Until this moment.

He looked at Ferro, and she looked right back at him. It was abundantly clear that she saw him.

"Oh shit," he muttered.

Ferro released a shriek.

With a loping, staggering gait, she raced down the hall toward him. Her body twisted and flailed and her arms swung out.

Her screams seemed to rouse the other Antennas. As she passed their open doors, the others emerged. Clawing at themselves and screaming, they galloped forward. They joined her, racing toward Tariq and the others.

It was a stampede through the hallway.

Screaming, charging, blood-thirsty inmates, suddenly freed from their shackles.

"Go, go, go!" Tariq yelled.

Joe and the others stood dumbstruck as the horde ran toward them.

Tariq pushed past them and ran to the stairwell himself.

He tugged on the door, but it wouldn't budge. Reaching into his pocket, he fumbled to get out his ID card. His hand wouldn't stop shaking as he slid it through the scanner.

Glancing behind him, the Antennas leapt onto Joe, Chuck and Hannah. They dragged them to the ground. Their hands clawed out, scraping out chunks of flesh from his coworkers.

Joe yelled, his voice seeming to come from a great distance. "Tariq! Tariq, wait!"

With a loud click and a green light, the door in front of Tariq unlocked, just as one of the Antennas reached out to grab his shoulder.

He slipped through and kept moving.

But in front of him was *another* locked and sealed door.

There weren't *two* sets of doors to the stairwell, were there?

A hand grabbed him by the shoulder.

Tariq turned and shoved whoever it was away.

He swiped his ID at the second door and yanked the door open.

The hand reached out and grabbed him again, but he managed to twist free.

"Tariq! What the fuck are you doing?" someone shouted.

But he wasn't slowing. He ran through the door and into the stairwell...

Only it wasn't the stairwell.

He expected to see a darkened, gray metal staircase rising up through a concrete chasm. Instead, he had to squint. Fluorescent light bounced off the white walls and floor.

Tariq stood there and blinked in confusion.

This wasn't the stairwell at all.

He was in one of the Antenna's chambers.

***

"Tariq! What the fuck are you doing?" Joe shouted.

The moment they had stepped out of the maintenance hallway, Tariq had started stumbling around as if he were some blindfolded kid being spun before trying to hit a piñata. And then he had taken off toward the nearest Antenna chamber, fumbling around to swipe his ID at the door.

They all shouted at him to stop, but he kept going.

It was when Tariq looked back at them from over his shoulder that Joe realized what was happening. He saw it in Tariq's eyes. The kid was looking right at them, but not *seeing* them. Tariq was seeing something else entirely, and whatever he saw filled him with fear. It was the exact same look of fear — true terror — that Joe had seen flash across Riley's face.

Joe ran after Tariq and tried to grab him before he could open the second airlock door, but Tariq firmly shoved him to the ground.

By the time Joe had climbed back to his feet, it was too late.

Tariq used his ID to unlock the door to Ferro's cell.

For a moment, time seemed to stop. Joe watched as Tariq stood in the cell. The kid looked around at his surroundings. A realization seemed to wash over him, but he appeared unable to fully grasp its meaning. This was *not* the room he thought he had unlocked. This wasn't what Tariq had expected at all.

As Tariq dumbly stood there, trying to force the puzzle pieces to fit together in his mind, Ferro threw herself on him.

Her weight knocked him into the door.

They collapsed to the ground together. The door tried to swing closed on them, but their fumbling bodies blocked it from sealing.

Tariq appeared to snap back to awareness somewhat. He tried to fight her off, but he seemed confused. His weak attempts to shove her away were no match against the fury of the hands that clawed toward his face.

The protective mitts were still strapped to Ferro's wrists, but the mitts themselves were in tatters. Her fingers reached out through holes in the mitts that she had evidently created by gnawing through the mitts with her teeth.

Within moments, those fingers found what they were looking for. Ferro latched her grip onto Tariq's oxygen mask and yanked it off his face. True realization and panic settled into Tariq.

Joe could see it on the kid's face — Tariq suddenly knew he was fighting for his life.

But by then it was too late.

Tariq had taken a few quick, fearful gulps of the room's toxic air. Even with the lines cut, the remaining gas in the room weakened his body. His arms flailed but struggled to make contact with Ferro or to put up any reasonable defense. He tried to shove her off of him, but his limbs didn't seem capable of fully communicating with his brain. His hands whiffed badly in their attempts to push, or even punch, her.

Ferro, meanwhile, laid into Tariq with a focused fury. The mix of oxygen and gas in the room was enough to cripple Tariq, but to Ferro, it seemed to be the most connected her mind had been to her body in years. She was seeing everything. She had been reunited with her senses and muscles. It gave her movements a speed that Tariq could neither match nor defend himself against.

It only took a few swings before she got her hands past Tariq's flailing defenses. She dug her fingers into Tariq's face.

"Help! Help!" Tariq managed to call out, although his words were already beginning to slur.

Ferro's fingers wormed their way into Tariq's eyes. She dug deep. Despite the air in the room disabling his muscles, he most certainly felt it. He released a violent, throat-searing scream. The kind of scream that Joe had only heard from the Antennas — on rare occasion — as they reached the pinnacles of the tuning process.

She lifted his entire skull through her vice-grip on his eye sockets, and then she slammed his head forcefully against the door.

Dead or not, Tariq stopped screaming.

It all happened so fast that Joe had barely been able to scramble to his feet before it was over.

Joe watched as Ferro, done with Tariq, grabbed the keycard from the kid's hand and rose off the floor. She lurched out of the cell and into the airlock chamber. She staggered past Joe, seemingly not seeing or caring that he was there. Her whole body twitched and swayed. Even as she regained control of her muscles, they seemed to have atrophied to the point that she could barely control them.

With immense concentration, Ferro steadied her hand long enough to swipe Tariq's ID through the sensor pad.

The green light flashed. Unlocked.

Ferro threw open the door and stumbled out into the main corridor.

Joe grabbed her arm to hold her back. She tried to pull away, surprising Joe with how much strength actually remained in her bony limbs. A tug-of-war commenced with Ferro's arm serving as the rope.

Joe yanked hard and to the side. A loud *snap* rewarded him as Ferro's forearm broke near her elbow. Even with her bone puncturing through her skin, the pain — which she must have felt — didn't cripple her as it would a normal person. She channeled it and fought through it. It was as though she were already operating at a maximum threshold for pain and any additional sensations were insignificant in comparison.

While ignoring the bone ripping through her arm, she forced her way through the door.

He released her broken arm and tried to grab her somewhere more substantial. "Hannah!" he called out down the corridor.

But then Ferro whipped around. Her good hand grabbed the edge of the door. She slammed it hard into Joe's head.

He collapsed to the floor.

His vision blurred.

All he could see was Ferro lurch across the hallway to the next cell. She swiped Tariq's keycard.

Joe tried to climb to his feet, but the moment he pushed himself off the ground, his legs wobbled, as if they were made of a frail rubber. He managed to push himself forward a single step before they buckled and sent him crashing back to the floor. He couldn't feel the tips of his fingers as his hands tried to push his body back up off the floor.

"Hannann..." When he tried to shout for Hannah's help, his tongue weakly twisted around his mouth as his numb lips struggled to form shapes. Even as he strained to push the words out his mouth, he could only hear them as though they were being shouted from a great distance.

As a grayness crept around the fringes of his vision, his eyes caught something. A line, running past his gaze. With his last ounce of body control, he focused his eyes on that line. It was a crack, traversing the length of his oxygen mask, precisely where Ferro had slammed the door on his head. His mask was compromised and whatever gas drifted through the open doors was sifting its way into his airstream.

With that sudden realization, he once again commanded his body to stand.

His mind commanded his arms to push himself off the floor.

His mind commanded his mouth to scream.

His mind commanded his eyes to stay focused and open.

As the blackness eclipsed over his senses, he wasn't sure which, if any, of those commands actually arrived at their destination.

**

Hannah watched in shock from the far end of the corridor as Ferro emerged from her cell and slammed the door into Joe's head.

"What the fuck is going on?" Chuck said from beside her. He angled his way toward the stairwell. Chuck certainly was no hero. He didn't seem like he was about to rush over to aid Joe or stop Ferro. And without Chuck's support, Hannah didn't much feel like doing it either.

And so, the two of them stood frozen by the stairwell.

"They got in Tariq's head," Hannah said.

"Huh?"

"They made him hallucinate. They tricked him into opening that cell."

"They can't do that."

"Well, they fucking did!"

"But how?"

"I don't know." Hannah's mouth hung open in wonder and fear. "This might be the most they've been off the gas. This is the most control they've had over their senses and bodies."

They stood and watched as Ferro limped to the cell across the hall. Her broken arm, the bone still visibly protruding from the skin and now dripping blood onto the floor, hung limply by her side. But she didn't seem to notice or care. With a clarity of purpose, she lurched up to her neighbor's cell. She swiped Tariq's keycard and then disappeared into the airlock chamber.

"We have to get Joe and get out of here," Hannah said. She took a few strides down the hall. Chuck begrudgingly followed behind. They didn't make it far before Ferro limped out, followed closely behind by *another* Antenna, "Crowe."

Ferro stumbled off to the next closest adjoining cell and began unlocking *that* door.

"She's freeing the others," Hannah said, a sense of realization evident in her voice. "That was their plan. They coordinated this. They needed Joe to get them all off the gas so they could move."

"Uh, Hannah?" Chuck pointed at Crowe. The Antenna was frail, like the others, but he was tall with a bone structure that must have once supported a strong build. Hannah sometimes tried to guess each Antenna's prior life and job; she ultimately felt that Crowe had been either a soldier or a professional athlete. He had *that* body. As such, those gangly, toned limbs and strong cheek bones — so high and pronounced that they formed deep craters around his eye sockets — made him the most intimidating of the Antennas.

And now, Crowe's eyes had locked onto them.

After so many years of observing the eyes of every Antenna roam aimlessly around their heads, to see a gaze transfixed and burning with purpose took Hannah's breath away. She instinctively put her hand up, as she might toward a wild animal. Not really knowing what to say, she opened her mouth anyway. Maybe she could apologize. Or calm him with a simple, *"Easy now..."*

But she couldn't form any words. There was no indication that Crowe's brain was capable of engaging in such a debate. When she looked into those sunken eyes, the only humanity she saw remaining was the human emotion of vengeance. She knew, looking into those eyes, that no explanation or apology would ever satisfy this man.

"Is *that* a hallucination?" Chuck said, jolting Hannah back to the moment.

"I don't know."

Another door opened. Ferro emerged, followed by another Antenna. This one a female. Latina. They called her "Vasquez."

This new Antenna joined Crowe.

Together, they stood in the hall and looked at Hannah and Chuck. The protective mitts, having been chewed apart, uselessly hung from their wrists in shreds. Their fingers stretched through the holes, like cats testing their claws. Thoughts seemed to pass between the two Antennas. Their movements seemed perfectly synced.

Then, at the exact same instant, both Crowe and Vasquez broke into sprints. With their hobbling, twitching stride, they raced toward Hannah and Chuck.

"Run!" Hannah yelled, turning to the staircase.

Chuck, his reflexes a couple beats slower, turned and followed.

The Antennas ran too.

Except for Ferro.

She had opened yet *another* cell.

CHAPTER 29

Joe's vision faded in and out.

At times, it was blurry, but he could make out shapes and shadows and light. But then, for moments, those blurry shadows would grow and consume his sight until there was nothing but darkness. It fluctuated like that for as long as he lay in Ferro's doorway. The gas still pumped through Level Two but was now dispersing into uneven pockets that drifted around Joe.

He was determined to escape from this hellish floor that seemed almost stuck to him. He concentrated. His mind firmly told his hands to lay flat on the floor so they could push his weight off the ground.

He thought it.

He envisioned them moving.

He went muscle by muscle, bone by bone, tendon by tendon, commanding each piece of his body to move.

And yet, his right arm remained curled underneath his body where he fell. His left arm moved a few times, but not in any coordinated maneuver. It instead chose to flop harmlessly at his side.

He tried commanding his legs to move. To lift himself up. To kick out. To twitch his ankle. *Anything*.

Maybe they did move. Maybe they were kicking wildly. He couldn't feel it as the darkness settled in again.

***

Joe's vision came back. How long had it been? There must have been a pocket of clean oxygen that moved through his system because the clarity was more than he'd had since his mask cracked. It was still blurry, but he could see the outlines of some shapes as well as a few muted colors. The thought ran through his mind that if he held his breath, he could use this moment of sensory freedom to scamper toward the stairs.

But then, one of those shapes, those strange hovering shadows, grew large as it moved toward him, darkening his path toward escape.

It was an Antenna.

Joe tried to figure out which one. Maybe it was one of the weaker ones. Maybe he could fight him or her off and still make it to the stairs. It seemed to be female. Caucasian. But his sight wasn't clean enough to make out the face.

His vision suddenly turned dark again, almost as if someone had a dimmer switch behind his eyes and was turning the knob down. The shape raced toward him. His muscles couldn't move.

His vision went hazy...

...hazier...

...hazier...

In his last faint moment of sight, he suddenly thought about the dream he had the night before. In it, he was trying to hide a body in a grocery store freezer. Kate had walked up to him, put an arm around his shoulder, leaned in and whispered into his ear. Joe finally remembered what she had said.

Her body had been tense, as though she was about to warn him of something important. But her voice came through relaxed. All she said was, *"I'll be gone for a bit. Watch Riley for me."*

And she left.

Joe pushed the dream from his mind and tried to focus his vision. He stared at the gray vinyl baseboard that connected the wall to the floor. He kept his eyes anchored to one particular seam in the baseboard, hoping he could will his vision to stay connected to reality.

But that gray crack expanded and blurred. It seemed to spread and grow until that seam of darkness wrapped itself around his eyes.

And then everything went black.

It was a deep blackness, unlike anything he had ever experienced.

When he was twenty-two, his appendix ruptured. He went to the hospital and they gave him anesthetic while they removed it. He remembered his eyes closing as the doctors told him to count backwards from one hundred. The next instant, when his eyes opened, several hours had passed and the surgery was done. He didn't remember a thing. It was as if his consciousness had been transported directly into the future.

This was different.

This time, even as his senses seemed suspended in the blackened abyss of a warm ocean, his mind stayed awake and alert. In the darkness, some gateway in his mind seemed to swing open and all his thoughts bubbled into his head. Thoughts of Riley. Thoughts of Bishop. Memories of camping. Dreams of Kate. They cascaded in, swarming and overlapping with each other.

He told himself to focus. He visualized closing the doors of his mind, shutting out the visions of Kate's brains splattering on the siding and the time his tent flooded during a thunderstorm.

He tried to count the seconds, hoping that having a task would allow him to concentrate.

One... two... three... four... five... six...

His vision returned.

The world was different. Bright. Very bright. He wasn't face-down on the floor anymore. No black-speckled linoleum. It was all white. Pure white. Bit by bit, the glowing whiteness began to tighten into focus. He could make out its edges.

It was the ceiling. He was staring *up* at the ceiling of one of the cells. Someone had moved him into a cell and flipped him on his back.

Was it really only six seconds that he had been out?

He told his eyes to look around so he could get his bearings. To his surprise, his eyes responded. The first place his gaze wandered, or rather *was drawn*, was down toward his chest.

Two Antennas huddled there over his midsection. Their hands and fingers flew with speed and viciousness in a digging, ripping movement. Chunky red liquid flew up into the air before coming down and splattering onto Joe's face. It took a moment for the fogginess to leave his mind and for him to realize the obvious — that it was his own blood and flesh being carved out of his body. But Joe didn't feel anything.

"Hello, Joe Gerhard," a girl's voice said. The voice seemed to be coming from inside his own head. He knew it as Riley's voice, but he also knew that it couldn't be her. "Welcome to *our* world," the voice said.

And suddenly, like the flipping of some switch... CLICK... *all* of Joe's senses turned on.

That's when he felt the pain.

Tyler cursed beneath his breath.

He didn't much like heights and he certainly wasn't a fan of darkness. And now, here he was, hurriedly climbing down one rebar rung at a time in the narrow, concrete access tunnel. It was a straight-shot down from here, about five floors, to the bottom.

Wearing an oxygen mask that restricted his vision and made his breathing loudly echo in his own ears didn't help with the sense of claustrophobia. Still, Tyler and his men hurried down those metal rungs embedded into the concrete wall, one hand and foot at a time. They quickly descended, trying hard not to step on the fingers of the guy below them.

Tyler couldn't move fast enough.

It had taken his team way too long to scale the barrier and gain access to the emergency shaft. The hatch on the shaft required a passcode that they needed to call into HQ to get. That alone took several minutes of various operators passing the phone (and the buck) from one to another.

With all the planning and redundancies and security protocols at this place, the one fucking thing that no one ever foresaw was the Facility supervisor locking out his own security team. The system broke down. All those security measures only served to hamper the actual security guards trying to perform an actual security mission.

And Tyler knew exactly where the blame for all this would fall. Certainly not on the bureaucrats and eggheads who designed this maze of hoops and procedures. No, they'd do what they always did. They'd find the highest-ranking grunt and say, *The head of security is the one who messed up. If he wasn't an incompetent traitor, all of our complex designs would have worked flawlessly.*

Tyler's entire body clenched in anger. If he saw Gerhard, he was going to fucking shoot him in the stomach. There was no time to day-dream about that, though. One hand at a time, Tyler led his team deeper into the shaft's black abyss.

After several more minutes of this tight descent, Tyler came across a number "1" painted on the side of the wall. He clicked on his walkie-talkie. "We're at the Level One access door," he said.

The men above him stopped their downward climb.

Tyler turned to his side. A hatch protruded from the wall. The shaft didn't provide any room to maneuver. It had been designed for maintenance in case an electrical failure disabled the elevators. It *hadn't* been designed for an armed incursion; there was no room to have one man open the door so another could race through with weapon ready. Tyler would have to open the door himself.

With one hand clutching the rung of the ladder, he reached out and grasped the crank that locked the door. He turned it. The unlubricated metal squealed loudly.

When the door unlatched, Tyler pushed it open. He drew his sidearm and crawled through...

Tyler emerged from beneath the large snack table in the Control Room.

He crawled out.

One-by-one, his men followed him and spread out through the room, their weapons held ready and their flashlights sweeping around.

The Control Room was dark and silent. The screens showed only black. An eerie silence hung over the room. Even when Tyler had performed late-night security sweeps, after most of the staff had gone home for the day, the Facility never felt as abandoned as it did now.

Tyler motioned for his men to follow him.

They gathered around the room's door. Tyler turned the handle and flung it open. His men fanned out into the Level One hallway. Tyler followed closely behind.

And there he saw the carnage.

Unlike the dim Control Room, the hallway was as bright as ever. Fluorescent overhead-lights reflected off the beige concrete walls. But the brightness only accentuated the butchery.

Judging by the fleshy Hawaiian-shirt-covered torso in the center of the hall, Chuck hadn't made it out alive. Someone had tackled him from behind. They had shredded his shirt from the back and ripped out sections of spine and rib, then flung those around. His arms, legs, and head had been pulled from his body and thrown to various ends of the hall.

The beige walls were splattered with his blood. Unevenly. Some wall sections and doors dripped with such a wet redness that it was as if they were coated with a layer of paint. The opposite wall — the one with several large posters reminding the staff of the importance of secrecy — ran thick with long drip marks.

A red pool crept out from that mound of Hawaiian-shirt-flesh. A series of footprints — bare footprints — had stampeded through the blood and run off down the hall and then back again, seemingly checking every door. The bloody floor prints had all the chaos of a Jackson Pollock painting — hundreds of prints from probably dozens of scurrying, twisted, human feet.

"Proceed with caution," Tyler said, not that anyone needed such instructions.

The men advanced down the hall.

"Check the doors," he said.

His men did as ordered.

Gobs of blood clung to many of the door handles. The Antennas, apparently after they had finished dismembering Chuck, had attempted to open the doors to the offices in the hallway. Tyler could see the streaks from where their blood-soaked fingers had tried to claw through the solid doors. They had thrown themselves against them, desperately trying to get to whoever was on the other side.

Dislodged fingernails lay at the base of some of the doors. The Antennas had clawed so wildly that they had ripped them off without noticing.

Tyler's men proceeded down the hall, trying door handles as they passed.

Locked.

Locked.

Locked.

Tyler tried the handle to the medical offices. Locked. He rapped his knuckles on the door. The sharp sound was amplified by the hallway's silence.

"Security," he whispered. "Anyone here?"

Nothing.

One slow step at a time, his head constantly swinging around to check behind them, Tyler led his team down the hall.

***

Hannah knew that she was probably in shock.

She huddled in a corner of the break room, thankful to have her back nestled against two solid walls. The rest of the staff — about thirty people in all — quietly sat at the tables or stood guard near the refrigerator that was barricading the door.

Nobody talked to Hannah.

Nobody talked at all.

Even the slightest shifting of someone in their chair caused a seemingly ear-piercing squeak of metal on linoleum. Thirty sets of angry, fearful eyes would then glare the culprit into silence.

Everyone did their best not to talk and not to make noise.

No one wanted to ask Hannah what exactly had happened out in the hallway before they heard her shrieking and banging on the door. Before they opened it to let her in. Before they saw her wide eyes, her blood speckled face, the gouge marks on her right arm from where she ripped herself free from someone's grasp.

Hannah had gone to the corner and sat. She barely moved since.

The things she saw them do to Chuck...

The things they would have done to her...

Chuck had been about three steps slower than her.

Three steps more vulnerable.

One of them had grabbed him by the shirt. The next thing Hannah saw was the swarm. And then the pieces of Chuck flying through the air.

They didn't just kill him. They wanted to hurt him. It was a fury and viciousness that didn't exist in nature. *That is what we have created*, Hannah thought. Something outside the bounds of nature.

Trying hard not to think about it, she instead focused on her hands.

They had developed a tremor. As much as she held them and massaged them, the tremor remained. Her breathing had become a constant ordeal. She would sit still for a few moments and then realize that she had forgotten to breathe. Then she would hyperventilate; her lungs would take massive gulps of air that were too big and fast for her body to process. She was unable to perform the simplest, subconscious, bodily function.

Focusing on her breathing, though, at least gave her something to concentrate on. She was thankful that it kept her mind from wandering to what she had just seen.

Suddenly, several people in the room looked up. Did they just hear something?

Everyone held their breath.

Yes. It was the sound of someone knocking on a door down the hall.

They heard a voice from out in the hallway, near the Control Room. "Security. Anyone here?"

A hopeful murmur rose from the staffers.

The knocking got closer. Help was arriving.

Some of the men near the door began sliding the refrigerator away from its place as a barricade.

"Be careful," Hannah croaked out. Her voice was weak. "Don't trust what you see or hear," she said.

Nobody really listened to her.

They all moved closer to the door. Closer to their rescue.

"Wait... wait..." she said. It felt like one of those dreams that she'd often had since her daughter died — she'd scream for help, but her voice wasn't strong enough for anyone to hear. But Hannah *knew* she wasn't dreaming. She knew she was awake.

She tried to pull herself up off the floor.

By this time, the refrigerator had been moved.

Nick Aguta — Hannah's young trainee in the medical department — cracked open the door to peek.

"It's Tyler," he said to the room, spying on their saviors through the narrow opening. He opened the door wide.

***

Tyler heard a sound come from the break room — the sound of a large object scraping across the floor.

He motioned for his team to advance in that direction.

As they neared, the door cracked a hair.

And then it opened wide.

Ferro burst out of the break room.

She rushed toward Tyler.

Her arms were outstretched.

Her eyes were wild.

Her hospital gown hung in bloody tatters from her bony, naked body.

Her mouth twisted open and released a banshee-like shriek as her clawing hands reached toward him.

On pure instinct, Tyler raised his gun and fired directly into Ferro's screaming, crazed face. The bullet burst out the back of her skull. She collapsed in a lump on the floor.

***

BANG!

Hannah watched the bullet burst out the back of Nick Aguta's head, taking a sizable chunk of his scalp with it. Her mouth hung open in dumb confusion as globs of blood splattered onto the beige wall, a chunk of brain flopped onto the floor, and Nick Aguta's body crumpled backwards.

On some level, Hannah knew exactly what the Antennas had done, and were *still* doing. But, like a broken hard-drive, her weary mind kept spinning, knowing that the answer was buried in there somewhere, but unable to access it. And so, for those crucial immediate seconds, Hannah simply watched, like everyone else in the break room who assumed it was all an accident.

Some of the staff put their hands up, seemingly believing that a startled guard must have mistakenly fired his weapon and that the safest thing to do was to simply stand still.

Everyone else stood dumbly.

The door swung wide open.

Tyler stepped over Nick Aguta's body.

***

Tyler stepped over Ferro's body and peered into the break room.

"In here!" he yelled to his men. "They're in here!"

Blood drenched the inside of the room. Bodies lay strewn on every table, in every chair. Every single Antenna was in there, attacking the staffers — clawing at one person's abdomen, sinking their fingers into another eye's, ripping the arm from the socket of another.

The staffers that were still alive screamed in agony as their limbs were torn from their bodies and thrown madly into heaps.

"Go! Go! Go!" Tyler commanded his men.

They swarmed into the room.

***

Hannah, like everyone else, had frozen in position.

The security team fanned into the room, their weapons held high and ready. Hannah could see their eyes through their masks.

These weren't the confident faces of rescuers. Their eyes were wide with the shock of what they were seeing. Their pupils darted about, taking in new horrors with each glance. Their breathing grew faster in just the half-second it took them to enter the room. Sweat began glistening on their faces inside their masks.

These men were terrified.

As all the other staffers stood dumbstruck, Hannah threw herself under a table. Then...

BANG! BANG! BANG! BANG! BANG! BANG!

A wave of bullets from half a dozen assault rifles sprayed out toward all angles of the room. They thudded into the men and women. The medics, the orderlies, the engineers, the janitors. The fury of gunfire erupted with such speed that some people were hit three, four, five, six times before gravity could send their bodies to the floor. And even then, another splattering of bullets thudded into their corpses with deadly, trained precision.

"Stop! Stop!" Hannah croaked out as bodies fell around her.

Hannah could see the expressions on her colleagues faces as they collapsed — shock and confusion, quickly replaced by pain and fear.

"Tyler, what are you doing?!" Hannah yelled, beginning to find her voice.

The gunfire swooped around the room, concentrating on pockets of people trying to run or cower. They found their targets quickly.

"IT'S A HALLUCINATION!" Hannah screamed.

***

Tyler heard Hannah's shout, but he still couldn't quite process it.

He looked around the room. His men were shooting Antennas in what seemed like droves. But when he looked to the floor, all he saw were bodies of coworkers. *Bullet-ridden* bodies of screaming, pleading, terrified coworkers.

"HOLD YOUR FIRE!" Tyler shouted. "HOLD YOUR FIRE!"

The gunfire slowed.

The sound of shooting echoed around the tight, concrete space. It took a few moments to die away. A thin layer of gun-powder haze lay draped over the scene. It too took a moment to clear.

As it did, reality finally revealed itself.

There wasn't a single Antenna in the room. Just dead or near-dead men and women. They lay in heaps on the floor.

Executed by Tyler and his men.

CHAPTER 30

"The gas is clearing again, Daddy. The pain will soon return."

Even through the darkness, Joe recognized the voice as Riley's. It had that same detached tenor to it, although, by this point, Joe could no longer remember a time when her voice had vibrancy. He knew she used to. She was such an energetic and bubbly child. Even during the hard times, perhaps especially during the hard times, Riley had a cheerfulness to her voice and mannerisms. A bounce to her step.

Joe barely remembered that Riley.

"Open your eyes, Daddy. You can see now."

His eyelids slowly crept open. A blinding light seared his vision, forcing him to scrunch them closed again.

"It will be alright," the voice said. "You should look now. I would like to talk. Before you truly feel the pain."

Joe forced his eyes open again.

It was so bright. Too bright to make out shapes or colors.

But the brightness began to subside. Despite the blurry, washed-out spikes of light and shadow that filled his vision, he could tell that he was still on his back, lying on the padded floor and looking upward at the white ceiling of one of the cells.

The shadows that surrounded him, he realized, weren't shadows but men and women standing, watching him. The Antennas. They swayed and twitched. Occasionally, one's arm would violently spasm. But mostly, they simply stood and observed him.

As his eyes adjusted, he could see that the remains of their gowns were streaked with blood. All except one. One of them didn't have the red-splattered gown. She had long brown hair, not a shaved head like the others. And whereas the rest twitched and swayed, this one woman — or girl — stood firm and erect.

It was Riley.

But Joe knew it wasn't Riley.

Her smile twisted into a gentle grin as his eyes focused enough to meet her gaze. The Antennas at her side contorted their mouths into what could only be described as "smiles."

"Do you feel it yet?" she asked. "Do you feel the pain?"

Joe rolled his head to the side and angled his eyes downward so that he could see himself.

"Don't look. Looking won't help," she said.

He did anyway. Despite the blurriness, he could make out the red, pulpy carnage of his own body. His clothes had been ripped from him. His skin lay in shreds around his legs, arms, and chest. They had peeled back his flesh, taking care not to dig too deep. They hadn't torn out his organs or nerves like they did to the others. They had carved around his arteries but didn't sever them. Despite all the blood, he wasn't bleeding out. He was alive. Very much alive.

As the view of his mangled body filled his vision, it seemed to reconnect him to his pain receptors. His intact nerve-endings pulsated signals back to his brain. Spasming waves consumed him. Overwhelmed him. Debilitated him. He couldn't scream or cry. It was too much.

His body and mind shut down.

Like flipping a switch, he retreated to the comfortable blackness of unconsciousness.

But he was only able to hide in that pain-free space for a moment.

The pale, searching faces of the Antennas appeared in the blackness. Those contorted, disembodied heads opened their mouths and emitted a screech — a high-pitched frequency that shook Joe's subconscious. The note stabbed his mind until his eyes opened and he was awake, yet again.

The pain flooded through him, like multiple dams bursting throughout his body. He clenched up and tried to ward it off.

As he did, Riley continued grinning at him. "You cannot hide from us in sleep," she said. "We can find you. We will always find you. Stay here. With us."

Joe bit down on his lip as he tried to absorb the convulsions rippling throughout his tattered skin.

"Thank you for setting us free," she said.

And then, like a faint headlight approaching through a stormy road, a thought penetrated his agony. A realization. As long as that thought hovered at the forefront of his mind, the pain, as unbearable as it was, seemed almost tolerable. A peace crept over him, like a warm blanket that numbed the fiery tide that rippled across his skin.

"Why do you smile?" she asked.

He hadn't realized he had been smiling. "C-c-can't you read my fucking mind?" he said, trying hard to keep his voice level.

She shook her head. "We've seen what you've seen. And we can make you see what we want you to see. Bishop built a gateway at the tip of your mind, the place where your sense of the world enters. When Bishop left, she gave us the key to the gate. We can see much.

But we cannot see what is *inside* your mind. So, tell us, why do you smile?"

"Riley," he said simply.

"What about Riley?"

"It was all a hallucination, wasn't it? She was never outside. The conversation in the pickup... it never happened."

"No."

"Th-th-the whole thing with her... gouging her eyes out... biting her tongue... it was all *you*. Wasn't it?"

"Yes."

Joe's breaths became easier and even. He could die now. He had been manipulated. His mind had been twisted and contorted. But he could die knowing that his daughter was safe. They must have implanted the same visions in Hannah. Or, perhaps, all those conversations with Hannah were also just hallucinations. Perhaps if he asked Hannah — the *real* Hannah — about her talk with Riley at the house last night, Hannah would look at him dumbly and swear that no such interaction occurred.

How deep did their lies run?

How long had they been manipulating his senses?

Had Riley's principal *actually* called to tell him about Kate's death?

Did Kate really die?

Had he really driven into town and picked up Riley from her friend's house?

All of those files that Chuck had sent about Kate's suicide... Was it all in his head?

But none of that mattered. All that mattered was that somewhere back at their home in Linville, Kate had probably just pulled dinner out of the microwave and set it on the table. Riley had surely just come home from softball practice, hungry and exhausted. Loose strands of hair would be escaping from her dual French-braids where they would be stuck to the dried sweat on her face and neck.

As they ate, they'd have a brief conversation during which Kate would only get a sentence or two out of Riley. Later that week, Riley would find out that her father had been killed in an accident at work. There would be a funeral. She would cry for him. And then, with her mother's help, she would move on toward college and life.

Joe's eyes glazed over. He could feel the blackness taking him, the life draining from his body, as if his life itself were only a puddle of water, slowly seeping down into the earth. There were so many things he had wanted to tell Riley. He had missed his chance.

But at least she was safe.

And so, he spoke out to the room, hoping that maybe somehow the sounds, or the thoughts behind them, might reach his daughter.

"Riley..." he said, his voice growing weak. "I'm so sorry. For everything. I should have spent more time with you. I should have been a better father. Be good to your mom. She loves you so much. It's right that you're with Kate. She—"

"What exactly do you think has happened?" the person who looked like Riley asked. "Your wife is dead," she said, matter-of-factly. "She killed herself."

Joe's vision began to blur again. He wasn't sure if he was dreaming the words she was saying. As his strength and life seeped away, he tried desperately to cling to his consciousness, to block out the pain and hold on just long enough to get some answers.

"Your daughter is where you left her this morning," she continued. "On the couch in your home."

It *had* been real.

Riley *had* endured Hell. Because of Joe.

"Why?" he stammered out. "W-w-why would you do this t-t-to her?"

The one who looked like Riley smiled and bent down. "Bishop saw your love for your daughter. It reminded Bishop of a daughter that perhaps *she* had also had. One that she couldn't remember but still loved. Riley was a bridge to you. You are the one who controls this place. You are the one who could set us free."

"She could have just... just gone into *my* mind. Why Riley? Why torture her? Why Kate?"

Joe blinked.

The vision of Riley vanished.

Only the Antennas remained.

"Why? Why do this to Riley?" Joe called out.

The response didn't come from any individual's mouth. Instead, a chorus sounded within Joe's brain. *"Physical pain is fleeting. The mind closes it off, as best it can. But some pain runs deeper. Some pain lingers. It sticks to you in the darkness, and the mind cannot push it away. Pain such as the pain of watching your family suffer. And the pain of knowing they suffered because of you. That pain will never leave,"* the voices said in unison. *"Consider it not a punishment, but a gift. The pain will be your foundation as you swim in the black. It will be your light. Use it to find your way, Joe Gerhard."*

The Antennas stopped swaying. They stood straight. They closed their eyes and tilted their heads upward. It was as if they were eagerly anticipating something.

Something that was about to arrive.

***

Tyler and his men exited the stairwell and advanced down the Level Two corridor. They could see that most of the cells were empty, although none of them trusted their eyes.

They stayed tightly formed in their group. Two men walked backwards so that they could keep a set of eyes behind them. Their cautious advance was painstakingly slow. They swept every which way with their eyes and their weapons.

As they neared Ferro's cell, Tyler could see through the window — all the Antennas stood in the cell, their eyes closed and heads tilted upward.

He motioned for his men to follow.

The door had been propped open. No resistance. Tyler led his men through the airlock chamber toward the door of the cell. It too was propped open.

On the floor lay Joe. Everything below his neck had been ripped and shredded, but his body still moved and moaned.

As Tyler paused in the doorway, the Antennas all turned, opened their eyes, and watched him. But none made any movement toward him. There was nothing aggressive in their posturing.

"Joe," Tyler called out, breaking the silence. "Is that really you?" He expected those words to shake the Antennas out of their stupor and perhaps give him an excuse to execute them all. But they only stood there.

"What do we do, sir?" one of his men said. He could hear the waver in the man's voice.

"Gerhard?" Tyler called out again.

"Ya think it's really him?" someone said.

Whatever was left of the man on the floor turned his eyes toward Tyler. They were sad eyes. It sure looked like Joe.

"Kill them," Joe said weakly. "Kill them all."

Tyler wasn't sure if the voice came from Joe or if it had been implanted in his own head. But suddenly, the only thing that felt real were the bullets in his gun.

Without another word, Tyler fired.

Single shots. Controlled shots. Head shots.

Bang!

Bang!

Bang!

***

Joe watched the blood splatter.

He watched as one-by-one, the Antennas fell.

He watched their eyes as their bodies hit the ground.

Peaceful eyes.

Thankful eyes.

Free eyes.

Soon, all the Antennas lay beside Joe. None of them moved.

That chorus of voices drifted into Joe's head again just as he lost consciousness.

"Goodbye, Joe Gerhard."

And then the voices were gone.

CHAPTER 31

Riley sat motionless on the stiff leather couch.

The sun had begun to set outside. Night was returning to the house again. Riley had lost track of the days since her father had walked out the front door. It had been awhile. She had definitely endured one full night alone on this couch. But maybe it was two or three by now. Memory and reality had blended together into an intractable blob in her mind.

She had discovered that if she didn't drink water, then she wouldn't have to pee. This meant fewer trips around blind corners in the house. Fewer opportunities for her to see things. Fewer chances to kill herself. And so, she ignored her thirst. She ignored her hunger. She ignored the overwhelming urge to sleep.

She hadn't seen anything out of the ordinary since her dad left, however long ago that was. But it only made sense that perhaps she hadn't seen anything *because* she hadn't moved from the couch. If that were the case, then she wasn't about to alter a working strategy. And so, she simply sat on the couch and tried to absorb herself with whatever she could find on TV.

The major story on the news was that the U.S. had killed some big-time arms dealer in Istanbul. It was some Russian guy who had supplied a lot of terrorist groups. Apparently, they found him just moments before he was able to complete the sale of twelve guided missiles, the type that can bring down an airliner from the ground. A major terrorist attack, perhaps *several* major terrorist attacks, had been averted.

The talking heads were debating whether carrying out an assassination on foreign soil was legal or just. Riley didn't much care. The world seemed a safer place without... what was the guy's name? Victor something-or-other. Some Russian name.

The U.S. had also just coordinated with the Mexican government to arrest the head of some drug cartel. The guy had escaped from prison and had been in hiding for three years. There was also a drone strike in Iraq that took out some guy who ran a terrorist propaganda site.

Although Riley never watched the news, this felt like a big news day.

The handle on the front door turned and opened. The alarm beeped, only for someone to enter the passcode and silence it.

Riley looked up, but she didn't move. It was the first abnormal sound she had heard in a while, and she didn't quite know whether or not to trust it.

Several tough-looking men stepped into the house. Some of the men went directly toward Riley on the couch. They clustered around and stood in front of her, as if they were standing guard over her. She didn't move anyway. She only traced their motion with her weary eyes.

The other men fanned out throughout the house. She could hear them thumping around, opening doors and checking rooms and closets. Someone shouted out, "All clear."

Again, Riley just stared off.

The men standing guard around Riley then relaxed their posture. They formed a slight path as a squat-looking mole of a man in a suit and glasses stepped into the house. He looked around, taking in the area, his eyes acknowledging Riley's presence before skimming past her to view the rest of the surroundings.

Appearing satisfied that everything was in order, he turned his head back toward the open door and tapped his hand against his thigh. "Here, girl. Come on," he called. One of the men handed a leash through the door. The squat man with the glasses took the leash and gave it a little tug.

Riley watched as a familiar black Labrador cautiously stepped into the house. The dog arched her back in a stiff showing of fear. Riley recognized the look. When Moby was excited, such as when she saw a squirrel outside the window, her head lifted and her tail became arrow-straight. When Moby was scared, like during a lightning storm, her head sunk to the ground and her tail curled beneath her quivering haunches.

It was clear to Riley that Moby was terrified of being back in this house. Moby's entire posture angled away, ready to scamper off if only not for that darned leash.

"Look who it is," the man said, pointing Moby toward Riley.

The dog lifted her head. She saw Riley on the couch. An excitement overtook the dog's fear and she scampered into the house, tugging on the leash until the man unclasped it. Then Moby, her feet moving so fast that they clacked and slipped on the hardwood, raced to Riley's side.

She propped her front paws onto the couch and tried to nuzzle her head into Riley's lap.

Riley felt the warm, furry head, but she barely reacted. Her weary mind couldn't calculate whether this was yet another trick. She gently pushed Moby down to the floor and kept her eyes on the man-with-the-glasses.

The man strolled over. He smiled warmly.

"She had been picked up by Animal Control," the man said, pointing to Moby. "It took them a day or two to pull up the information on her chip. They called it into your dad's office only a little while ago. They said she was found about five miles from here. Must've been quite a journey."

He spun around her dad's recliner and helped himself to a seat. "Hello, Riley," the man said pleasantly. "I am so terribly sorry that we left you here, unattended, for so long. It's been a busy couple of days and we're still in the process of sorting things out. Tying up the loose ends. My name is Javier Aguirre. But my friends call me 'Javi.' I work with your father."

His eyes seemed to be observing Riley, waiting for any response or acknowledgement from her. She provided none.

"You can relax. I'm one of the good guys."

He took off his glasses and polished them on his shirt. "How long have you been here alone?" he asked.

Riley just looked at him.

"A little shy, huh?"

She didn't respond.

"I have some tragic news," he said, his eyes turning downward. He seemed to realize the abruptness of the transition. Creases then formed on his forehead and his lips twisted into a frown. Even to Riley's exhausted eyes, these expressions felt like a forced display of sympathy.

"There was an accident at your father's office. Many people were killed. Including your dad."

Riley had no reaction.

"Did you hear me? Your father is dead. I'm so sorry."

"Hannah?" Riley whispered. "Can I see Hannah?"

"Dr. Chao died as well. Again, I am so, so sorry." He said.

She finally looked up at him.

"We're all saddened by the loss of your father," he continued. "And with your mother's passing, I know that this has been a very stressful time for you. I'm here to clean up this whole mess. I want to make things better, as much as I can. Do you think we can work together toward that?"

Riley's head gave the slightest indication of a nod.

Mr. Aguirre smiled. He reached into a bag at his side and pulled out a computer tablet. As he tapped a few notes, he glanced up at Riley. "Your friend, Silvia Vargas, and her mother have been very concerned about your health and welfare. They hadn't heard from you and have been very assertive in contacting the local police to do a wellness check. Now, you understand that your father's work was very sensitive. I think it would be best for everyone if we move past these last few days and didn't get the authorities involved. Police investigations just slow things down. They don't fix anything. It just feels cleaner and better for everyone, don't you agree?"

There was no answer from Riley, but that didn't seem to bother Mr. Aguirre.

"I see you have grandparents on your mother's side. From everything I've read about them, they appear to be trustworthy, simple people. I think they would take good care of you. Would you like to live with them?"

Again, Riley had no response.

"In my medical opinion, this is a simple case of stress. All you need is a good night's sleep."

He reached into his satchel and pulled out a small, unlabeled bottle. He held it out to Riley and gently shook it. The pills inside rattled around.

"If you take one every twelve hours for the next three days, you'll sleep like a rock. I guarantee it." He smiled. "One of the side effects is that it may make your short-term memory a little fuzzy. You might forget details of the last few days. The things you remember might seem more like the whispers of a dream before it slips away. Nothing harmful. Take my word for it. We've come a long way in our understanding of the human brain. Science is always improving. In a few days, you'll forget all about this experience and you'll feel great."

Riley looked at the pill bottle. Then she looked at Aguirre's smiling face. The strain of his smile. The glistening of the nervous sweat on his brow. She made no move to take the bottle.

"There's another option, of course," Aguirre said, letting his smile drop. "With your dad's health plan, we can send you to a *special* facility. Free of cost. I personally know of several places. They offer excellent, round-the-clock care. We can keep you under observation and really dig in deep on what's going on *in there*," he said as he pointed to Riley's head. "We'll inform the Vargases and your grandparents, and, well, anyone else in your life. They'll all know that you're... resting. They may try to contact you, and it will be a hassle, but we'll make sure they stop trying to bother you. We'll see to it that you get plenty of peace and quiet. One way or another. Personally, I think this—" he shook the pill container, "is the better option for everyone. But it is all up to you."

It was at that moment that Riley heard it.

A voice.

Not the woman's voice.

A *man's* voice.

It was the voice of her father.

The voice didn't speak words, per se. It sounded more like an impulse, or an emotion, that spoke into her head, cutting straight through all the cluttered, half-formed thoughts that were swirling around. The voice beat back the haziness that shrouded her tired mind with a clarity that Riley had forgotten existed in the world.

She could *feel* him begging her, pleading with her. His terror, his desperation, his sadness. But Riley refused to trust it. She concentrated on forcing the voice back into its silence.

A memory then began playing in her mind, as clear as if someone had flipped the "on" switch of a projector and began to showcase a movie in front of her eyes. She couldn't turn it off, she couldn't push it away, and she couldn't ignore it.

It was the memory of waking up in a large bed. She was beside her mom who let out a sleepy groan before snuggling deeper beneath the fluffy blankets. As she stood within the dream, the world felt distorted and strange. She recognized the house and her parent's room, but she was seeing it differently than she ever had before. It was then that the realization struck her that these weren't *her* eyes through which the memory was occurring, but those of her father's.

Through those eyes, she watched as he tiptoed out of that bedroom and down the hall. When they arrived at the dining room, she saw herself, a freckle-faced five-year-old, twirling in a sparkly evening gown as she jumped excitedly at the breakfast display she had created, complete with a homemade "Happy Father's Day" card.

Within the memory, Riley felt a hand gently grasp her waist. She turned and saw her mother. She wore an old t-shirt and red flannel pajama pants, her standard sleep outfit. Her long dark hair was uncombed but fell gently onto her shoulders in an elegant, effortless beauty.

Riley's mom smiled and hugged Riley's father.

"Happy Father's Day," she said.

A sense of joy bubbled up through Riley. Like a long-simmering pot that had finally reached its boil, the emotions flowed from Riley in soft tears. Soon, she was sobbing on the couch as a dozen armed men cautiously stood guard over her.

The voice, as wispy as a breeze through the trees, said, *"Take the pills. Forget it all. Please, Riley."*

It was her father. Of this she had no doubt. The voice filled her with a sense of love deeper and more real than any imaginary trick or horror.

She looked down at Moby sitting intently on the floor. The dog's ears were perked and her head was cocked to the side. She had seemingly also heard something, but Riley detected no fear in the dog's reaction. Just familiarity.

Riley reached out and petted Moby's head, allowing her fingers to feel the smooth, soft hairs. She believed that this was the dog she had known for years. And she believed that the voice she heard was also one that she knew.

With that, she took the pill bottle from Aguirre's hand.

She undid the cap, took a pill, and put it in her mouth.

She meant to look up and gauge Aguirre's reaction. Whether his face betrayed relief or impartiality. But her eyes suddenly drooped closed and she fell asleep, right there on the couch.

CHAPTER 32

"Riley Gerhard," the speaker announced.

Riley walked up the steps and marched to the center of the stage. Principal Green handed her a diploma, or at least the empty case for one — the real one would arrive in the mail in a week. She shook hands with the principal, turned to the side and paused as — *click!* — a photographer snapped their photo.

"Justin Greggory."

And just like that, Riley's moment was over. She continued to the opposite side of the stage as Justin Greggory now received his applause.

Her eyes drifted out over the audience as she walked. Somewhere, Grandma and Grandpa were clapping for her... unless they left to use the bathroom. Her friend Silvia and Mrs. Vargas were out there clapping somewhere too. But other than that, Riley didn't have many friends at this graduation.

The "ordeal," as she came to call it to her therapist, had set her back a year in school. When she returned to complete her senior classes, it was with kids who had been a grade below her. Behind her back, they nicknamed her "Schizo," which eventually became "Schizzy Gerhard," before the kids, their cleverness having reached its limits, finally settled on "Schizzy G."

It actually wouldn't have been a bad nickname — it kinda sounded like a rapper name — if it didn't contain the ounce of truth that, yes, Riley had had a mental breakdown. And everyone knew it. Not that Riley remembered much of the events of when both her parents died in the same week. The whole episode in her life was a haze, punctuated by some vague, but terrifying dreams.

Riley proceeded off the stage, went back to her seat, and sat down. Alone. Around her, jubilant seniors cheered for their fellow classmates. Riley didn't really know any of them. She didn't care to either.

When the time came, she rotated the tassel on her cap in sync with the rest of the class. Then she threw her cap in the air and hooted and screamed with the others. But her exuberance felt forced and empty.

Afterwards, she went out to lunch with her grandparents and Silvia. Silvia had been a good friend, but Riley could feel the distance growing. There just wasn't much to talk about, and Riley didn't much feel like putting in the effort. Besides, Silvia had already moved on to college. She had a whole new group of friends and experiences. Whenever they hung out, Riley felt like a pity case.

When lunch ended, and Silvia drove back to her dorm at UVA, Riley borrowed her grandparents' car. Not that they cared; they took two hour naps every afternoon. Simply sitting in the high school auditorium had used up all their energy for the day.

Moby hopped into the car with her. Even for an old dog, Moby was always ready for a trip if it meant that she could stay by Riley's side. Together, they rode off to Riley's favorite spot, the *only* spot where she felt comfortable these days.

Up the highway she drove, climbing up Shenandoah Mountain.

June was a beautiful time of year, as the days were sunny and the world was a vibrant green, having not yet been browned-out by the impending summer heat. The further she went, the thicker the tree cover became until it formed a full canopy over the road. The sun occasionally shone brightly through the cracks in the canopy, creating a blinding glare that made some of the tight turns feel dangerous.

But it was worth it for the view.

As she neared the summit, she pulled off the road and onto a gravel overlook. The parking area was deserted, just as she preferred. She liked to be alone these days. Ironically, she felt less lonely when she was by herself.

She lifted Moby out of Grandpa's old Buick and together they crossed the parking area toward the High Knob Trailhead. Her dad always liked to point it out on their many drives between her parents' two houses. He always wanted to be a forest ranger, or a scoutmaster, or some job that would allow him to be free in the woods. He constantly mentioned how much he wanted to get her into hiking and backpacking, starting with this trailhead.

They never got the chance.

But now, it was her favorite place in the world. Whenever she was alone on the trail, she felt closer to her parents.

It was a short hike, mostly uphill. The mountain straddled the border between Virginia and West Virginia and along the trail a gorgeous view of the valleys of both states would occasionally open up through the trees.

"Hey, guys, it's me," she said out loud to the swaying trees and dirt path.

Riley liked to talk as she walked. Always to her mom and dad. She would tell them about her life, her school work, her friends. About Grandma's slight hints of dementia and Grandpa's complete unwillingness to stop eating sugar and carbs despite his out-of-control Type 2 diabetes.

And she always told them how much she missed them.

"I just walked at graduation," she said, strolling along and listening to the gravel crunch beneath her feet in response. "I need some advice about college." She took a pause to catch her breath as the trail grew momentarily steep. "I'm just not feeling Gonzaga. It's so far. It's cold. I won't know anyone."

She hiked a bit in silence, the only sound being Moby's tags clinking against her collar as she trotted along at Riley's side.

"Silvia said that I could take a gap year and then maybe reapply to UVA. It's a good school too. It's pretty close, so I could check in on Grandma and Grandpa a lot. I could take care of Moby. And... and I have so many friends there." In truth, she knew that they weren't really her friends anymore.

"I... I just kinda wanna..."

Riley didn't finish the thought, although she knew what she wanted to say. She wanted all those friends — well, *former* friends — to see that she was just a normal college girl. She wanted to prove to them, and also herself, that she wasn't crazy. That she wasn't "Schizzy G."

But she didn't want to admit that out loud.

Not even to her dead parents.

She rounded the corner and hiked the final steep yards. The tree line fell away behind her and the trail opened up to the gray, hazy evening view of the rolling green hills of Virginia. Atop this stony clearing stood an old fire watchtower. It rose twenty feet off the ground and was built entirely of gray and brown granite which helped it blend into the hilltop.

Riley hiked over to its base. Then she clomped up the brown, wooden staircase that wrapped its way around the tower, her boots clunking and echoing on the planks. Moby hopped up the steps one-at-a-time right behind her.

At the top, Riley leaned against the decaying, weather-beaten wooden handrail. Moby, not at all interested in the view, plopped down at Riley's feet, taking the moment of rest as an opportunity to lick the inside of her leg.

Riley closed her eyes, leaned forward, and allowed the gentle wind to caress her face and slip its way through her hair. It was then that the voice came to her, as it often did when she spoke aloud on this hike.

"Go. Go far away," the voice said.

And there it was. She would go to Gonzaga.

She opened her eyes and glanced down at Moby. The dog had stopped licking. Her ears stood straight and her head cocked to the side, seemingly recognizing the voice drifting through the wind.

"Cool," Riley said. "Thanks."

The voice was never vague. It rang inside her head with a firmness and clarity. The words always came in short syllables. A word or two here and there. Often little more than a yes or no.

Riley dared not tell her friends or grandparents about the voice. It would only open more Schizzy G rumors. And she certainly wasn't going to tell her therapist. Her dad's death benefits provided for a lifetime of medical care, but the only catch was that she had to use specified providers. She didn't particularly like the therapist that her dad's work set her up with. And she didn't trust him at all. There was just something about him that made the hairs on Riley's neck stand up, as though she were being observed and spied on.

Perhaps the voice was right. Perhaps it was best that she left this side of the country. She could make a new start at Gonzaga, away from all her fake-smile doctors and therapists.

She would listen to the voice. It never led her astray.

After her dad's closed-casket funeral, several lawyers from his company presented her with all sorts of N.D.A.s, waivers, and confidentiality agreements. In exchange for her signature and promise that she would never speak about her father's death or job, they granted her a hefty settlement. Enough money to keep her comfortable for life.

She hesitated signing. She still had questions. So many unanswered questions. How exactly did he die? What exactly was his job? Why wasn't she allowed to see the body?

The voice came to her then too. It told her to sign. To take the money. To stay quiet.

And so, she did. It all seemed to work out well. The money appeared in her account, and she never heard from the Company again.

The voice was her secret. She assumed it was her subconscious guiding her toward the best, most rational decisions. It made sense. But she liked to believe that it was something more. A guardian angel. Her parents had gone to Heaven — or wherever people go when they die — and now they protected her from afar.

As long as she had her angel, she never felt alone. Whenever she needed guidance, the voice was there. And that comforted her.

"Be careful," her father's voice said. "Be safe."

With a satisfied nod, Riley turned and walked down the steps. Moby followed behind.

She didn't know if she was going to like Gonzaga University. She didn't even know what her major would be. But there was plenty of time to figure that out and hopefully have some fun and some parties along the way. It was a chance to start anew. To reinvent herself. She knew that much.

But mostly, Riley knew that she had parents who loved her. They never really said it. They didn't need to. She *felt* it.

And that was enough.

Riley smiled. "I love you, Mom. I love you, Dad."

A faint response drifted over the hills.

The voice simply said, "Too."

Then Riley hiked back to the car. She felt a sudden excitement for this new opportunity and adventure in her life. Now that the choice had been made, Riley was determined to make the most of it.

EPILOGUE

Javier Aguirre stepped into the Control Room.

The Facility Supervisor, Janet Hawthorne, closed the door behind him. She pointed toward the two men seated at the control stations.

"You remember Adrian, our control operator. And that's Phillip, our chemical specialist," she said. The guys at the controls turned and made like they were about to stand and shake his hand.

Mr. Aguirre smiled warmly as he motioned for them to return to their seats. "Don't let me distract you. I'm just here to observe a session."

Janet motioned him toward the platform that overlooked the room. "Can we get you a water? Coffee? Soda?"

"I'm fine, thank you."

He went up to the platform and took his seat. He pulled out his tablet and began jotting down notes, pretending not to be keeping an eye and ear on the proceedings.

"Load stimulants for Case 31198," Janet announced.

"Loading stimulants for Case 31198," the man at the controls responded. "Who's our Antenna?"

Mr. Aguirre's eyes glanced up at the big screen which was tiled with video feeds from the various cells. The Antennas, seven of them, lay on their mats in their hospital gowns. Their sunken eyes gazed out of their shaved heads. Their mitted hands pawed at the air.

Janet looked at the screen. "Let's use Antenna-307," she said.

The control operator clicked around and a video-feed popped up of Antenna-307 — an Asian female.

As the preparations went into motion, Janet took a seat beside Mr. Aguirre.

He could feel her glancing at him, waiting for an opportunity to start a conversation. She'd probably drop in a hint or two about how her team hadn't had a weekend off this month. Something about the workload and being understaffed and how equipment requests slipped into the HQ void. Blah-blah-blah.

Mr. Aguirre stayed fixated on his tablet. He liked Janet. She was good at her work. Her colleagues respected her. But she was just another local that they kept promoting because it was always easier to hire from within, much like the supervisor of the last facility, Site B. Hopefully, if he looked busy enough, she wouldn't bother him.

He missed the first facility, Site A. That one was only an hour from his office in D.C. There were many kinks in the system back in those days. It was all still so experimental. No one had any clue how to do anything, but they were all learning and troubleshooting together. Back then, there wasn't the pressure from the higher-ups to deliver intercepts quickly and clearly. They could take their time and really get things right. In those days, Javier Aguirre felt like part of the team. He considered those people his friends.

It was too bad they had to close it and scrub it.

He loaded up the profile of the supervisor from that facility. He really liked her. She was a spitfire. Incredibly sharp and resourceful. West Point grad. Best supervisor that Aguirre ever worked with. He missed her.

He looked at her photo. Her long dark hair and strong face.

She was dead now. Her name was Claire Thompson.

But Aguirre actually admitted that the name "Bishop" suited her better.

Site A felt like a long time ago now.

Heck, Site B, the West Virginia one, also felt like ages ago. Time had a way of moving super-slow *and* super-fast at this job. The long days and weeks, with all the traveling and report-writing and having to be the bad-guy to the supervisors, crawled by. But the years were gone in a flash. He couldn't believe how much they had accomplished in so short a time.

He also couldn't believe that they were already onto Site C. Now he was travelling all the way to South Carolina to view tuning sessions. Soon, he'd have to begin overseeing the construction of Site D and Site E. They were already scouting locations in Florida and New Mexico. There was never enough money for staffing or upgrades, but there was always plenty in the budget for expansion, expansion, expansion.

But this meant the travel would only get longer and longer.

So many hours on the road.

Oh well. Aguirre actually liked the travel.

As the work proceeded around him, Aguirre scrolled over to the profile picture of the supervisor of Site B — Joseph Allan Gerhard.

Joe was a good guy. Friendly, professional. That is, *before* Joe bashed a computer into Aguirre's head and tied him to a chair. Asshole.

He wondered how ol' Joe was doing these days.

"Let's use Antenna-301," Aguirre said, looking up from his tablet.

Everyone in the Control Room hesitated.

"I, uh, I don't know if that's a good idea," the supervisor, Janet, said.

"And why not?"

"We use him so much, I'm concerned with burnout. I mean, yes, Happy definitely provides the clearest, most detailed intercepts..."

Mr. Aguirre cocked his head to the side. "*Happy*?"

Janet gulped. She cleared her throat, knowing that she slipped up. "Um... yes. When they arrived at this facility, they were only identified by number. Communication between the medical staff became a little confusing. And so, um, we gave them call-signs."

"I see. And the call-sign 'Happy' came from..."

"Well, there are seven of them. And so—"

"The Seven Dwarves. Of course. Very clever. And why, pray tell, did you choose 'Happy' for Antenna-301?"

"Because... because despite his extensive injuries... he's always smiling."

"May I see?"

The screen clicked over to the video feed of Antenna-301. He didn't wear a gown like the others. Instead, extensive bandages were wrapped around his body. Any sign of flesh that peeked out from beneath the bandages showed long, jagged scars. In many places, three or four scars ran parallel to each other, the exact width and distance that clawing fingers would make as they peeled away skin.

Yet despite those miserable conditions, the fringes of Antenna-301's mouth curled up into a smile. Almost as if he knew that they were watching, Antenna-301 tilted his head and looked directly at their camera. His eyes didn't roam around his head like the other Antennas did. They remained focused.

That smile stayed on the Antenna's face.

It was a natural, relaxed smile. Not the sinister, twisted smiles that crept across the features of the other Antennas. This was a smile of contentment.

The smile a proud father would have as he gazed upon a daughter who just graduated high school and had been accepted into a very good private college. A daughter who had endured so much, and yet overcome it with a remarkable strength and self-confidence. A daughter who had every right for self-pity and crippling remorse but refused to indulge in such emotions. A daughter whose father had failed her, but despite those failures, she had become a better, stronger person than he ever was. A daughter he would love forever, across all physical bounds of the earth.

He would find his daughter always. He would watch over her, as he promised her mother he would. He would love and protect her until his final breath.

It was a smile of pure bliss.

Mr. Aguirre had to turn away from that smiling Antenna. The smile unnerved him. He gently set down his tablet, removed his glasses, and tilted his head toward the floor. He reached up and massaged his temples and then the back of his neck.

Maybe it was from staring at the screen of the smiling Antenna. Maybe it was from too much work and not enough rest. Maybe it was the stress of the job. Whatever it was, a pressure pushed against the back of Mr. Aguirre's eyes.

He hoped it would soon pass because he was experiencing the *worst* headache of his life. Strange.

THE END

Thank you for reading!

I hope you enjoyed *Intercepts*.

Please consider leaving a review on Amazon. It doesn't need to be a book report or anything long. Just a sentence will do. Reviews are an important way to support authors and I greatly appreciate them.

Plus, I love hearing from readers!

If you enjoyed *Intercepts*, I invite you to check out my other books:

In My Father's Basement: a serial killer novel

Just your average father/son story...
but with abduction, torture and murder.

A *"deeply disturbing page-turner"*

The Venue: a wedding novel

Amy never expected to be invited to Caleb's wedding. And now, she
doesn't expect to get out alive.

"Rollicking dark, twisted fun!"

ACKNOWLEDGEMENTS

When I published my first novel, *In My Father's Basement*, I was blown away by all the support and encouragement from my friends and family. My writing can be quite nasty and cruel, and I know it is not a genre that many of you seek out, but my dreams would never have stayed afloat for this long without you. I am very fortunate to have so many wonderful people in my life

I want to thank my brilliant editor, M.A. Your work ethic, attention to detail, nose for writing, and commitment to story propelled this novel forward in innumerable ways. You catch things that my eye just doesn't see anymore. You have a skill for knowing what the narrative needs and when it needs it. Thank you for your tireless work and for inspiring me with your talent as a writer.

Also, I need to give a special thanks to my wife. Transitioning my career toward novels is an immense risk, and yet, our life together is so wonderful and joyful that I feel no apprehension in taking such risks in my career. You inspire me, you stabilize me, and you push me to be better. Thank you.

And thank you to everyone who takes the risk to commit time from their busy lives to reside for a little while in my sometimes-twisted imagination. I could not be a writer if there were no readers. Thank you, and I hope you continue to enjoy my work!